"You win tonight," she said. There was always tomorrow night.

"So what's my prize?" he asked.

His prize? If he expected what she had just denied the wolves, she would slay him right here and now, and be damned if she fell to her death.

"I can't ———— said, dashing his tongue along one ————————— 've got that damned collar. To ——————————-gives me a thrill. But I can do this."

And ————— her. Hard and urgent, forcing his sweet breath into her mouth. The vampire persisted, pressing his body against her knee, challenging her to hurt him, to deny him this stolen prize.

Training had not covered this sort of attack. She could feel his fangs pressing into her lip, but not cutting. Insanity! Never would she—

Suddenly the hard crush of their mouths softened. Lark dropped her knee. And like —— moth with tattered wings surrendering ——————me, she granted the vampire h————

BEAUTIFUL DANGER

MICHELE HAUF

MILLS
BOON

First published in Great Britain 2013
by Mills & Boon, an imprint of Harlequin (UK) Limited,
Eton House, 18-24 Paradise Road, Richmond, Surrey TW9 1SR

© Michele Hauf 2013

ISBN: 978 0 263 90407 9
ebook ISBN: 978 1 472 00671 4

089-0713

Harlequin (UK) policy is to use papers that are natural, renewable and recyclable products and made from wood grown in sustainable forests. The logging and manufacturing processes conform to the legal environmental regulations of the country of origin.

Printed and bound in Spain
by Blackprint CPI, Barcelona

Michele Hauf has been writing romance, action-adventure and fantasy stories for more than twenty years. Her first published novel was *Dark Rapture*. France, musketeers, vampires and faeries populate her stories. And if she followed the adage "write what you know," all her stories would have snow in them. Fortunately, she steps beyond her comfort zone and writes about countries she has never visited and of creatures she has never seen.

Michele can be found on Facebook and Twitter and at michelehauf.com. You can also write to Michele at PO Box 23, Anoka, MN 55303, USA.

The music from the cello-rock band Apocalyptica inspired this story so I want to thank them for filling my brain with fantastical images of beauty, danger and love.

And those who were seen dancing were thought to be insane by those who could not hear the music.

—Friedrich Nietzsche

Prologue

Smoke billowed and clouded the halls and rooms in the Levallois pack complex. Werewolves, in both animal form and human form, retreated from what had once been their sanctuary.

The alarm sounded a droning cry but didn't coerce the pack leader to work more swiftly. Remy Caufield, pack principal, stuffed a valise with valuable financial records taken from the safe, along with other documents he was unwilling to leave behind. Sure, the safe was fireproof. But he could not guarantee he would be first on the scene following the fire's devastation to claim what was inside the safe.

The door to his office slammed open, and thinking the flames had raged this far, he held up the leather valise in a protective manner to block his face.

What stood in the doorway was not flame or a fellow werewolf.

The haggard creature who bounded into the office, right leg dragging limply, and wild black hair tangled about his head so only his eyes showed, was the pack's pet vampire.

Well, *pet* defined the man ironically. They'd had the longtooth for countless months, and had used him well. The thing just would not die. It had become a sort of experiment to see how long the creature would cling to life. He had defeated every opponent put to him in the circular steel cage kept in the compound basement. And remarkably, the UV sickness, while it maddened the creature, only seemed to make him stronger in the ring.

The werewolves had made a mistake last night. Remy hadn't known the vampire they'd matched against this creature was a phoenix. The phoenix was a powerful vampire who decades ago had survived a witch's blood attack, which had once been poisonous to vampires. Drinking his opponent to death must have infused their pet's blood with the nearly indestructible phoenix's blood.

Domingos was his name. Maybe. Remy didn't care.

"You've gotten loose?" he asked stupidly.

The vampire slapped his filthy hands on the desk before him and growled, showing his bloody fangs—blood that could only have come from Remy's men.

"You will pay for this!" the creature raged. "I will return!"

Remy scoffed, but his heart cringed. The vampire's eyes were black as hell and yet bright, so frighteningly bright. He looked into a strangely lucid madness.

"Serve me your worst," Remy said bravely. "You won't make it beyond the flames."

The vampire grinned maniacally. For a second Remy thought he would leap the desk and attack. But instead the longtooth grabbed the office chair and tossed it toward the window. Glass shattered.

Leaping to the windowsill—they were three stories up from the concrete courtyard—Domingos turned and saluted. "I will kill every wolf in the Levallois pack."

And then he jumped.

Remy slapped the valise to his chest, knowing he would see the vampire again.

Chapter 1

One month later

The pack complex had not been rebuilt after the fire. The pack principal, Remy Caufield, had created a sort of family home in an eighteenth-century town house at the edge of the sixteenth arrondissement, close to the forested Bois de Boulogne.

Or so Lark had been briefed an hour earlier by her supervisor.

The Order of the Stake tendered a fragile relationship with werewolves. Knights in the Order exclusively slayed vampires, but there was nothing to keep them from tracking and killing a werewolf should it prove a threat to mortals. The Order, populated exclusively by mortals, allied with none from the paranormal nations.

"Ah?" The principal of the Levallois pack looked up from his desk as she approached to stand quietly before him. His dark eyebrows furrowed curiously. "I hadn't expected a woman. I thought the Order was strictly men."

"You thought wrong," she answered curtly. "You have a job for me?"

"No introductions? I'm Principal Caufield." He offered his hand to shake across the desk.

Lark did not accept the offer but instead returned an acknowledging nod. Best to keep him appeased. She didn't like paranormals of any kind, but her training had taught her diplomacy.

"You can call me Lark."

"Lark. Pretty, in a…" His pale eyes took in the sleek black cleric's coat she wore, tight black leather leggings reinforced with Kevlar on the thighs and high leather jackboots. At the collar of her coat gleamed the bladed edging designed to keep away vamps looking for a thick, juicy vein. "Well, you seem to fit the bill, Miss, er…Lark. You've been knighted?"

"As are all who serve the Order. If you need reassurance that I can do the job, Principal Caufield, you've only to check with Rook, as I'm sure you have. But I am here now, and I assume you wish little time wasted. A third of your pack has been slain?"

He nodded and exhaled as he settled back in the office chair. "Yes, a third. Utter insanity. Eight of my pack slain in a month's time. The culprit is the vampire Domingos LaRoque. He is mad."

"Truly?" Lark hated to think of madness overtaking any man, yet while her tone professed lacking belief, her heart believed. Too deeply. "Or is he merely angry over crimes the Levallois pack perpetrated against him?"

The principal leaned forward, eyeing her with some concern. "You show pity toward a vampire?"

"Not at all. I simply want to deal with the facts. Lies complicate things. So tell me the truth."

"Very well. To cut through the bullshit, it is no secret the pack engages in the blood sport."

Illegal fights that pitted captured vampires against one another to the death, but those fights only occurred after months of starvation and forcibly induced UV sickness. Such callous disregard for the sanity and welfare of those not their breed was a good reason for Lark to not let down her guard around werewolves.

"Domingos was an odd one," the principal continued, thumbing his chin in thought. "Normally the vampires we engage in the sport last a round or two before expiring. But LaRoque lasted six months. That vampire possessed a twisted will to live. Even the UV sickness could not defeat him. Although I believe it made him mad—literally. He's a dangerous opponent. Can you take him out before he murders the remainder of my family?"

"Of course." Lark nodded once and then, before turning to leave, said, "The first time I lay eyes on Domingos LaRoque will be the last time he takes a breath."

The pack had spread out as he'd thinned the herd. Heh. He'd stood good to his word upon breaking out of that hellacious complex. But no time to celebrate. He had a werewolf to track—if he could just keep the music in his head from distracting him. It wasn't even a song. More like a gathering of distorted violin chords, like a cat in heat yowling for attention. That, and the slithery whispers that never left him alone. He never understood any of the words, if they were words; it was just an eerie constant murmuring. It was enough to drive a man mad.

"Been there, done that. Still doing it," Domingos muttered.

He banged the side of his head against the brick wall where he hid in a dark alley. That helped. Joggled his brain. Focused him. Until the cacophony resumed.

Clenching his teeth, he smacked a fist to the side of his skull. Ah, silence.

"Finally," he muttered, and snuck forward through the night.

Cool shadows calmed him and relaxed his muscles. Always tense lately. Ever on guard. A man couldn't find peace with so much to tend, both mentally and externally.

Didn't matter. So he was mad. He dealt with it as best he could. Besides, the madness proved an advantage when he leaped for his prey and ripped out its heart. Yet that wasn't Domingos LaRoque who stood holding the pulsing heart. That was the phoenix inside him.

That other vampire. The one you drank dry in order to survive.

Heh.

A clatter focused him on a mangy scent on the dark Paris streets. The werewolf was not using stealth. The dogs were not known for grace or silence.

Feeling his veins tighten in anticipation of the deed, Domingos crept forward. He would have his revenge. Again.

The wolf spoke with someone. Female, and…mortal. He scented her blood, sweet and tainted with floral perfume. Good thing he'd fed an hour earlier. But damn, the last thing he needed was a mortal witness.

Domingos turned and looked down the alleyway he'd come from. He clasped his fingers over the brass-framed goggles that hung from around his neck. He wore them always; be it day or night, he never ventured outside without them. If he so much as looked toward UV light, his vision went completely white.

What was that? A shadow moved not half a block away. Had he passed someone without realizing? Did another wolf follow him?

Never let down your guard. Stay alert. They are everywhere. Snap out from nowhere to grab you and take you back. Don't go back!

Disregarding the werewolf putting the moves on the mortal, for he hadn't yet verified if it was from pack Levallois, Domingos slunk back the way he had come. Inner whispers forced him to snap his head back and forth, as if he were a headbanger with Tourette's. The move was not successful. Yet in between the clamor of distorted musical notes and hideous whispers taunting his brain, he managed to pick up a heartbeat. Calm, yet aware.

Casting his gaze across the rooftops—two stories up—he ran a short distance and made a leap, landing on the slate tiles with ease, for his bare feet gripped the smooth tiles and held him there. Squatting, he clasped an arm about his tattered leather pants and leaned over, much like a gargoyle, seeking the mysterious shadows below. Yet unlike the gargoyle, he was not positioned— and had no intention—to protect.

Down the alley, the werewolf laughed counter tempo to the click of the mortal woman's heels. His prey had hooked up. Lucky bastard.

You don't need a woman. You seek only the blood from those who tortured you.

He wasn't sure the wolf had been Levallois, and he wasn't about to take out the wrong wolf.

The violin scratched at the inside of his skull. Domingos made to slap his head but paused. A curious shadow moved below. And he wanted a closer look.

He could do this to a sound track—even one that screamed like a burning cat.

Leaping, Domingos descended with a grace that loosened up a chuckle. He sometimes forgot that his inner madness manifested in voice. The shadow, alerted by his laughter, dashed between buildings as he landed on the cobbled street crouched, fists to the ground.

Another chuckle echoed into the night. Domingos laughed at himself from the grandstand. His other self—that sane self—could never quite manage belief in the antics perpetrated by the phoenix, the true darkness within him.

But he'd given himself away.

Quickly, he slipped into the shadows, becoming but a heartbeat. He listened, straining to hear the mysterious other over the insistent skull clatter. Cars rolled by, exhaust fumes billowing into the night. The werewolf's scent lingered, yet he knew that ship had sailed. Pity the mortal woman should she not expect an animal in her bed tonight. The moon was half crescent, so the wolf needn't shift, unless that was his thing.

Forget the wolf, Domingos thought. *I want to play with the mystery shadow.* He scented her now. Yes, female. And close by. As if it was her intent to remain. Could she have been tracking him?

Interesting.

He hadn't gone to Club Noir tonight. The erratic thrash-metal bands they featured provided an escape from the noise in his brain. When he was there, females hung on him, attempting to get his attention, to entice him into learning their salacious secrets. He hadn't the interest.

They all need to die.

So what was he doing now?

Playing with the shadows.

Right.

Slipping past the open doorway of an abandoned building, Domingos moved swiftly. He made out the shape of her now. Her back to an old iron street pole, she stood tall and slender. Alert.

He moved like the wind, and just at the moment he sensed she knew he was behind her, he grasped her around the neck and pulled her spine against the pole. One hand pressed across her throat, choking her, while the other moved to the hand she slashed back toward him.

His fingers grazed cold metal. He clamped his hand about hers, sliding his fingers up along the metal cylinder. He recognized the shape of the weapon only from a close encounter years earlier. *Fuck.* She held a— She couldn't be!

Her free hand gripped the pole and while her body moved slightly forward as she kicked back with one foot. Something sharp on the back of her heel tore through his pants and thigh. Domingos cried out at the pain of it, but he didn't release her.

No, he wanted to play with this prize.

Blood scent blossomed as he squeezed his fingers about her trachea. Blades? He wasn't about to let go, despite the icy sharpness cutting into his palm.

He felt her grip on the cylinder loosen and snatched it from her. Slamming the blunt end of it against the back of her shoulder, he growled, "You want to die, hunter?"

"You first!"

This time he avoided her kick but released her as he backed away. Chuckling, and wielding what he knew was a deadly titanium stake, he lunged and wrapped himself about her back. The force of their collision knocked her to the ground, facedown with her palms to the tarmac.

Straddling her, Domingos shoved the stake against the base of her skull, execution style. He'd never slain a mortal, but he'd make an exception this night.

"Why are you following me?" Stupid question. If she was a hunter, the answer was obvious. "Where'd you get this fancy stake, eh? The Order doesn't hand these out as Halloween treats."

"It's mine!" Her hand slashed backward, cutting across his forearm.

The blade she held cut deep, and Domingos jerked his fist away from her skull. Forcing up a hip, she managed to twist onto her back beneath him, and slashed the blade again. He slapped a hand about her wrist to contain the flailing weapon. It looked like brass knuckles, with a blade cupped in the palm.

Strong and determined, this one. Dark bangs hung to eyes of a color he could not discern in the darkness. Dirt blushed her cheeks. She smelled like brightness and courage. At her neck the blades on her collar glinted with moonlight.

In Domingos's brain, the phoenix performed a maniacal jig to celebrate his stolen survival instincts.

"You're Order of the Stake," he said. "Good for you, little girl. I didn't know they were knighting chicks these days. Too bad you die tonight."

"If I die, I'm taking you with me."

The violin ceased tormenting his brain. The sound of her heartbeat thundered into focus. And suddenly— Domingos heard his own heartbeat, which he hadn't noticed for weeks. Why was that? The woman's fierce gaze didn't mesmerize, but instead pierced his heart without aid of a weapon. That pain he felt more deeply than he had the knife.

He crushed her wrist and gave her hand a shake, and

the blade looped about her fingers dropped to the cobbles with a clatter. Still she resisted, willing to fight to the end. He liked that. Most women would scream and beg for mercy. And he wanted to hear her beg.

"Mercy," he hissed. "Ask for it."

"Fuck you, longtooth!"

"You're one tough mortal. Why are you after me? I thought the Order didn't stake vamps unless provoked? I have done nothing to bring harm to mortals."

"This conversation is over."

He took a blade in his back. She'd kicked him with those nasty boots. And now she wrestled to get the stake from him. Domingos released his prize and propelled himself over her head, landing deftly on the tarmac, and ran out into the main street.

She twisted up to a running pursuit, slashing the deadly stake toward him. Moonlight gleamed on her long black hair queued in a ponytail and at the bladed collar. Focused grit tightened her face, yet her lips were so red. Sensual.

Domingos stood but a kiss away from death.

He didn't have time for death.

"Adieu, my pretty little hunter." He bowed, danced a few steps to the side and just as the stake whisked the air near his cheek, he leaped to a rooftop.

Standing at the tiled edge, he looked down over the frustrated hunter. She flipped him off. He made a motion to capture the gesture and smashed it against his heart.

"Until we meet again!" he called, and hurried across the tiles until her heartbeat faded from his senses and only the violin caterwauled in his brain.

Chapter 2

Lark marched purposefully north. The vampire had gotten the better of her. And how had that happened? She'd had him. And then she had not.

This was her first failure since she'd been knighted into the Order six months earlier. The night wasn't over yet, so she wasn't about to call this one in the vampire's favor.

He might be tracking across the rooftops now, but he had to come down sometime. And he'd taken off in this direction. She couldn't see or hear him, but so far, the line of same-level houses with mansard roofs continued.

Stake held firmly at her side, she kept her head up, and ears honed for noises above and behind her. The titanium cylinder housed a spring-loaded stake. She had only to slam the cylinder against the vampire's chest, right over his heart, click the release paddles and *wham*. Dead vampire.

This kill would be number seventy-two. She was less than a third of the way to her goal.

"Three hundred sixty-six," she muttered sharply.

He'd had opportunity to use the stake on her when she'd felt the cold metal pressed against the back of her neck. Stupid creature. He would regret not using that one and only chance.

The block ended, and she looked around, scanning the rooftops populated with bird droppings, sooted gargoyles and ancient slate tiles. Paris at night was crisp, dry and noisy with traffic. There were stars above, somewhere, but the City of Light dulled their twinkle. He couldn't have gotten down, crossed the street and disappeared.

Well, he could have, but she would have noticed. He had been chuckling to himself, for heaven's sake. The vamp was not in any way stealth. And he'd been barefoot. What was that about? Truly, he must be mad, as Principal Caufield believed him to be.

Didn't matter. One vampire, be he tattered and barefoot or cloaked in finery and charm, was the same as the next to her.

Crossing at a light, Lark holstered the stake at her hip and insinuated herself into a crowd of hipsters that lingered outside a nightclub blasting out technopunk loud enough to frizz her eyelashes. If the vampire wanted to lose her, he'd go where the crowds were.

Lark didn't like rubbing elbows with all these free and happy drunk people, so she slipped into an alley. Near the end, puffs of smoke signaled someone standing alone sucking on a grit.

She walked swiftly, head up, and fierce mien carrying her slender frame as if she were a quarterback headed for the end zone. No one would mess with her. Until a man flicked the half-smoked cigarette and it careened through the air and landed on the cobblestones before her steel-toed boots.

Lark stopped before the smoldering ember and slammed her hands to her hips. Her forefinger touched the stake. In her left hand she'd concealed brass knuckles that were bladed on the palm side.

"Hey, demoiselle, you are lonely." It wasn't a question.

Lark rolled her eyes. Smoke and whiskey shrouded the man. The scent was obnoxious. But beyond the normal smells she'd expect from a patron lingering near a nightclub, something deeper clung to him. Wild and feral.

And then she sensed others. Two to her right and one to her left.

Shit.

"What do you say, boys?" the whiskey-scented man asked. "We need a little fun before we go for a run, eh? Too bad the full moon ain't out."

Lark bit her bottom lip. Werewolves? They gave off a distinctive aura that she sensed, more alpha than most mortal men were capable of. They had better not be from the Levallois pack, or she would insist on double her pay for enduring these half-wits when finally she had slain the longtooth.

"I'm not into dogs," she said, and turned quickly, backing up to hold a firm stance with the open alley behind her.

A pack of four stood before her. *Double shit.* All of them looked like bodybuilders, arms flexed out at their sides, and wearing muscle shirts and blue jeans that enhanced their meaty, rugged builds. Wolves were rowdy but usually never gave her problems. They couldn't know what she was—that she was trying to help them.

She didn't need them to know.

Holding out her hand, she revealed the blade tucked

against her palm, and bent it in a come-get-me gesture. She didn't go so far as to say "bring it," but she was thinking it.

"Oh, she's spunky! Henri, you hold her down."

"With pleasure." A brutish blond wolf lunged for her.

Lark slashed her blade across his cheek and stepped aside to avoid the blood spatter. The wolves saw the gaping wound on their buddy's cheek and charged all at once.

Not too proud to save her ass the smart way, Lark turned and ran down the alleyway but paused when she felt the breath of one at her back. Times like this she questioned her sanity.

She spun on one foot, swinging her leg up into a high roundhouse, and clocked him against the skull with the hard rubber sole of her boot. It was never easy to bring down a behemoth. The wolf grabbed her leg and toppled her off balance. She hit the cobbles, back and shoulders first, an unladylike grunt forced from her lungs.

She should have kept running. Panic had distorted the calm she had been trained to maintain.

Kicking at the next wolf who lunged for her, she slashed his jaw with the blade that sprang from the toe of her boot. Using her hands as springs, she jumped to her feet.

"She's armed to the teeth!" one growled. "What are you, lady?"

"She's a walking death wish," one said.

"I like 'em feisty," another said, revealing with a smirk his thick canines made for tearing meat.

Lark felt a beefy arm wrap about her waist. The *shing* of talons grazed her Kevlar vest. Another of the wolves shifted out his claws. Not good. She didn't want to deal with four fully shifted werewolves. Did they dare shift in the city? So close to mortals?

"You don't want me enough to risk exposure," she said, and drew her blade across the wolf's wrist, which granted her a howling release.

Lark stumbled against a brick wall, and realized the alley was fenced off with wrought iron topped by pointed spindles, a dead end. Four wolves stalked toward her, bleeding and flexing their muscles, each with a hunger for something she wasn't willing to give them.

"I say we rip her limb from limb," the one commented as he sucked at his bleeding wrist. "She's too nasty to screw."

"Me first!"

The big blond one named Henri charged her, and when Lark wasn't sure what her next move would be, she slashed blindly through the air—yet impact of wolf to her slender frame did not happen. The wolf howled and landed up against the brick wall to her left.

And before her stood Domingos LaRoque, his back to her, standing tall, with arms out as if to shield her.

"Come on, puppies," he said. He whistled, short and quick, as one would to call in a dog from the yard. Twisting his head to the side, he flipped back his wild tangle of hair. "Pick on someone your own size."

"A bloody longtooth," one growled.

"Get him!"

And the battle began.

Wrestling only momentarily with the weirdness of the vampire protecting her, Lark found her bearings and pulled out a stake. She preferred not to kill werewolves unless it was life or death, but she would do what was necessary to save her own life.

The vampire tossed one wolf down the alleyway as if it were a rag doll, and followed by crushing another's face into the brick wall. His moves were erratic yet swift.

Though tall, he was much leaner than the wolves, and anyone watching would have laughed to see the werewolves get their asses kicked by the slender vampire.

Henri grabbed Domingos from behind. Lark swung around her arm and stabbed the werewolf in the back with the stake. The wolf yowled but didn't ash. She hadn't expected him to. Only vampires were reduced to ash with a death punch to their heart. But the wolf did bleed and whimper at the well-placed strike that had, no doubt, pierced a lung.

Disengaging the stake, she swung toward the next attacker.

The vampire ducked and yelped, "Watch that thing! I'm trying to help you here!"

"Sorry." But she didn't mean it. If she could take out the vampire amid the ruckus, then bonus points for her. The stake landed in the skull of another wolf, and she had to tug hard to reclaim it. "Thickheaded beast."

She kicked the slumped wolf aside, and turned to catch the vampire against her chest. The last two standing wolves had tossed him at her.

Hanging over her shoulder, his face close to hers and his breaths panting, he suddenly licked her cheek. "Mmm, tasty. But I knew you would be."

Before she could shake off the disturbingly sensual shiver that tightened her nipples and react by plunging the stake into his heart, he pushed away from her and charged both wolves.

The vampire was truly insane, because the wolves were twice the size of him and surely twice as strong. The only advantages a vampire had against a werewolf were speed and stealth. Which he was utilizing to his maximum capability. But was it enough?

Domingos tossed one wolf over his shoulder, and Lark

lunged to draw her blade across the wolf's throat. Hot blood sprayed her legs and dripped down the shiny woven Kevlar that reinforced the thighs of her pants. Protected the femoral artery. A fashion must when slaying vampires.

A wolf yipped, and, being the last one, he smartened up and took off down the alley. Three wolves lay groaning on the ground, not dead, but one or two could be close.

Domingos scooped her into his arms and ran toward the wrought-iron fence blocking off the alley.

"What are you—?" She kicked the air but couldn't manage to get free.

"You don't want to stick around for those dogs to get their second wind, do you?"

He leaped to the top of the fence, and then the roof, as if he had wings and carrying her was no burden.

Lark pressed the stake against his shoulder, though it would do little more than damage muscle and bone. A direct hit to the heart was required for death. "Put me down!"

"More distance," he hissed, racing across the rooftop. "Quiet the music!"

"The what?"

She struggled and managed to jump from his hold, but he tugged at her and tried to pick her up again. Lark's boots slid on the tile rooftop. Trying to place the stake on his heart and maintain purchase on the slate tiles was impossible. She lost her balance.

The vampire grabbed her wrist and shoved her around against a chimney. "Ungrateful wench."

"Bloody insane vampire. I don't need your help."

"Yeah?" He hooked his thumbs into the pockets of his leather pants, which were torn in spots along the outer leg seams, the hem shaggy. Blood glittered from where she had stabbed him in the thigh earlier. "You like being puppy chow?"

"I could have handled them."

His laughter echoed across the rooftops. And he said nothing more, only squatted and eyed her through the tangle of his dark hair. Disturbing, to say the least. His silence prodded at her confidence. Lark scanned her periphery. Nowhere to run without experiencing a punishing fall.

"I'll give you a head start," she said. Where had that come from? Clinging to the chimney, she marveled at his ease of keeping traction on the slick tiles. Of course, the man was barefoot. "Five seconds. Then I come after you."

He remained, defying her with a curious tilt of the head and a smooth of his fingers over the ill-shaven goatee and stubble that scruffed his jaw.

"Run!" she warned.

He spread out his arms and stood. A bend of his fingers defiantly invited her closer.

Lark stepped forward, but her boots slid on the tile. She wouldn't be able to run across two feet of this roof, let alone attack the longtooth. And what if she fell?

"I win," he said. "That means I get a prize."

He lunged for her, pinning her hips against the chimney and clamping her wrists to the brick so the stake was directed skyward. He smiled widely, revealing descended fangs. A pair of goggles clacked around his neck, small ones, like something out of a steampunk novel. And he smelled like smoke. Not cigarette smoke, but rather a sweet firewood scent.

"You're pretty," he said, again giving her that curious look, much like a boy looking over an insect he'd crushed in the backyard. "And deadly."

"You win tonight," she said, hoping to appeal to the sane part of him that would have compassion and let a woman go. There was always tomorrow night.

"So what's my prize?" he asked.

He pressed his body against hers and she could feel his hard muscles pulse with movement. Not bulky like the wolves, but sleek and dangerously strong. A predator to the core.

His prize? If he expected what she had just denied the wolves, she would slay him right here and now, and be damned if she fell to her death.

"I can't bite you," he said, dashing his tongue along one fang, "because you've that damned collar. Too sharp. Though pain gives me a thrill. But I can do this."

And he kissed her. Hard and urgent, forcing his sweet breath into her mouth. She didn't like it, and twisted to get away—he slapped a hand to her head and held her still. Lark struggled, and shoved up her knee into his groin. The move hadn't the punishing force she'd hoped for. The vampire persisted, pressing his body against her knee, challenging her to hurt him, to deny him this stolen prize.

With her heartbeat thundering, Lark's rationale scrambled for a solid hold. Training had not covered this sort of attack. What to do? How to… She could feel his fangs pressing into her lip but not cutting. Insanity! Never would she—

Too long since you've been kissed. If you're going to fall, shouldn't it be like this? Less painful than splattering on the street below.

Suddenly the hard crush of their mouths softened. Lark dropped her knee. And like a moth with tattered wings surrendering to the flame, she granted the vampire his prize.

Because nothing in her life made sense anymore. And everything was opposite what it should be. Now she dealt with strange paranormal creatures on a daily basis, when once she'd never even believed in them.

And because it hurt her heart to remember the last time her husband had kissed her.

A regretful protest rumbled in her throat, and the vampire pulled away from her. The city was bright with the glow of neon and streetlights, and the eerie illumination fell upon his handsome yet deceptively brutal features. Too much facial hair to decide if he possessed true beauty.

The vampire studied her face and touched her cheek, drawing away to inspect the droplet wobbling on his fingertip.

A teardrop? She had become a mental case herself!

"What's this from?" he asked, pointing the tear-soaked finger at her. "I am so awful to you?"

She nodded. That was as good a reply as any. Not the truth, but she needed that lie right now.

He licked her pain from his finger and nodded. "Of course. I can be nothing more to one so beautiful as you."

And then he turned and ran across the rooftops, leaving her clinging to the chimney like a bird without wings. And Lark wondered how in hell she was going to get down from this aerial perch.

Chapter 3

He felt freest and safest walking above the city, but Domingos sensed the sun was not far off, and exposed on the roofs was the last place he wanted to be for that terrible event.

He leaped, landing on the tarmac, and moved sinuously up into a walk, but he turned as he did to spy the hunter. She was rappelling down the side of the building. Must have pulled some rope from her utility belt. *Heh*. Wasn't that what vampire hunters wore? Some kind of superhero belt to hold all their crazy weapons?

"Smart chick. Pretty, too."

And vicious. He sucked at his palm where the blade had cut deep. Almost healed, it wouldn't scar, but there was humiliation in actually taking the cut. From a woman. Yet it hadn't been her deft punches and kicks that had hurt him most. Her rejection following his kiss had hit him in the one tender spot remaining within him after all he'd been through.

"No, it didn't," he argued with what little clear conscience he could find. The whispers slithered accusingly. "Stupid hunter. Not pretty."

A chuckle burst from his mouth. He hated the part of him that did that, but it wasn't a reaction he could control.

Yet he remained, watching, to ensure that she landed on the ground safely. The werewolves would not give up. They had her scent and would retaliate like dogs to her bones. But if distracted they'd forget the bone in favor of another more meaty treat.

The hunter wasn't meaty, by any means. But she'd done the one thing that would ensure that the wolves didn't lose her scent—she'd stood up to them.

And for that Domingos could overlook her nasty rejection and applaud her moxie. "Too bad it's going to get her killed."

But better the hunter than him, eh? *Heh.*

She headed west. Drawing up the goggles over his eyes and tugging his sleeves down over his hands, Domingos decided to parallel her, for the heck of it.

Lark slammed the apartment door shut behind her, dropping her weapons on the gray leather sofa and stripping off her coat and shirt as she made way toward the back of her home. Dawn was not far off, yet the apartment was dark. She navigated the murk with ease. In the bedroom, she unlaced and pulled off her boots and pants and beelined into the black-and-white-tiled bathroom to turn on the shower.

Tonight had been a complete failure.

Standing before the vanity mirror in a black lace bra and panties, she stared at her reflection, assessing the damage. The months-old brand of the Order marred her left shoulder, the design of four stakes within a circle pink and rough. Part of the knighting ceremony, the branding had hurt like a mother. She was proud of it, though; she'd endured a lot to earn it.

She'd taken a nasty bruise from a werewolf's fist on her right arm, and it had already blossomed deep purple and red. Studying a thin slice dashed under her jaw, she realized one of the wolves' talons must have done that. With the adrenaline pumping at the time, she hadn't noticed the cut.

Pulling out the band from her ponytail, she shook out her long, stick-straight hair. Her eyeliner was smeared up on one corner, giving her a half-cat's-eye look.

Staring at her pitiful reflection, she wondered when she had last cared. Had she ever cared?

Yes. The world had been different two years ago. Dreams had felt fluttery and fun, ambitions solid and achievable. Fashion and beauty had been important to her, because she'd known she was pretty and liked to look her best. Music—oh, music—it had been more than a hobby. Despite working nine-to-five for a local attorney's office as a file clerk, her real passion had been her music, and she'd been practicing to audition for a seat in a small community orchestra. But she'd abandoned the fine arts after falling in love.

During a trip to Paris, she had fallen in love and married Todd Cooper, knowing what he was. And, okay, so the falling-in-love part had come after the marriage. After four months of dating, she'd discovered she was pregnant and Todd had gotten down on his knee and promised to take care of her and their family. She'd been ready to plunge into the unknown of family and the new known regarding his profession, but only because fear had motivated that readiness.

And that fear should have forewarned her of this dangerous future in which she now existed.

Fool, she thought now. To have thought she could change a person? That had been her mind process as she'd said "I do." She hadn't liked Todd's profession and had hoped a new family would lure him out of it. Yet she'd quickly learned people didn't change; they only grew more deeply into themselves, altering imperceptibly, minutely, but at their core, ever remained the same.

While she waited for the water to warm up (she could brew a cup of tea faster than it took to summon hot water from the pipes in this old building), she wandered out to the living room to get her coat. Best to keep it hung when not wearing it. The Kevlar vest and pants she let lie on the floor. She was too tired to do housecleaning right now.

No, not tired. More like annoyed. Yes, by that irritating vampire!

She selected a hanger from the movable rack she'd pushed against the back door, because the iron staircase that climbed the rear of her building was unsafe and coming loose from the outer wall so she never used it.

She heard a knock outside. On the back door that sat atop a dangerous staircase that only someone very stealth might navigate.

"Shit." Lunging toward the end of the bed, she grabbed her pants and shuffled them on. Then she ran into the bathroom, shut off the water and grabbed a stake from the linen closet. She kept weapons hidden throughout the apartment.

Returning to the door, she slowly pushed aside the hanger rack but didn't get it moved all the way when the door burst open, shoving the rack of clothes toward her. She stepped aside, stake raised—and recognized Domingos LaRoque behind the funky brass goggles.

The vampire remained on the threshold, his palms flat before him, pressed against…nothing. A vampire could not enter a private residence without permission. That he'd been able to push the door inside surprised.

Lark exhaled but didn't let down her guard. She wasn't safe by a long shot.

"Save it for later," he said, eyeing the stake held aloft by her shoulder. "The wolves are at your front door."

Without taking her eyes off him, she tilted her head but didn't have to try to hear if someone was at the front door, because it also smashed inside. Wolves did not need permission to cross any threshold, private or public.

"This way!" Domingos yelled.

Tempted to go after the nuisance wolves, Lark checked her bravado. They were more than merely nuisance. Apparently, the brutes wanted to punish her for showing them up. And when weighing her chances against two or three wolves or one vampire, she'd go with the better odds.

She stepped toward the threshold and gestured that Domingos move aside. Once her hand crossed over the threshold, that was all he needed. The vampire grabbed her hand and tugged her outside, lifting her over his shoulder like a sack of flour. She beat a fist against his back, directly over the kidney, but that didn't stop him. He didn't take the stairs to the ground, but instead went up the rickety iron staircase.

"Let me go!"

"They're in your bedroom."

He tossed her up to land on the roof, which was shingled, and since she was barefoot, she had better hold than if she wore boots.

With a deft jump, he landed beside her and pressed a finger to his lips. "Quiet."

A wicked clatter preceded the entire iron staircase landing on the small, private courtyard below. Lark moved to look over the edge of the roof, but Domingos tugged her back and shook his head in admonishment.

Below, a werewolf said, "They went down and took the stairs out behind them. Let's go!"

The vampire eyed her breasts, the nipples peaking beneath the thin lace bra fabric. "No treats for the puppies this morning."

"They think we went down, but they'll figure it out as soon as they pick up my scent. They'll find us up here."

"That's why we're not going to stick around. Come on." He stood and offered her his hand.

She should stake that hand and then plunge the stake through his heart. But she'd dropped the weapon when he'd pulled her over the threshold. And going anywhere with a vampire was out of the question.

"I'll be fine on my own." She took off across the roof, thankful for lacking shoes because that softened her footfalls and provided traction.

Lark crossed two rooftops with ease because the buildings in Paris were so close together, and by the third rooftop she was congratulating herself for her agility and finesse. But she knew she was not alone. The vampire followed, silently, mocking her with his easy stroll. Hands behind his back and head bowed, he merely stood there each time she looked over her shoulder, as if a child's game and if she saw him move that would mean he was playing.

Wolf howls echoed from below. They either hadn't figured where she had gone, or else they were tearing her place apart. She didn't mind losing her things to raging wolves. Save the violin she valued, and perhaps a few photos she'd tucked away in a drawer.

Now if she could just lose the vampire.

As suddenly as she had the thought, she turned and the vampire crashed into her, sweeping an arm around her back and lifting her as he took the twenty-foot leap to the next roof. They landed softly, with a grace that only a winged creature could possess.

Lark knew vampires could not fly, nor did they have wings, but he presented curious evidence that the mythology the Order had taught her may be incorrect, or perhaps incomplete.

Tugging her along behind him, Domingos ran toward a roof door. They descended a concrete staircase into an empty loftlike space, floored in rotting hardwood that reeked of chemicals and coated with what looked like centuries of dust. A former factory long vacated of workers and industrial equipment?

Here they would be safe. Unless they turned on each other, which Lark wasn't beyond doing should the vampire have the same thought.

At the far end of the loft a circular window boasting a ten-foot span looked over the rapidly brightening city sky. It reminded Lark of the rose windows found in cathedrals, yet without colored glass.

"So," she said after catching her breath and moving to position herself near the window. A door stood to her left. An escape. "You've saved me twice tonight. Though I guess it's morning now."

"That means I get another prize." Shoving the goggles to the top of his head, Domingos walked before her, pacing in a random circle, his bare feet leaving trails in the dust. "What shall it be this time?" He conked the side of his head as if trying to dislodge something. "Tell me!"

Lark startled at his shout, and reminded herself that no matter the kindnesses he'd granted her, he was a monster.

Hell, she didn't need an excuse to label him monster; he simply was, end of story.

"No more kisses," she stated flatly.

"Of course not. You find my kisses disgusting."

"Absolutely."

He lifted his head and eyed her sharply, giving no sign that she'd offended, but perhaps his tight jaw was the signal. His goatee was scruffy, a match to his disheveled hair. Looked as though he hadn't combed it in a month. And perhaps he had not. Despite the lean muscles she had noticed while fighting with him earlier in the alley, he was too thin. So incredible that he'd defeated those hulking werewolves.

His gaze fell to her chest. She wasn't embarrassed by her lacking top. But that she'd raced across the rooftops in but a bra and pants might have raised a few eyebrows if any early risers had been gazing out their windows, coffee mugs in hand as they contemplated yet another day.

"What time is it?" he asked.

"I don't know. About five in the morning?"

"Sun's up soon."

Lark smirked. Sometimes the stake wasn't necessary. The sun would do her work for her today, if she could just keep him talking a little longer...

"How about...as my prize," Domingos suggested, "you don't kill me today?"

Lark bristled. She slapped her palms to her hips. She'd intended to kill him hours earlier. And the longer she went without killing him, the worse it damaged her record. But she did owe him. And tomorrow was officially only nineteen hours away. She believed in reciprocation, damn her soul.

Yet if the sun got to him first, she couldn't be held responsible.

"Deal," she said.

Oh, really? Inwardly, she cursed her hasty reply. She was tired, that was it. Not thinking clearly.

"How are you a hunter?" he asked. Another hit to the side of his head. "Damn it! Stop!"

"I didn't do anything."

He leveled her with a vicious sneer, and Lark backed toward the window, pressing her palms to the cool dusty glass.

"It's in my head. Skull clatter." And then he laughed that thoughtless chuckle Lark was beginning to associate with madness. "Don't go!"

"I'm not leaving. You're the one who needs to get the hell out of here if you want to beat the sun."

"I will." He thrust out a placating hand while shaking his head as if fighting whatever it was inside his skull. "But I need your name first. Only fair."

"I've already given you nineteen hours. That should be enough—"

"Name!" he shouted.

Lifting her chin, Lark stepped forward, daring to approach a man she suspected would lunge for her neck at any moment. No protective coat to keep him from her carotid. Yet he was not capable right now. She sensed he waged an inner war, and she'd never been one to walk away from a damaged individual.

As she approached him, he still held out a hand as if to keep her back. He yowled and pounded his head, then stomped the dusty floor. She reached out but retracted as if burned when he looked at her. That fanged grin was too sharp to be kind.

"I can't watch this," she decided, and turned away from what could become the beginning to a very bad day filled with memories she had thought to lock away when joining the Order.

"You don't want to watch the insane vampire go through his contortions?" he hissed. "Because torture is not pretty, is it?" He leered, and leaned toward her. "You don't want to see inside this." He pounded the side of his head with a fist. "Pretty girl, look away!"

"Lark," she offered, breaking into his tirade. "That's my name."

Domingos tilted his head. "Sounds like a bird. Can't be your real name."

It wasn't. She'd shed Lisa Cooper when entering the Order. That woman no longer existed. She couldn't exist and survive.

"Listen," she said, pacing back to the window. "You know where I live, but if you value your life, don't return."

"Not even to keep away the wolves? Damn it!" He stomped the floor, then bent forward to catch the back of his head with both hands. His hair swung across the dusty floor.

Get out of here, Lark! Don't look at this. All those wonders you had about what Todd suffered? This vampire can show you. You don't want to see!

And yet his apparent pain touched her profoundly. While she wanted to avoid experiencing it at all costs, at the same time, the man was like an accident you slowed down to gawk at.

"Why didn't you kill those wolves?" she asked, curiosity gaining the better of her discretion.

Domingos straightened and smoothed a palm down his shirt, which was only buttoned once in the center. He lifted his chin proudly. "I'm not a killer."

"You've slain a third of the Levallois pack."

"I am only taking the justice owed me!" He rushed her, pinning her against the windowpanes, which creaked with their weight. "Is that not my right? You've been hired by the Levallois pack to stop me, haven't you? Stop me from claiming the justice owed me."

"Murder is not justice."

He shook his head violently, brushing her cheek with his hair. "Can't tell me that. Stop the violins!"

He smashed a fist through the window beside her head, and Lark reacted by putting up her fists. Domingos saw her defensive pose and shook his head that he would not hurt her. He put up his hands in surrender. Blood trickled down his fingers, yet she watched the cuts heal instantly.

Vampires are creatures. Do not forget that.

"We have a truce for the day," he said. "You don't kill me. I don't hurt you. Too bad. You smell sweet. Your blood would taste delicious."

"You bite me and you die."

"Fair enough. But that doesn't mean I won't keep trying."

"Why? I'm a hunter. You know I want you dead. Why don't you run away from me?"

"Pretty little hunter without weapons to protect herself?" He laughed quietly now and tapped the floor with his toes. A flick of his fingers unbuttoned his shirt. "You are the sweetest thing I've known since before I was taken by the pack. I will crave you even as you plunge that metal stake into my heart, Lark. And yet you've not a lark's song, which pleases me. Don't like music."

"Is that the violins in your head you were talking about?"

He nodded and bowed his head. Their distance remained but a hand's width apart.

Lark exhaled shallowly. She didn't want to know—yes, she did. "What did they do to you?"

No. You don't want to know!

"Blood games," Domingos muttered, and bent forward, clasping his arms across his chest, as if protecting his heart. "Very bad. Not stuff for pretty girls to know."

He shook his head side to side violently, then murmured deep in his throat. And Lark reached out to stroke her fingers down his hair. It was ratted and tangled, but he closed his eyes and moaned softly as if her kindness eased a balm to his inner struggles.

Questioning her own sanity, she retracted. *Don't pick up another stray.* "I should leave. The wolves will be gone by now."

"No, they'll linger around your apartment to see if you return. Give it a day. Or better yet, find a new place to live."

He squinted and turned from the window. The sun flashed a sharp orange line on the horizon.

"How will you get home?" She didn't care. Number seventy-two? Coming right up.

He pulled the goggles down over his eyes and slipped off his shirt.

"Most vampires can walk in sunlight for a few minutes without harm," she stated. "But your goggles—"

"No!" He pounded his head. "UVs. They burn me. Cannot look at the light."

Lark recalled that the pack principal had mentioned UV sickness. It resulted when the vampire was kept imprisoned under harsh UV lights. She wasn't exactly sure of the results, beyond burns and sensitivity to light, but Domingos's strong shoulders actually shivered now.

It was too close to home, seeing a man cower from torture. *Get away from him, Lark. You don't need a plunge back to memory now.* She must stay strong, and make a call to Rook to secure a safe house for a day or two.

"Take it!" He thrust out his shirt, not meeting her eyes.

"I— No. You'll need protection from the sun."

"I've ten minutes."

"If you're lucky and you move right now." What was she doing? She wanted the bastard to get fried.

"You shouldn't be walking through Paris in your bra like that. I don't want them to see you."

"Them?"

"All of them. The men. They will look at you wrong. Take it!"

She grabbed the shirt to appease the agitated vamp.

"Now go!"

Startled into motion, Lark hustled through the doorway near the shattered window. When she stood on the other side of the wood door in a stairwell that descended to the ground floor, she flinched when feeling the thud against the other side. He stood there, body slammed against the door. Listening? Waiting?

Shirt clasped to her chest, she placed her hand on the door. "What did they do to you?" she whispered.

But she wasn't asking about Domingos's torture; rather, she had never dared to ask her husband about his 366 days of captivity.

She had wanted to know. The vampires had changed him. Irrevocably.

Domingos held in the yowl clawing inside his throat until he dashed across the threshold to his home and plunged against the wall. Alone in the cool, quiet darkness of his sanctuary, he released the scream that had been building.

His fingers clawed into the wall painted a calming

slate-gray. He banged his forehead against it to redirect the icy pain. He smelled burned flesh. The sun had flashed across his bare back, searing the already scarred tissue. He could see whiffs of smoke from over his shoulder, and he beat a fist against the wall, which had begun to crack, the thick layers of paint flaking off.

Tugging off the goggles he tossed them aside and then dropped to his knees. Rocking forward, he assumed the all-too-familiar rhythm, back and forth, arms clasped across his chest, to distract his mind from the pain.

He'd given his only protection to the hunter. "Lark," he whispered.

The sacrifice had been worth it.

Chapter 4

Lark picked through the remnants of her life in the living room. The smell of rank wolf seemed to linger on everything. Actually, it wasn't so much a smell as a feeling. They'd touched her things, violated her sanctity. In the bedroom, she fit the back door into the frame as best she could. Under her bed, she located the violin she'd owned since she was thirteen, still in its case, safe.

The plan was to take away only what was important and leave as quickly as possible. She couldn't trust the wolves wouldn't return. And this place was no longer livable. It needed to be physically cleaned and warded.

Gathering her valuables was easy. She pulled a manila envelope from the safe at the bottom of the linen closet. Inside were bank numbers and some credit cards and stock certificates. She should have put them in a security box at the bank, but she didn't trust banks.

The violin was too large to carry around with any

stealth, so she had to trust leaving it behind and, again, tucked it under the bed. Everything else was expendable. Save the picture in her bureau drawer. She retrieved the folded photograph and tucked it in the envelope without looking at it. She remembered his face. But the face she remembered was much different from that on the glossy photo paper. The image in her memory had hardened and grown thinner, desperate.

"Stolen," she whispered as she tucked the envelope into a backpack. A soul stolen in a slow and methodical way that tortured her to consider what he must have endured.

The vampire LaRoque was living, breathing evidence of such torture. She hated looking at him. And at the same time she couldn't turn away from Domingos's crazy gyrations and manic actions. That bedraggled soul needed some tender attention.

In a way, coming en garde with the vampire might prove her penance. She deserved to pay for the suffering she had not been able to stop. And what better way than to stand up to it and face it in all its horrid and terrifying glory?

Changing into a pair of leather pants, gray T-shirt, the Kevlar vest and her cleric's coat, she then gathered her weapons. Half a dozen stakes, some blades, brass knuckles and a retractable garrote that hooked at her belt. A vial of holy water also fit in a loop on her belt.

Pausing in the kitchen, she picked up the black shirt Domingos had given her and, without thinking, pressed it to her nose. Smoke was the only scent she could get off it, and yet the soft fabric tempted her to hold it pressed against her cheek longer than any sane woman should.

How many times had she done the same with one of Todd's shirts after he'd been away a few nights on a job? Her husband's leather-and-pepper scent had always made her smile.

The vampire didn't have a scent, beyond smoke, and that disturbed her only because she wanted him to have a telltale odor. Something to remind her…

Lark shoved the shirt away from her face and dropped it as if it were suddenly on fire.

"Don't think like that. You are not attracted to a vampire."

Even one who would offer the shirt off his back with the sun glinting on the horizon?

"Even so," she chided her thoughts.

Grabbing the gear she'd stuffed into a black nylon backpack, she locked her front door because it felt right— even though the back door was off its hinges—and shuffled down to street level. She dialed Rook as she hailed a cab and slid into the backseat, telling the driver to "Drive until I know where I'm going."

The phone clicked and a gruff French voice answered. The second-in-command to the Order's leader went only by the single moniker, which Lark suspected was a code name and not his real one.

"Rook, I need a safe house for a few days."

"You are having trouble with the assignment?" he asked in thick French. He never used English, though she knew he spoke it. He looked down on Americans, of which, she was an expatriate.

"No, I stumbled onto some werewolves last night. Pissed them off. To thank me, they trashed my place."

"I'll send a cleaning crew and ward master immediately."

"Thanks." The ward master would provide the plastic seal, so to speak, over her newly cleaned apartment. Should make it safe to return without fear of intruders.

"Were they Levallois?"

"I don't think so." She hadn't a physical ID on the entire pack, but noted that Domingos had not killed any of them, which led her to believe they had not been his target wolves. "So the safe house?"

"I can manage one for a couple days, which is all you'll need. It's located in the fifth arrondissement, tucked along the Jardin des Plantes. But tell me your progress with Domingos LaRoque. He has been eliminated? You haven't reported in, which is very unlike you. Are you sure you're not having trouble with this one?"

Lark sighed and tapped her fingers upon her knee. It had begun to rain, darkening the morning sky through the water-streaked cab windows. Somewhere out there a vampire who needed to wear goggles to protect his eyes against the UV rays must be rejoicing over this weather.

"I ran across him, but the situation with the wolves aggravated it, and I wasn't able to make the kill."

She heard Rook's soft yet admonishing tut on the other end.

Always an astute student, no matter what the study, Lark had taken to the Order's training program with zeal and a determination that had surprised even herself. She'd always been a girly girl who liked fashion and partying, and, well, the idea of exercise and martial arts, and honing her muscles and fighting skills had never been on her radar. But tragedy had altered that girl, changed her into something adamant. Something Lark still didn't recognize in the mirror.

After being knighted into the Order of the Stake, she'd proven herself a ruthless hunter. When she went after a vamp, it was dead less than twenty-four hours later. Nothing could dissuade her from her quest.

"I've got the situation under control," she said.

Oh yeah? What was that stupid "one day to live" deal you made with LaRoque? A vampire! You don't deal with them. You slay them.

Every hour she allowed the vampire to breathe, she let Todd down a little more.

"Expect to hear from me tonight," she said. "What's the address?"

Rook gave her the address to a safe house, along with a digital entry code, and after hanging up, she gave the cabdriver directions.

The safe house was clean, the walls bare of decoration, and the modern furniture a plain beige leather accented with uninspired black pillows. Lark didn't like it. She needed personal things around her to make her feel…

Admit it, Lark. You don't feel safe here.

It was called a freakin' safe house for a reason. But nothing she looked at reminded her of home. *Of him.* Yet would anything ever bring back that feeling of safety, of feeling loved and cherished?

Had it ever been love? Or simply her clinging to the *idea* of love, marriage and happily ever after?

Shoving away doubt, she sighed. She wouldn't be doing this if it hadn't been love.

"Only a few days," she said, and dropped her backpack on the floor by the beige sofa.

Even the rug was uninspired, no texture or color. At home she'd liked to dig her bare toes into the thick, soft pile of the sapphire rug before the gray leather sofa. More than a few times she and Todd had made love on that rug.

Shaking her head rattled at the intrusive memories. Looking over the rug, she decided flat and no color was best for her now.

At that moment a knock on the door startled her hand to her hip, fingers glancing over the stake. Perhaps it was

Rook come to check on her? Made little sense. The man oversaw the Order from his office and the training facility; he didn't often go out in the field. If contact was required with a knight, the knight went to Rook. And forget ever casually running across King, the leader of the Order. It never happened.

"Lark," called from the other side.

The skin at the nape of her neck tightened. How had he found her here?

She strode to the door and jerked it open, not fearing that he would rush inside to attack her. They'd made a deal. And besides, he needed an invite.

The scruffy vampire leaned against the door frame, goggles pushed onto his forehead and head bowed. He wore a turtleneck beneath a hooded jacket, and leather gloves. The only skin visible was on his face, and the scarf hanging about his neck clued her in that he used that as a mask.

"Did you track me?" she asked.

He nodded.

"Why? What's wrong with you? Most people would put distance between them and the one person who had explicitly stated she's of a mind to kill you."

"It's afternoon," he said. "I've still got a good eight hours before our deal expires. May I come in? It's raining out."

"The rain won't make you sizzle."

"Actually, it feels great on my skin." He tilted up his head to show the side of his jaw where the scruffy beard revealed red skin, as if plunged into hot water, yet not beset with a boil. "It was sunny when I set out after you."

"Is that why you keep a beard? To protect as much of your face as you can?"

"No. I hate this stuff." He stroked the thick black facial hair. "I just haven't gotten to a barbershop lately. They don't keep the same hours as I do." He rapped the air in the exact position of the threshold, and his hand did not penetrate the invisible barrier to Lark's side. "Pretty please? I promise I won't bite. And I'm getting soggy."

"I thought we had a truce? Me not stabbing you. You not biting me."

"It makes me feel special to know you intend to hold good on that." All kinds of snark in that statement.

The vampire winced as heavy raindrops spattered his face.

Lark sighed and stepped back. She would not invite him in. That was insanity. Yet he looked so pitiful. Like a wet kitten scamming for a pat on the head. If she even began to relate him to the homeless menagerie she'd helped in the past...

"You're not hearing tunes right now?" she wondered.

"I'd hardly call them tunes. But no, no cats screeching in my brain. The whispers are there. Always prodding me. You going to invite me in?"

"I have no reason to."

"Can't we be civil to each other during the truce? I want to get to know you, Lark."

"I don't understand why."

"Because you're pretty, and feisty. And maybe I came so I can get my shirt back from you."

"It's not here. It was torn and—" had no scent beyond the smoke, which had frustrated her "—not wearable."

"It's one of few I own."

Struck by that confession, Lark swallowed back surprising guilt. Maybe the guy *was* homeless? And she'd taken his best shirt? Because what he was wearing now didn't look much better. The linen scarf and turtleneck looked thin. Though there were no holes in the jacket and he didn't smell like smoke now.

"Please," he said. He shook his head like a dog against the wet, yet it was that erratic shake that clued Lark he battled inner demons. "She's dangerous!" The vampire chuckled lowly, and slapped his arms across his chest as if to stave off the insane mirth.

"I am dangerous. And you…" she started.

Baffled her. Yet at the same time, the man's presence tugged at some inner threads that coiled about her heart, threads she'd thought severed and the ends singed.

Before her better judgment could strangle her conscience, Lark invited the vampire inside. Because he looked pathetic standing there with his goggles and burned skin and dripping hair. Damn her, but she'd never been able to walk past a stray kitten, either.

Rook would have harsh words for her if he discovered she'd invited a vampire into one of the Order's safe houses. Hell, the man would speak with his fist. He had never been averse to punching her while training.

Lark closed the door but clenched the doorknob, clenching her jaw as tightly as her fist. What was she doing? Had such merciless training taught her nothing? Getting friendly with a vampire—not even with the excuse to cozy up to the subject—was strictly forbidden. Vamps were known to charm and manipulate, yet beneath the sometimes sexy—or crazy—exterior, they were nothing but deadly predators.

Domingos wandered to the couch, but before he could sit she asked him not to. He flicked her a wondering look over his shoulder.

"You're filthy," she stated. "Your clothes look like something you dragged out of a Dumpster, and your hair… Hell. Why don't you clean yourself up?"

He shoved his hands into his pockets and, head down, simply stood there.

And Lark's shoulders wilted. Why must she be so cruel? The alley cat only wanted to be picked up and stroked, not scolded for his appearance. The man wasn't all there in the head. He probably didn't even comprehend his tattered attire. Fashion couldn't be a concern if he had in mind only to slay werewolves and, hell—to survive.

Lark straightened. This knight wasn't going to abandon her hard-earned training at the first pitiful meow from a stray. "Don't you have wolves to slay?"

"Thought I'd enjoy my free day," he muttered, looking longingly at the couch. "I'd clean up if you wanted me to."

Lark crossed her arms. "Is that so? You going sweet on a hunter, vampire?"

He shrugged. "I don't know the meaning of that word. Sweet. Heh. Only dark and heinous in my world lately. I am getting a bit scruffy. Call it camouflage. Helps me blend when I'm stalking wolves."

His chuckle was maniacal, and it set the hairs upright on Lark's arms. He jerked, as if with Tourette's, trying to shrug off the strange outburst.

Once, Todd had brought home a stranger who, due to his tics and constant shouts of nonsense words, she suspected had that very disease.

Oh, Lark, what would a little water and soap hurt?

It was apparent he was here for a visit, and she couldn't shove him right back out into the rain. And conversation was not tops on her list, especially not with the enemy. Best to put him to work.

She marched into the bathroom, grabbed a razor and strolled back out to hand it to him.

Why did she care?

She didn't. But this offer felt…familiar. As if she

was doing something that she was supposed to do—
something she'd once done willingly with her husband
at her side.

"I get it," Domingos said. "You need to clean me up
before you stake me. For reasons beyond my ken."

"I'm just offering a kindness, vampire. Take it or leave
it."

He snatched the razor and pointed to the bathroom.

"There's shaving cream in there and you can use the
towels. This place is stocked for men, so you'll find everything you need."

"An Order safe house?" he wondered as he strode into
the bathroom.

"I'll never tell. But you were never here. You know
nothing about this place. We didn't even talk. We've
never had a conversation. Got that?"

Silence.

Lark waited, listening for the water to run, or for some
sound that he was shaving. She slapped her arms over
her chest, and now her conscience jumped up from the
bleachers in revolt.

*What are you doing? Rook will banish you from the
Order. Todd would hate you for this. And you! Don't you
care about yourself? Because every moment you allow
him to intrude on your life he pulls the emotional threads
tighter and makes you...*

Feel.

Sighing, Lark remembered the stray kitten she'd
nursed for a few months when she was a teenager, only
to have it die from feline leukemia on her lap one rainy
fall evening. At least it had died safe and cared for.

And really? Todd wouldn't have hated her for this act
of kindness (though he would have raged to know the
benefactor of her kindness was a vampire). If Lark had

been the kitten magnet, it was Todd who had attracted the homeless. He had often taken in strangers. He'd bring them home, offer them a shave and a hot meal and then he'd send them off with a few crisp ten-euro notes in their pocket. Lark had always protested. They left a ring in the bathroom sink. They could be scoping the place out to later return and rob them. Todd would always dismiss her complaints, and later kiss away her protests and coax her into bed.

So here she stood. Razor secured in the homeless man's hand. Assuming her husband's role.

Dead husband. *He's not really your husband anymore, because he can't be if he no longer exists on this mortal plane. Right?*

Why did she cling to that label? *Husband.* It gave her no comfort to remember his last breaths. Nor did questioning whether or not she had truly loved him appease her aching heart.

She glanced down the hallway. Yesterday she had scuffled with the wily creature now lurking in her bathroom, and had almost taken a stake to the back of her skull. And today she was playing house with him?

Tilting her head back to prevent tears from spilling down her cheeks, Lark noticed Domingos stood in the bathroom doorway holding out the razor. Shaving cream frosted his chin and jaw.

Bother. "What's wrong?"

"I can't do this myself."

"Why not?" She walked into the bathroom and found he'd set out the shaving cream can on a towel draped over the sink. He moved in behind her and she looked up in the mirror. And saw nothing. "Oh."

The Order had taught her about a vampire's lacking reflection. She'd even used a compact mirror on a few occasions while out in the field to verify her marks before slaying them.

"Will you do it for me?" He offered the straight-edged blade that most barbers would sharpen along a leather strap.

She snatched the razor and looked along the keen edge. Sharper than the blades edging her coat collar. And a fine weapon, that with just a flick of her wrist—

"You would trust me with a blade to your neck?"

"Eight hours," he countered.

"Closer to seven now."

He sat on the toilet seat and lifted his chin. "I trust you."

"Me. A hunter?" She approached, hand to one hip, blade hand held up in challenge. "What if I'm a liar? Best way to lure the enemy to his death is through deception. That's Order rules 101."

"You're not lying to me now. I can feel you are impeccable in your manner and word." He tilted back his head and waited.

If only she had as much confidence in herself. Yet lies were a bane she despised. She lied rarely, and would never trust a person who she felt could lie to her.

Todd hadn't lied; she'd just never wanted to believe his truths.

For reasons beyond her grasp, Lark leaned forward and stroked the blade across Domingos's jaw. The steel glided smoothly over his skin, softened by the spice-scented shave cream. Turning to rinse the blade in the sink, she returned for a few more swipes. She was half finished before he spoke again.

"You've done this before."

"My husband used to let me shave him. He said it was a symbol of his trust."

"Just like I said. I trust you."

The blade wobbled near his bottom lip, but she avoided nicking him. The vampire grasped her gaze and Lark noticed an oddity. One eye was golden-brown, while the other was completely black.

"What happened to your eye?" she asked.

"I think my pupil got blown out, or something like that. UV light. Fuck, I hate it."

It must have happened when he'd been in captivity. "Does it hurt? Can you see out of that eye?"

"I can, but it's the first eye to freak out if I don't time the sunlight correctly. When the UVs hit my eyes, feels like a hot stiletto getting pushed through the pupils."

She didn't know what to say to that. *Details. You wanted details.*

No, she hadn't. Maybe? No.

Lark tended the other side of his jaw. He was still and calm; she was surprised at his composure after witnessing his ticlike behavior and his raging at the inner voices.

"You're not hearing voices now?" she wondered. "You seem pretty calm."

"Strange, isn't it? I'm not going to question. Though, as always, the whispers are present."

"Just don't start banging your head when I have the blade to your neck. Or do. It's no biggie to me if your death is accidental."

"You cutting my throat won't kill me. You know that, hunter. But maybe you like taking a vampire's blood, eh? Watching your victims bleed before you end their life?"

"Not at all. My kills are clean and quick. Never bloody, if it can be avoided. A well-placed stake reduces the vampire to ash."

"I'd expect that from you. Efficient and graceful when granting death."

She was about to protest that assessment. He didn't know her. She didn't *grant death;* she took out predators using skill and stealth, plain and simple.

What are you doing, Lark? Just get him shaved, stuff the euro bills in his pocket and send him on his way.

The vampire tilted his head to allow her access and closed his eyes, humming a few notes that she recognized as Mozart. *Eine Kleine Nachtmusik?* Interesting. And did his fingers tap the precise beat on his leg?

"Tell me about your husband. What happened to him?"

Startled by that question, Lark firmly gripped the curved metal handle of the blade before it could slice his skin.

With a deep inhale, she resumed calm. "Why do you assume something happened to him?"

"He's dead. Otherwise he'd be protecting you right now. That, I know."

A lucid assumption. This vampire was not crazy. Did he use the madness act to deflect from his true evil? If she had thought to keep her enemy close, he could be utilizing the *make them think you're not all there, and then strike* method.

Suddenly Domingos grabbed her wrist and thrust away her blade hand. She struggled, planting her feet and lowering her hips to focus her strength at her core. She'd guessed his plan exactly—but when a ragged moan came from between his gritted jaws and his eyes closed tightly she realized he was having another manic episode. Music in his head? Didn't sound so terrible if it was Mozart. But he'd said something about constant whispers. That sounded creepy.

"Damn it!" He kicked out a foot and clutched the sink with both hands, struggling against what seemed like his body wanting to rage and flail. "Get out!"

Lark backed toward the door.

"No! Stay! The voices—" He gasped and hung his head, heaving and breathing deeply. And with a chuckle that danced a rigid insanity, he looked up, then straightened, tilting his head up to expose the unshaved side of his neck. "Gone now."

Closing her eyes and breathing through her nose, Lark vacillated between tossing the blade into the sink and finishing the job. She didn't need this. Todd wasn't even alive, so what could he care if she showed kindness to a homeless man on his behalf? The vampire probably wasn't even homeless. He might own a fine estate and just didn't buy new clothing or have a care for his appearance.

"Please," Domingos said, "I'm good now. Finish?"

Heartbeat thundering, Lark exhaled and forced her body to stand upright from the defensive stance. Another inhale and she drew out the breath slowly as Rook had taught her to find her calm.

"You try me, vampire, and I will cut you."

"Fair enough." He tilted back his head.

And Lark returned the blade to his neck and slid it through the shaving cream. She wanted to do this more than she knew why the want existed. And the challenge of that ineffable desire kept her from ending this tense tête-à-tête with a rough dismissal.

"Your husband," he prompted. "You were going to tell me about him."

No, she was not.

And yet…

"Do you want me to arrange a visit with a psychiatrist? To talk about his death?"

Rook hadn't waited for her answer before nodding and suggesting the option was always there. The implied message had been that if she'd taken him up on his offer, that would prove her weakness. Women were not meant to be knighted into the Order.

She hadn't needed talk. Action had always worked best to soothe her aches, both physical and mental. Even after the horrible event early in their marriage—no, that was one thing she would not mentally revisit. She had enough on her plate as it was.

"He used to be in the Order," she said quickly. And then more words spilled out before her heart could rule against the confession. "Todd Cooper was one of the best hunters the Order had. Until vampires captured him and tortured him for a year and a day."

"Captivity hurts," Domingos said, emotionless and still.

"Yeah? So does sitting at the edge of a big bed every morning, looking over at the undisturbed side and wondering if your husband is still alive, or if he'll ever be set free."

She drew the blade across the last narrow patch of stubble and then tossed it into the sink with a clatter. "I'm done. Wash up. Take a shower, and toss out your clothes so I can burn them."

"I'll have nothing to wear."

"There's men's clothing in the bedroom. Help yourself. But don't linger in the shower. This is not your wake. I want you to leave as soon as you're dressed."

Chapter 5

The cool shower felt so good, Domingos had lingered, his scarred back facing the shower stream, but not more than twenty minutes, he suspected. On the other hand, who knew? He'd lost the ability to gauge time without a watch since his adventure in the pack complex had damaged his innate sense of place—his very sense of self.

Or maybe it was the phoenix who raced through his blood, urging him toward the crazy train, which required no ticket but guaranteed him a lifetime pass. Just thinking about that other part of him made him chuckle.

Rubbing himself dry with a towel, he wrapped it about his hips, then slipped down the hallway to the bedroom. Rain drooled down the windows behind sheer white curtains. He was disappointed not to find Lark in the quiet, undecorated room.

Wanting to find a woman lying on the bed in wait for you? You really have slipped a cog, LaRoque.

"All my cogs, actually," he muttered. "Heh."

He listened and heard her moving about in the living room.

Why was she being so kind to him? He was still amazed she'd invited him in. He could now enter this safe house whenever he wished. It was bizarre that she would offer such compassion when not long from now she'd wield a stake against him. Of course, she had mentioned something about luring the enemy in with kindness.

Didn't matter. She'd lose. He wouldn't like killing her in defense. Maybe he wouldn't have to. Perhaps he could injure her enough to keep her away from him. Because he wasn't ready to die when their daylong pact ran out at midnight. His death mustn't come until the rest of pack Levallois had suffered his wrath.

And after that? Come what may.

Wincing, because he hadn't been concentrating on blotting his back carefully he'd dragged the towel across the tender flesh, Domingos gritted his jaw to prevent crying out.

Shaking his head back and forth, he tried to hold off the screeching that always accompanied his pain, but he wasn't fast enough. His head filled with the horrid noise. So he shook his head harder, faster, trying to race the madness over the edge.

Slamming a palm to the closet door, he yowled.

Letting loose his voice allayed some of the dizzying noise. He waited, wondering if Lark would check on him after his outburst, but didn't hear movement.

No one cares about you. Get over it, vampire. Slay the rest of the pack, then disappear. That's how you have to do it.

Right. But he couldn't do it naked.

Domingos touched the clothing hanging in the closet. All the items were fashioned in black and dark gray fabrics. Suit coats and slacks. Sweaters and a few crisp, ironed shirts. There had been a time when he'd possessed fine things and had taken care for his appearance. He'd liked deep purples and forest-greens for shirts, colors of royalty and wonder.

Wonder had fled his life.

Even after he'd been transformed to vampire against his will five years ago, he'd continued the personal care regimen and had slowly accepted vampirism, inch by inch, confidently growing into the creature he'd become.

Thanks to Truvin Stone, who had taken him under his wing a month after his attack, he'd learned all he needed to know about vampires. Truvin had hooked him up with tribe Zmaj, and they had taken him in within a few months of his transformation. He'd almost felt a semblance of family and companionship for his fellow tribe mates.

Monsters? No, his kind were simply a breed apart from mortals. He had been *this close* to grasping pride for his vampiric condition.

Until he'd walked right into a pack of smirking werewolves.

Pressing his face against the fine clothing, Domingos wondered over his thoughts. They were so clear. The mind-creasing whispers had left as if on tiptoes. Rarely did that happen, unless he was focused on tracking a wolf. Focus was the key to touching sanity.

Did Lark's presence alleviate the cacophony? Did it somehow enter his brain and push out the rubbish and twisted shrapnel?

"Can't be that easy," he said, clutching at a shirtsleeve. "Never that easy."

A black shirt loosened from the hanger, and he decided to go with it. He fumbled with the tiny pearlescent buttons, but managed to get it halfway buttoned from neck to midchest. He searched for a pair of jeans, but the most casual he could find were a pair of black leather pants, which fit him well, though they hung low on his hips. He'd lost weight while in captivity, and didn't feel quite like the man he'd once been.

Make that *vampire*.

When tossed in the ring and surrounded by bloodthirsty werewolves, he'd learned to scrap, to fight dirty in order to preserve his life. No man would claim pride for the things he had done to survive. Yet he must own the heinous acts he'd committed. Besides, he'd gained the strength of a phoenix, and so he'd worry about his physical shortcomings some other time.

Back in the bathroom, he claimed his goggles, draping them around his neck, then decided to comb through his hair. It took a while, because even though he'd shampooed, his hair was horribly snarled. Bet he'd scared the shit out of Lark kissing her last night.

No, she's a hunter. Tough girl like that can take anything.

Even your unwanted kisses.

He wished she hadn't reacted so offensively to his kiss. But why should he have expected anything even close to acceptance?

"Well, that's a one hundred percent improvement." Lark leaned against the bathroom door frame.

He set down the comb and spread out his arms for her to inspect. "I feel like a new bit of tatter."

"You look great."

He rubbed his smooth jaw, momentarily forgetting

his real life, and taking on the suave he'd once possessed around women. "You think I'm handsome?"

Her dark brow quirked above eyes that were so dark he couldn't determine if they were midnight-blue or moss-deep-emerald. Lark, of the sparkling eyes and naturally rosy lips.

Not a bird. Don't crush her. Or do! Yes, crush the mortal hunter—

"I'll give you handsome," she said, and strolled back into the living room.

"Really?" Had she just pronounced him attractive?

Domingos followed eagerly, a puppy that had been tossed a bone, and then he realized he was acting like a puppy that had just been patted on the head and he assumed a nonchalant, careless posture, not meeting her eyes. He could do casual with the best of them. "How much time left?"

"Six hours, give or take. Enough to give you a good head start. You going to leave?"

"Do you want me to?" *Please say no. Don't reject me.*

"I need to shower, eat and…get things in order."

That was a yes. It sure as hell hadn't been a no.

"Now that I'm clean it'll be harder to track my scent. Or wait." He sniffed the air, noting the fruity scent. "Now I understand. You had me shower and use that smelly cherry shampoo so now you can track me even better. Well played, hunter. Very clever."

"Leave, Domingos. I can't do this."

"Do what?"

"Be friendly with the guy on my hit list. It's not working."

"I think it is working."

"It's not supposed to work!"

"And you are losing your cool."

He stepped up to her, his bare feet landing on the rough, flat rug before the sofa. He stood but inches from her body, defying her to look him in the eye, to see that he had once been like her. Human. Capable of emotion and—hell, all those other things he couldn't grasp at the moment.

"Don't do that."

"Stop me," he defied, not sure if she would stand good on her word, but prepared to go on the defense if she did not. "Does the big bad vampire with the broken fangs scare you?"

"Nothing scares me anymore."

"Anymore? What used to scare you, Lark?" He took another step, and she didn't back away, boldly holding position. He liked the challenge of her. It kept back the whispers. "Monsters under the bed?"

"Please."

"Snakes? Spiders? Creepy crawlies?"

After a thoughtful pause, she said, "Falling."

He noted her cool composure. Truly, not scared. She was a trained killer, through and through. And yet he'd just peeled back a thin layer from her hard exterior. "So, on the roof last night?"

She nodded.

"That's the only reason I was able to kiss you. Because you were afraid of falling."

"You think I'd ask to be kissed by a man with fangs?"

He ran his tongue along a fang, cursing the fact that he could not will them up as any normal vampire could. UV sickness had really worked a number on him.

A violin screeched in his brain. He caught his head against a palm.

"What is it?"

"Nothing but my own madness. Time to leave you."

As if mocking him, the violin played a series of notes that mimicked what he'd just spoken. "But not without one final plea for my life."

Domingos slid his arms around Lark's back. Pulling her to him, he bowed to kiss her. He wished his fangs were not down, but so be it. He was bruised, broken and beyond repair. The hunter would have to deal with it. He did not want to risk cutting her and tried his best not to let the fangs graze her lips too hard.

Warm in his embrace, her body felt liquid and bright, something that would never again be his to own. Tender, yet strong, she was a prize he had not earned, could never rightfully own.

When she gasped, he opened her mouth with his, but did not dash out his tongue. Too presumptuous. And the danger of poking her was real. He pressed a palm to her jaw and bowed his forehead against hers.

"Too sweet," he murmured. "Never again mine."

Dashing for the door, Domingos fled the temptation of softness that had been stripped from his life by the werewolves' heartless blood games.

"He said he didn't know what sweet was," Lark said as she stroked a finger over her mouth. The rasp of his parting words had brushed her jaw and she still felt the tingle of that touch warming her skin.

Twice now the enemy had kissed her. And she couldn't deny that her curiosity for the enigmatic vampire was growing stronger.

A kiss could be used to manipulate—by both of them. But she sensed no untoward intentions from Domingos. And that worried her. Because she liked a challenge. She *needed* that challenge to feel pride for a job well done.

If the vamp was just going to stand back and let her at him with stake at the ready, what was the thrill in that?

As well, it mattered little whether she liked him or despised the very marrow in his breed's bones; if the vampire wouldn't stop kissing her she'd never be able to stake him. Never would she be able to move on to number seventy-three, and seventy-four, and so on. She'd be stuck, paused.

Because a kiss…? Well. Such intimacy. Their bodies needn't even touch, only their mouths, breathing, tasting, granting permission. And in such a startling manner. She honestly did not know how to deal with it.

Lark closed the door and leaned against it. "What do I do now?"

Rook would slap her soundly and tell her to get a grip. If Todd were still alive he would—

"No," she whispered. "He's gone. When can I finally bury him so that my heart can move on?"

Only after she'd achieved her goal. A goal that had suddenly stalled at number seventy-two.

Chapter 6

Lark snapped upright on the sofa. The digital alarm on her cell phone played the opening notes to the Brandenburg concerto. Earlier in the evening she'd set it to go off at midnight, knowing she was tired and would probably doze after she'd showered and ordered in Greek.

With the stoic resignation she'd gained during her training, she turned off the alarm and padded into the bedroom. Behind a secret door in the closet she found full Order gear: Kevlar-lined leather trousers, Kevlar vest over a T-shirt, cleric's coat and leather gloves. Inside the coat and around her belt she wore three titanium stakes, a syringe filled with holy water (worked on baptized vamps), a pistol with silver bullets (would kill a werewolf but only slow down a vampire) and numerous nonstandard-issue blades that she'd used more often than any of the other weapons.

She had no idea whether or not Domingos had been

baptized. Didn't matter. The physical fight was her strong point. Up close and in their face was the only way to bring vampires down. Rook often chided her for taking the risk of putting herself so close to the opponent, but she'd argued that staking required close contact anyway, so why stake them and make it easy when a fight served to ignite her need for vengeance?

The physical struggle actually soothed something deep in her soul. It was the only way she could do what she did. And if she began to question her motivations, then she'd be lost.

She pulled her straight black hair into a tight ponytail and fluffed her bangs. A little eyeliner and some lip gloss (just because she was on the hunt didn't mean she had to look like a pale ghost), and then she stepped into the pair of running shoes she'd packed. The soles on these had better traction than the Doc Martens she normally wore. The boots were outfitted with hinged blades she utilized often during the fight, but tonight she wanted stealth.

Because she knew exactly where to look for Domingos LaRoque.

She locked the front door and strode down the outer walkway that hugged the building, and headed back inside to the main hallway. Smoothing away a strand of hair from her mouth, she touched her lips and experienced a flash of kissing the vampire, of feeling his seeking mouth against hers and of not at all reacting defensively to the hard slide of his fangs. He'd had to be careful not to cut her. At the moment she'd felt the fangs her blood had run cold, and yet the kiss had been too amazing for her to want him to stop.

As had been their first kiss up on the roof. After her initial horror, that is.

Lark sighed and shook her head miserably. It had been

too long since she'd been kissed if she was thinking vampire kisses rocked. Either that or crazy was a communicable disease.

She tugged open the roof-access door and made her way up the rubber-padded concrete stairs, stealthily, a stake gripped at her side. She emerged in the warm summer night air. Moonlight sparkled on the tin eaves, but Lark didn't admire the beauty. Instead she strode over to the man sitting on the mansard roof, leaning back on his elbows, bare toes jutting over the edge.

"Thought I'd find you here."

"According to the last church bells I heard, it's past midnight," he said without looking up at her. "Time's up."

Now the moonlight would not allow her to ignore the beauty surrounding her—and that right in front of her. The vampire had cleaned up well. Lark had never been interested in men with long hair—or vampires, for that matter—and had always preferred clean-cut blonds. The fresh-from-the-beach-volleyball-game and I'm-so-healthy-I-beam look appealed to her standards for health and fitness. Maybe it was Domingos's straight nose, or the way the shadows played across his newly shaven jaw? Couldn't be the fangs that peeked out between his lips. Nor could it be the pale, almost translucent skin that reminded her of pearls and fine things Lark had once liked to lay against her skin.

Something about him…

Then again, this one would never enjoy the sun on a sandy beach anytime soon.

"You're making this too easy." She stalked over to him, straddled his outstretched legs and crouched, slamming the flat base of the stake against his chest. The knights called their stake the death punch. She liked that term.

Lark peered into his unflinching gaze, not expecting him to return a defiant look, and he did not. "Say good-bye, vampire."

"Goodbye, vampire."

"I'm serious. I thought you wanted to live."

"I do. I have over a dozen werewolves left to take out."

"Then what if I promised not to stake you if you promise to leave the rest of pack Levallois alone?"

What was she saying?

"Can't do that," Domingos said. He eyed the stake. "I stand by my word, as I would expect you to stand by yours."

Lark gritted her teeth, gripping the stake more firmly. All it required was one squeeze of her fingers about the paddles and the spring-loaded stake would eject out from the cylinder. The power of the release was so forceful it always bounced her fist upon the victim's chest. It needed to be that strong to permeate fabric, flesh, bone and finally, the thick, sinewy heart muscle.

Once the vampire's heart burst, it was dead. There was no coming back from a stake through the heart. She certainly didn't believe the urban legend about the one vampire who had survived a stake by keeping it in and allowing it to slowly heal, thus pushing out the stake.

"Lark?"

Why she had given him her name was beyond her reason. Too intimate, that. Almost as intimate as a kiss.

Domingos's eyes were soft, glittering with the gorgeous moonlight that managed to clear a way through the leftover rain clouds. Feeling her neck and throat flush hotly from his insistent regard, Lark strained to move her fingers. To squeeze the paddles. To finish him right here and now.

If only he wouldn't look at her like that, with just the

hint of a curve to his mouth to reveal fang and a decidedly wry smirk. Only one other man had possessed such a devastating smirk. It had been enough to cloud her eyes from his dangerous profession and fall blindly into his charms. To give up her plans to become a professional musician touring with a symphony. To believe that they could do the family thing and make it work. To hope that they could simply exist for one another.

Never again would charm seduce her. Not to the same end she'd had to bring her husband. It hadn't been right, she being forced to such a thing. And it was all because of creatures like Domingos.

"Ah!" She thrust herself away from the vampire and, turning, sat, clasping the stake to her chest. Todd's charming smile was right there, so close she could touch it, feel it, remember the way it had made her heart go pitter-patter. Until his smile had been lost, stolen by torture.

She was right there now, in the middle of the kitchen, kneeling on the tiled floor next to Todd. He'd been left at the doorstep an hour earlier. The man she had worried over for a year and a day writhed in agony on the floor, his clothing in tatters upon his emaciated form. Wounds on his forehead, arms and legs angered Lark. He'd been lashed. Over and over.

But those weren't the most troubling wounds. Two puncture marks on his neck told her what the pain would not allow him to put into words.

Until he did speak—and then it was to beg.

"He begged me to kill him," she gasped out.

"Your husband?" Domingos guessed. He hadn't moved, and looked out across the rooftops that featured jagged spines silhouetted against the sky. "Why would he beg for such a thing?"

"Because they'd bitten him," she said tightly. "He was

going to transform into a vampire. The blood hunger was too strong to fight. To become a creature who feeds upon human blood was the last thing he could bear. So he begged me for hours to stake him, to end his agony."

Todd's moans had wended through her veins, cringing into her bones, until she'd crouched against the wall and had covered her ears with her hands. She hadn't been able to look at him, and so he'd crawled up to her and slapped the titanium stake into her hand.

"Did you?" Domingos asked softly. "Stake him?"

Lark bent her head against her knees and squeezed her arms about her legs, not willing to voice the obvious reply. Tears did not come, because she'd cried more than a lifetime's worth over the year and a day that her husband had been in captivity. Yet her body shuddered, racked by the pain that could not manifest.

She didn't deserve forgiveness. Rook and the Order certainly hadn't given it to her. She didn't need it, didn't want it. She'd done what had to be done. The cruel act had become her cross to bear, and she understood that.

But that didn't mean it didn't torture her as much as she believed her husband had been tortured. All as a means to prove to the Order that they, the vampires, would not stand for the Order's brand of vigilante justice.

But if the Order did not police the vampires, then who would? The Council? The little Lark knew about that organization of paranormals who oversaw the paranormal realms was that they watched, and rarely intervened. They would never act against one of their own simply because he'd slain a mortal to feed his blood lust.

Lark felt a hand on her arm. Or maybe Domingos brushed the end of her ponytail. The vampire's touch didn't land on her for long, just testing, making the briefest yet cruelest contact.

The longtooth bastards had never touched Todd so gently.

She flipped her hair over a shoulder and pounded the slate tiles with a fist. Through gritted teeth, she growled, "Would you get the hell away from me?"

"You don't own the roof. I can sit where I want to." Domingos leaned back on his elbows, stretching out his legs and crossing one ankle over the other. He wiggled his toes. The Order clothing fit him well, and— She wasn't going to admire him. "Do *I* bring all this bad stuff up from inside your tender little soul?"

"Tender?" She scoffed. "It has nothing to do with you, vampire."

"You're lying."

"You think yourself far more important than others do, obviously."

"I am the least important thing to walk this world. Insignificant."

"Save me the self-pity. We all have our crosses."

"And yours is dragging through my path to salvation."

"Poetic."

"Just making an observation." He rapped the tiles smartly. "I don't like to see you sad."

"You don't even know me."

"You are my death," he said softly.

His words fluttered over her skin like something fragile, too delicate to hold without breaking further.

"Yeah?" Lark dismissed the ridiculous image. "If I'm your death, you don't look too worried. I can take you out, vampire. I'm just a little…off…tonight. I'm tired. I've only slept a few hours."

"Then we should reconvene tomorrow night. Same roof? Same stake?"

Lark smiled wearily, then tucked her head against her

elbow, looking over her arm at him. His crazy smile wasn't so much insane as charming, and charming promised nothing good for her.

"I can't figure you out," she said. "I can see the madness. But I also see a soul behind your fucked-up eyes."

"I bet you've never looked into the eyes of your victims before you stake them, eh?"

"It's not very smart. Track 'em and take 'em out. That's the way of it. Live to serve. Serve until death. Die fighting."

"Is that the Order's motto? Special. You gotta love an organization that has its own kick-ass yet self-sacrificing motto."

Lark was amused but couldn't manage a smile. It was true. The knights kicked ass and sacrificed all for the cause. Rarely did the knight have a family and friends, though certainly Todd had tried. He had known his job demanded all. He just hadn't realized a family life would demand as much of him. Nor had she.

"How'd a chick ever get accepted into the Order?"

"By proving I was worthy."

"I wager you had to go above and beyond to do that. Even the most pro-feminist of men have a hard time accepting that a woman could stand as his equal. I heard a rumor that a real king heads your little death club."

"That is a rumor. His code name is King. That's it. And the Order didn't want to accept me—they knew the story with me and Todd—but I barged in on training one day and wouldn't leave even when I was forcibly removed. I just kept going back, until finally they tolerated me. I was determined. Still am."

"To make all the vampires pay for what happened to your husband?"

"Damn right."

"Even though none of the ones you kill are directly related to his death?"

"Vampires are ruthless killers. Present company included."

Yet Lark's fingers flinched on the stake as she said that. That hadn't been a lie to herself, had it?

"I will accept that I have become what the werewolves have forced me to become—a broken bit of fang and flesh. A monster," Domingos said with a confidence that poked at Lark's heart. "But I was not always this way. I had embraced my unasked-for vampirism and had been living without suspicion among the mortals. Yet now, unlike you, I am only taking revenge against those who were directly related to my capture, imprisonment and torture."

"And that proviso redeems your heinous crimes?"

"We were talking about your heinous crimes, Lark. The last time I heard of a group dedicated to exterminating an entire race, well…"

He let the accusation hang. Lark knew what he insinuated. It was a cruel comparison. But was it? She'd never given the idea of exterminating an entire race much thought before. And to do so now…

Was the Order a death club?

Don't let his big sad crazy act get to you. You weren't able to stake him tonight because you got too close. You should have never looked into his eyes. Step back. Distance yourself and get Todd the hell out of your brain or you'll never accomplish this challenge.

"So, until tomorrow?" Domingos held out a hand for her to shake.

Lark stared at the offering. *Don't cross that line. He's manipulating you. You're smarter than that.*

When she didn't reach to shake his hand, he leaned in, grasped her hand and shook it. Lark tugged away.

Domingos moved swiftly, lunging over her and pinning her back flat onto the roof with his body, one knee to her thigh, but not so roughly that she couldn't shove him off.

Lark did not push the predator away.

He gripped her by the head, and she saw her death by broken neck flash before her eyes. Better than the fang, she thought wistfully, because that would be too much to live down should the Order learn she'd been taken out by the tooth.

The vampire kissed her. Hard. His fangs cut her lip, and as the minute pain and blood trickled into her mouth, she struggled against him. She did not want him to taste her blood. He would not relent, deepening the kiss, invading her with his tongue and making her want what she should not want—the hardness of him, the utter urgency, his desperation.

So like you. Too much like you? Or just close enough to understand?

Ceasing her struggles, Lark clutched at his borrowed shirt, pulling him onto her and hooking a leg over one of his. He moaned at her rough acceptance. It was too easy to fall into the moment, to take what she needed. Connection. Unrelenting desire. A slap in the face to those who hadn't believed in her capabilities.

She'd always made the right choices. Her decision to marry Todd had been encouraged by her mother after she had learned he'd graduated summa cum laude from Princeton in the States. (She'd not told her mother she was pregnant.) Todd had told her mother he had studied to be a lawyer. All lies. But she'd had to get married. It hadn't been a necessity, but a surprise pregnancy had prompted a proposal, which she had gratefully accepted.

She hadn't wanted to face life and all its struggles alone.

Why had she allowed that lie to linger over her life?

Charm, a tiny voice whispered. *You're not a nun, and just like any other woman, you can be won with seduction and promises of a happy future. He was going to keep you safe. Keep your family safe.*

Even after the miscarriage, Lark had played the devoted housewife. She'd loved Todd. But the choices they'd made within the marriage had not involved her life. She'd done everything for Todd, to accept his secret job, to put up a smiling face when he returned home after two, sometimes three days' absence, to simply please him. And he had been pleased.

But the right choices regarding her pleasure? She didn't even know what that meant. Because she'd known the truth of Todd before marrying him and, despite her reluctance, had gone through with it. For family—a family that had never been given a chance to begin.

Domingos's breath was hot upon her lips as he kissed the corner of her mouth. She devoured what he gave her, pulling him closer, drawing him down and begging him with a silent acceptance. He pulled her out of her irritating need to do right by others and plunged her deep into the unknown. The forbidden. The impossibly wrong.

Kissing down her chin and to her jaw—he hissed and retracted from the intimate exploration. Blood dripped from his lip. The blades at her collar had served their purpose.

Gripping her coat, he pulled it open and pushed back the lapels to expose her neck. Eyes wild, he caressed her skin, tapping her carotid with a fingertip. The glint in his eyes spoke of something completely different than passion. Had the madman emerged? Or was it simply the vampire who needed human blood to survive?

"Give me a day," Lark hastened out.

He tilted his head, wondering. Blood from his cut lip trickled onto her throat. The creature temporarily subdued, wanting to hear her out before tearing open her neck.

"A day without biting me in exchange for another day without staking you," she offered.

"Deal." He kissed her hard and quickly.

Too quickly Lark's dangerous plunge into the unknown, the free fall into the forbidden, ended.

Pulling away and standing, Domingos stepped over the top of her head and ran along the spine of the roof, an aerial acrobat of the night. He was off to hunt werewolves. She knew it as she knew the taste of her own blood in her mouth.

A crazy new torture had entered her life.

And she had opened the door wide and invited it in.

Chapter 7

The wolf didn't see him coming. The idiot dog stood outside at the back of an SUV, arms crossed over his chest, eyes closed. He was probably dozing on his feet, waiting for a passenger or not.

Domingos had tracked him from the fifth quarter rooftop, where he'd left the female knight, to this dark street behind a redbrick warehouse with few windows, and those windows were barred with iron rods. He didn't want to think about what could be contained behind those caged windows, but he suspected captive vampires a likely possibility.

If so, they needed help.

Domingos wasn't a superhero. He couldn't save anyone but himself. And he'd never get back to saving himself until all in the Levallois pack had fallen.

For once the whispers in his head agreed. The wolves needed to die.

Lunging for the wolf, he slashed the silver blade he'd pinched from the hunter through the air and brought it down hard across the wolf's chest, diagonally from shoulder to hip. The blade sank in deep and he felt little resistance as it cut through rib bones. The silver would enter the bloodstream, and before the wolf could even open his eyes—

The phoenix inside Domingos let out a maniacal chuckle and reached inside the wolf's gaping wound, punching through rib bones, and gripped the moon-dog's heart. He jerked out his hand and thrust the slippery organ to the ground, where it landed beneath the SUV's front grille.

The creature clasped at his chest and growled. He swore at Domingos, and stepped forward once, but that was the last step the wolf could manage.

The cut gaped and the wolf bent over backward, arms flailing madly. Then its body collapsed and began to boil from inside. Within minutes the silver poisoning would reduce the dog to nothing but a mass of goopy flesh and bone. The heart on the ground had been spared the silver poisoning and would remain intact.

Nasty mess for the mortal police to find, but that wasn't Domingos's problem. Most good paranormals called in a cleaner to take care of their messes. He'd never claim even a portion of good.

Wiping his bloodied hand down the front of his shirt, he kicked a stone at the SUV's tire, then peered inside the vehicle. No other wolves. But this was a pack car. He could smell the mangy scent indicative of Levallois. It was something he'd never get out of his head, that horrid feral odor of twisted entitlement and the thirst to watch blood be spilled.

He eyed the warehouse. What he hadn't noticed when

reconning from the rooftops, he did now—smoke billowed out from a barred window.

"No," he whispered. The utterance wasn't out of fear, but rather in answer to his rising conscience to protect those inside who were weaker. "Not my place to consider a rescue attempt. Never again."

Stringed instruments howled inside his brain, doubling Domingos over before the warehouse. He clutched his hair and tugged, gritting back the yowl that he wouldn't give the dying werewolf the satisfaction of hearing. Slamming his head against the brick wall, he pounded his skull with a fist.

The phoenix wanted to turn around and kick the wolf, rage at the indignities it had been served.

The vampire in him pleaded for the compassion the mortal man he'd once been had possessed—and won.

Domingos ran inside the building. Smoke siphoned into his throat, making him choke, but he pushed onward and passed a man who was on his way toward the open doorway. The wolf didn't notice him as he raced out to the car, yelling about a fire.

Go get him!

Domingos paused inside the threshold, smoke fogging about his legs and hands. *One more kill,* the phoenix whispered. So close. So easy. He could jump the wolf from behind and slash its throat, then roll it over to dig out the heart.

A yowl from inside the warehouse skittered up his spine and annihilated the screeching violin chord that had haunted him for months. Twisting down and pressing the crown of his head against the wall, he clutched at the wall and tried to press his skull through the wood.

There were others inside. Vampires, he suspected. Fire

would not kill them, but the flame would damage them irreparably. Drive them mad, surely.

No man deserved the madness he carried in his soul. A quick death—hell, the stake—was preferable to madness.

Domingos turned and ran through the smoke until he collided with iron cage bars.

Curiosity had prompted her to follow the vampire after their rooftop bargain had sealed their fates for another twenty-four hours. Lark had watched him kill the were-wolf with unflinching grace. Not a blink, nor a wince. As if dashing a mark in the air, he'd drawn the silver blade down the wolf's chest. And then he'd torn out its heart and tossed it aside. Cold. Unrepentant.

It's how you *do it.*

How she used to do it before she'd met Domingos. Never had it taken her so long to accomplish an elimi-nation.

"I'm losing it," she muttered. "He's throwing me off my game."

He, being the vampire she seemed to prefer kissing over staking. What was her problem? If watching him rip out some werewolf's heart wasn't enough to fortify her determination to slay him, then nothing else could.

Yet she'd watched Domingos vacillate about approach-ing the smoking building, and when finally he'd walked toward it, her heart had beat faster and her fingers had clasped about the iron railing in anticipation. He'd paused at the threshold, thrashing his head about and fighting some inner demons that she couldn't understand, and then he'd rushed into the flames.

He'd been in the burning building five minutes. Fire engine sirens trilled about a mile off. Would they find a dead vampire inside? Fire couldn't kill a vampire, only melt off his skin, a wound that would probably never completely heal, even though their breed was known to regenerate masterfully and could even regrow a severed limb, according to the Order's teachings.

Lark believed that as much as she believed vampires had a moral compass.

Yet her gasp stifled her harsh thoughts. A tall dark-haired man stumbled out from the burning building, dragging two men behind him by their arms.

"Domingos. He rescued them?"

Clasping the cold railing to keep from rushing down the iron stairs to hug him, Lark chided her ridiculously romantic heart. Heroes did not exist. They belonged in movies and books, not real life. The vampire must have an ulterior motive for doing something so selfless. She had just watched him murder without conscience!

He dropped the men on the sidewalk and rushed back inside, disappearing into the black smoke that raged like storm clouds. The men on the street managed to stand, and one of them grabbed the other and they ran away as the sirens loomed closer.

"Vampires?" she wondered.

That could be the reason the werewolf had been standing outside, like a posted guard. The Levallois pack? Made sense. Domingos had been set on killing only members of that pack. For revenge.

Just like you, Lark. How can you fault him?

She didn't fault him. But that didn't mean she condoned his actions. So he'd saved lives. *Vampire* lives. Vampires who should have burned, for all Lark cared.

A twinge of remorse pinched at her spine. When had she become so cold?

"Stupid question, Lark."

Domingos emerged in a cloud of dark smoke with a

man's body draped across his shoulder. He set him down on the sidewalk and slapped his face, rousing the vampire who must have inhaled smoke, yet who seemed to rally with a few deep breaths of fresh air.

The fire truck rounded the corner, and both men took off, Domingos tugging along the one he'd rescued. Wouldn't be wise, or easy, to explain to a fire brigade why the smoke hadn't killed them, or at the very least, knocked them out. And most certainly vampires would have to refuse mortal medical care.

And then there was the mass of dead werewolf on the ground before the SUV—and that still-beating heart.

"He's not so crazy, after all."

Tugging out her cell phone, Lark dialed up Tor, the Order's spin doctor. Generally, when a crime scene contained remains, such as the werewolf, or in other cases, partially ashed vampires, the knight contacted Tor and he arrived to smooth things over with the public and any reporters who might be nosing about.

The dead werewolf—and the heart lying under the truck—would definitely require some spin.

Lark returned to find Rook waiting inside the safe house. His salt-and-pepper hair that teased at gentle curls was slicked back over his ears, and a scar at the corner of his left eye lifted it higher than the other, giving him a shifty appearance, even though she knew the man was all about honor and integrity. Armani business suits, always, and shoes so highly polished she wondered if he spent more time on those than, say, waxing his car, which was something ridiculously expensive and probably rare. She had learned he appreciated the finer things in life and could afford them easily.

She didn't like the guy, but she didn't hate him, either.

Respect was due, and he had earned that from her. Rook had not once given her a break during her training—not that she'd expected one. The man was the only means for a member of the Order to speak to King. You had to go through Rook to get anything, and he kept a tight fist on all operations. He had a way of looking at her—at anyone—and seeing her truth. She suspected he wasn't mortal, yet she had never dared ask him what he was or how he was able to divine truths.

She'd been knighted by King but hadn't been personally introduced to him during that brief ceremony. Didn't know the founder's name, beyond which, she again suspected, was code: King. Didn't know if in fact he was or had been a king, as was the rumor. The other rumor whispered about the Order was that their leader was actually a vampire. She always stopped herself from trying to figure out if it was truth. To know she was working for the one breed she hated most? Well. It just didn't jibe.

She'd only just spoken with Tor, so she suspected he wouldn't have had time to report to Rook yet, and so decided to keep the information about the fire need-to-know right now.

"Rook."

He set down the cup of coffee he'd brewed. *Sure, make yourself at home.* Wasn't as if it was her home. He'd probably already searched the closet and the bathroom, inspecting for God knows what. Good thing she'd cleaned the shower, washed the towels and adjusted the clothing in the closet after Domingos had left. So she'd never lost her domestic bone; sue her.

Lark sat on the sofa and slid the coat off her shoulders.

"Hard night slaying?" he asked.

"You could say that."

"You smell like smoke." The man didn't miss an eyelash. But he had to be mortal. On the other hand, mortals weren't always what they appeared. That much she had learned while studying the paranormal breeds during training. "Kill Domingos LaRoque?"

"Couldn't find him."

The lie didn't make her feel as awful as she expected it should, and yet Rook's tense jaw clued he might suspect her deception. The vampire had performed a heroic act not an hour earlier. He deserved a little slack. And she intended to stand good on her word, regardless of how crazy making a bargain—twice—with a vampire had been.

"I intend to go out after I've had some rest," she said. "If he's so allergic to daylight, he'll be holed up somewhere soon enough. Might give me a chance to stake him when he's down. Did you find any known addresses for him?"

"Research turned up some interesting stuff, but no address after five years ago. He disappeared off the face of the earth after he became vampire."

That was interesting. He'd not been vampire even a decade? And had he alluded to being made a vampire against his will when they'd spoken on the roof? "What does the research show?"

"You've never asked for details before. Why this time? Why is this particular vampire eluding our best hunter with an ease that is embarrassing?"

"I'm not embarrassed. He's giving me a good chase. For once. Most vampires are too easy. Spot 'em and smoke 'em. I rarely break a sweat."

Rook smirked. "I'll give you that. But I am embarrassed for myself, the Order and you. I trained you, Lark. You're better than this."

Yes, she was. *You never should have looked into his eyes.*

"Before he became vampire," Rook continued, "Domingos LaRoque was a musician."

A musician was giving her a good chase. Okay, now she was a little embarrassed. "What did he play?"

"Is that important?"

She shrugged. "No." But she was a musician, and the tidbit intrigued.

"Cello," Rook offered with disinterest. "He was a much-sought-after guest with symphonies and had worked on some sound tracks but never achieved a fame that would have made him a household name. Seems he preferred anonymity when working with others."

"Music. Interesting."

Lark thought of her violin she'd had to leave behind, and how she desperately wanted to pick it up to play. It was her one escape from reality and a sure balm to her aching soul. She hoped if the wolves had returned to her apartment they hadn't smashed it. That would prove plain vindictive. "I just got a call from Principal Caufield a minute before you arrived here."

Why was everyone up and about in the middle of the night?

"And?" She knew what he'd say and tucked her head against her chest to avoid eye contact.

"LaRoque has killed another pack member."

Yes, but she felt sure the pack leader had neglected to mention that wolf had been standing guard before a smoking building filled with vampires.

"I don't need to tell you how angry Principal Caufield is. He thought he'd hired a professional." Rook leaned over her. His breath reeked of coffee. She could feel the tension in his fingers, gripping her knee. "*Did* he hire a professional? Or did he hire a little girl who likes it when her prey leads her on a good chase?"

Calling her "little girl" was how he'd taunted her throughout training. The little girl hadn't strength to stand up to a vicious vampire. Little girls don't like to get their hair mussed. Little girls should go play with their dolls and makeup and leave slaying to the men. Little girls cry over dead husbands.

That had been the last teardrop she'd allowed any man to witness.

"I'll get the job done." Lark straightened and lifted her chin.

"Good. I know you are a woman of your word. Your apartment has been cleaned and restored. It's warded against werewolves, vampires and witches."

"Witches?"

"Thought I'd throw that in as a bonus. Though I personally have nothing against witches, they can be terrible to deal with. So you can return. Which is fortunate. I need this place for a visiting dignitary."

"Give me five minutes to gather my things and I'll be gone."

"I'll give you one more day, Lark, before I pull you off this job and replace you with Gunnar."

He walked out, leaving the door open.

Lark swung a fist after him. The one man she wanted to punch in the nose was the only man she had to respect. But she had to put up with him only until her revenge was complete. Then she was hanging up her stake and leaving the country to start a new life.

Chapter 8

Hood pulled over his head and goggles in place, Domingos squatted behind a chimney on the shady side of Lark's rooftop. The rain kept the sky gray, but it was morning and he was prepared should the sun suddenly peek out. Not ten feet away from where he stood, the roof door was open a crack.

The risks of exposure outweighed ignoring the call to be close to Lark. Yet he couldn't seem to keep away from the sultry hunter whose mouth tasted like a treat he'd never before imagined tasting and whose skin smelled like a brightness he could never again view. Such dalliance with the enemy wasn't proving a problem. He'd managed to slay the wolf last night, and gotten a few vampires to safety to boot. He was on top of his game.

Heh.

The game was swallowing him whole. But he wouldn't allow himself to become a pawn. Instead he'd control the board and go down screaming at the voices in his head. It was the only way to win.

Here on the roof he felt some solace. The strangled music in his head was eerily absent, which he associated with being near Lark. Had to be. His thoughts hadn't been so noise-free in months. And if she truly was the reason for it, he was damn well not going to stray too far from her.

She'd moved back into her apartment hours earlier, and Domingos could sense the wards against him. So long as there were also wards against the werewolves, he didn't mind so much. It was the smart move to make, and she was no idiot. Unless he counted fraternizing with him, which really blew her off the scale of Not Smart.

He could pick up her heartbeat below as she moved from where he knew her bedroom was and into the living room. He wondered what she was wearing. The night he'd grabbed her from her bedroom to keep her from the wolves, she'd worn nothing but pants and a bra. The hunter was hot. Sexy. Agile and deadly, yet sensual and soft like one of those fantasy paintings that depicted a warrior woman with an impossible weapon.

He wanted to have sex with her, to bring his skin tight against hers and feed off her warmth, her sleek, toned curves and wanting moans. Because he knew she would moan in his arms, gifting him sweet murmurs of pleasure to feed his desires.

But more so, he wanted to taste her blood beyond the droplet he'd tasted during their rooftop kiss. Would it be as sweet? Dark and thick? Perhaps fresh and bold like a young wine? Blood tasted vastly different from person to person, depending on diet and lifestyle. Domingos imagined Lark's blood would be not too thick and not too thin, sweet, but perhaps laced with a bittersweet edge like fine chocolate.

Both urges—sex and blood—were stupid. He was sane enough to reason that out.

And then he didn't care. And the whispers inside him segued to an abrupt chuckle.

It was never stupid to want a connection with another being. To finally know that which he desperately craved. Because since becoming vampire he'd been missing the implicit connection between two people. More than skin on skin, or blood to tongue. It must go deeper, permeating skin, muscle and bone, to the very soul.

Yet his broken soul wasn't worthy, he knew that much. So he must be satisfied with seeking to appease the lesser urges of touch, sex and blood. Fortunately for the hunter, he'd fed on a vagrant sorting through a garbage bin before coming here. He required blood daily since his escape from the blood games. Just one more thing that cursed him a crazed monster.

Pressing a palm flat onto a roof tile, Domingos closed his eyes and wished he could project his desire to the beautiful, smart woman below. If only he had some means to express what he wanted beyond grabbing her and awkwardly kissing her. She couldn't like that, especially when he must be so careful with his fangs.

Though last night up on the roof she'd pulled him to her body. For a few moments they had both taken what they'd needed from each other. Lark had wanted the crush of his mouth against hers, his skin brushing her skin and a hard body limning her curves. It must have killed her to take those wants from a vampire.

"I wonder if she wants soul-deep love. To simply…"
Be loved.

He'd never known love. Not between two people. Sure,

when mortal, he had dated women and had gone steady with one for over a year. But to experience a love so deep and abiding it burrowed to his very soul? Not yet.

He had once loved music so deeply it had been his voice; he had defined it as the voice of his soul. Music had not been stripped from him by vampirism as had his humanity. He'd willingly given it up after transforming to vampire. Music was too perfect to be touched by a monster such as he. Which was why he now only frequented the loud, raucous nightclubs. Couldn't allow himself to enjoy a symphony or even a quiet melodic love song. Though Mozart's *A Little Night Music* did have a tendency to interpose over the murderous cats on a few blessed occasions.

A musical note played a wavering vibrato between his ears. It drew out so long, he clenched his teeth and his fangs threatened to pierce his lower lip. Banging a fist aside his head didn't knock out the torment as it usually did. So he leaned forward and pounded his forehead against the roof—just once.

Pausing, Domingos spread his fingers over the cool tiles and listened. The music was not coming from inside his head, but rather *outside* it. Pushing up, he scanned beneath him. Had Lark turned on the stereo or television? It wasn't so awful; in fact, the notes were beautifully clear. A violin testing the beginning bars of a solo originally composed—

"For cello," he said angrily.

Domingos launched himself over the side of the roof and landed on the narrow ledge of the back door with ease. His toes hung over the wobbly threshold that had loosened when the iron stairs had fallen, but pressing his back to the door, he balanced. The door had been repaired, as he assumed her apartment had been fixed up.

Music echoed through the wood door and into his body, spiraling up his spine and into his skull. Preparing for the torture—it did not come. The tune was melodic, in perfect 4/4 time and not the clatter of disharmonic cat screams that normally tormented him.

And that angered him to the very blood of the phoenix he'd stolen to survive.

Domingos pounded on the door, feeling an electric shock zap through his veins and spark throughout his system, pinching every nerve as if in a vise. *Youch!* That was not from the music.

"Stop it!" he yelled, beating relentlessly, even though contact with the door continued to shock him.

The door swung open and Lark, hair unbound and falling lushly over her shoulders, holding a pale, unvarnished wood violin and bow, glared out at him. "What the hell are you doing?"

"What are you doing? No music! It's not yours."

She clasped the violin to her chest and protested, "It doesn't hurt me."

"It's not yours!"

"Go away if it bothers you so much, you annoying vampire."

"No. I want to be near you."

Lark exhaled and made a show of glancing at the digital clock near her bed. "Not many hours left on our deal."

Domingos held his position by pressing both palms flat against the door frame. The ward electrified that touch, but he wincingly maintained contact. "I'm not leaving."

"Are you going to stop shouting? I can't risk the neighborhood hearing your crazy tirade."

"If you stop playing, I'll stop shouting."

"I will not—" Heaving out a surrendering sigh, she

gestured with her bow hand. "Hell, I know by now that you're never going to leave. Come inside. And don't make me regret my kindness."

Released from the shocking repulse that zapped through his system, Domingos was thrust inside and across the threshold. Moving swiftly, he grabbed the offensive instrument from Lark's hand and lifted it over his head.

"No!" She lunged to claim the precious violin, so he held it high out of her reach. "That's mine! You can't break it. How dare you?"

"It hurts me," he seethed. He swung the instrument before him, defying her to grab for it.

"No, please, Domingos." Putting up her palms placatingly, she softened her tone. "It was my father's. It is precious to me!"

Her shout defeated the raging chorus of insane instruments orchestrating in his brain that insisted on being heard over the gorgeous melody that had invoked his anger. Lulled by her pleading dark eyes, Domingos stopped, violin clutched to his chest, his breaths heaving with anxiety.

At the sight of Lark's desperate expression, he closed his eyes. Didn't she understand? Music was sacred to him. He'd banished it from his life to protect it. To hear it now only reminded him of what he'd once been, and could never again have.

"But it hurts me," he said quietly. "The music. I've told you."

"I promise I won't play it again. Not when I know you're around." She reached for the violin but moved cautiously, unwilling to push him into another tirade. "I didn't know you were near."

"Needed to be close to you. Makes me feel safe," he

said. The maniacal chuckle escaped, but he cut it off abruptly. "Until you started to play. It's too sweet. Stirs up the dark anger in me. Makes me remember what I was like as a mortal man. No more. I'll never be that man again."

"No playing, then. Promise." Her smile didn't look forced, only worried. "You know you can trust my word, Domingos. Yes?"

Twice now she'd stood good on her word. A hunter who had granted her prey life only because she wished to. Truly, this woman was too good and was not maneuvering him into a ploy to let down his guard to allow her to attack.

He nodded and turned his head down and away from her. The sane part of him chastised the madman for scaring her with such a cruel threat. He knew the value of a musician's instrument—it went beyond currency.

Thrusting out his arm, he offered the violin.

Lark claimed it, carefully setting it in the leather case that sat open on the bed. Her fingers danced respectfully over the wood body, tracing a faint scar as if remembering its origin.

"It's over two hundred years old," she said. "My grandfather's. He handed it down to his son, who then gave it to me. It sounds like a Stradivarius, at least to me. If any damage came to it, it would feel as though I'd been cut in my soul."

He understood that, and felt her words tap against his soul, yet Domingos couldn't determine if the tap wanted to wound or heal. This madness fogged his heart beyond recognition. How to know if these feelings were real or just a facade designed to further torment his tattered soul?

"It looks fine," her soft voice said calmly. "You didn't harm it."

"I'm glad for that."

Lark turned and sat on the bed beside the violin case, drawing her palm up and down her opposite arm as if she were cold. "I wish I could understand your need to constantly be near me. It's not healthy. And I know you're not all there in the head, but— Sorry. That was cruel to say. Why are you here? Why me?"

Domingos, head bowed in shame, clasped his hands to his chest. Without a second thought, he spoke a new yet deep and desperate desire. "I want to bite you."

A startled gasp fell from her perfect red lips. So beautiful with her loose hair and barely there makeup. Natural, unbound, like pages of musical notation strewn across the floor in wait of discovery.

Recovering her obvious shock with a regal tilt of head, Lark said, "So what's stopping you?"

"We had a deal."

"Right. No biting. No staking. For another four or five hours. I should have added a clause about keeping your distance, as well."

"Just makes it easier when you need to find me, yes?"

"There is that. You seriously need to get a hobby if all your spare time is spent following me."

"I have one."

"Right. Leaving slain werewolves in your wake. And… ripping out their hearts."

Exactly. And let no hunter judge him unless she could prove to walk on higher ground. Yet how did she know he ripped out their hearts? Caufield must have reported that detail to the Order.

"Lark, I need to— I wanted to…" Heaving out a wilting sigh, Domingos said quietly, "Forget the bite. Will you…let me hold you?"

Now he cast his gaze upon her and attempted to radiate his need from within the tattered and torn muscles that pulsed about his heart. He sensed she felt the same need. *Please, let her be receptive to me.*

"Promise I won't bite," he rushed out. "I just want to smell your brightness. To listen to the blood rush through your veins."

She stifled a wince. Not exactly turn-the-girl-on date chatter. Hell, the last time he'd been on a wine-and-roses date he'd been mortal.

Idiot. Domingos turned away and clasped his arms across his chest, giving himself what she would not.

"If you think chumming up to me will change my mind—"

"I'm not doing that. I just wanted…" He caught his head in his palms. "I just…wanted."

He just wanted.

Never had a man been so open with her, so blatantly bare and truthful. Not even—no, not even her dead husband. No games with this one. He hadn't time for silly mind games. She respected him for that.

They were similar, which was difficult to admit. As Lark drew in a breath her body shivered with undeniable need. *You want, too. You've denied that want for over a year.* Too many other things to deal with. When would she let it come to her?

Could she risk it this once? If she was going to take a chance on anyone, it made sense to do it with a crazy vampire because soon enough he would be dead, and would take any confession of their shared embrace to the grave with him. Best way to keep her dirty little secrets safe was to ash them to oblivion.

It sounded good in theory.

Go with it. You've got all the power. You can stop it as soon as it feels wrong.

Dismissing the irrational thoughts, Lark opened her arms and embraced Domingos from behind. Solid and sure, he didn't feel like the broken creature she had come to learn he was, but instead muscular and strong. The vampire turned and tucked his head upon her shoulder, his nose snuggling into her hair. He squeezed her against his lean form, and it felt like something she'd never had before—unconditional acceptance.

Because there had always been conditions. *You mustn't tell. Keep my secret.*

She threaded her fingers through his hair; it was silken soft and still smelled of cherry shampoo from the safe house. But he also smelled dark and smoky and like a treat she had always denied herself because that was the right thing to do.

How long will you make yourself suffer? Does the length of time you suffer equal the amount of perceived pain you should feel for a lost one? Why do you not miss your unborn child as much?

Lark gasped as he drew his nose along her neck, taking in her scent, perhaps feeding his need for the aroma of her life pulsing beneath her skin.

Take it all, she thought, *while I am able to give it.*

They stood there for several minutes, longer than five, maybe ten. She wasn't counting, but she knew she didn't want to break the embrace. To push Domingos away would feel sacrilegious. The two of them fed off each other's need for skin contact. He wasn't as cold as the grave, which was something she'd never known about vampires. Shouldn't they be cold and clammy? Well, she'd never been so close to one before.

And he was solid and muscled, contrasting with the slender form she assumed could not possibly be strong. Strong enough to slay werewolves. Strong enough to hold her so firmly she felt as if nothing could ever again harm her. Safe.

Safe?

It was a fantasy that she wanted to play through, toy with and tease to see if it would last. At least, for the length of this embrace. They shared pain, and though hers was not so personal as his, she had experienced as much.

Hell, her pain was as personal as it got.

Yet the last person in the world she needed to be around was another man who had survived torture. It couldn't be good for her broken soul. And yet, as she held Domingos, it was as if she were holding the one person she hadn't been able to offer comfort to while he'd been in captivity.

"What's wrong?" he whispered at her ear. "Your heart is suddenly thudding. Are you afraid? You want me to let you go?"

"No." She grasped his arms before he could break the connection. "I don't know what it is. I'm not afraid of you. I...like this. You holding me."

She studied his gaze, wincing at the black iris that had been damaged by the werewolves' cruelty. And the lost little girl named Lisa Cooper who had wanted to play music and dance about in frills with not a care asked, "Can you make it better?"

He let out a soft rumble of laughter. It was not the crazy laugh, though, and that was the important thing. "I don't think I can touch the pain you feel, Lark. I've got too much of my own to wade through."

"You've already touched it. And believe me, I don't expect anyone else to be an agent to my healing. That's my cross to bear. Just know that I appreciate this. Between us. Whatever it is you want to call it."

"It's not a gift," he said, offended. Yet she clutched his arms when he attempted to pull from their embrace. He looked at her clinging hands. "I give you nothing, hunter. You take what you will from this. I'm serving my own selfish desires."

She nodded. "I know that. But we both know there's something more here. This thing between us. You…you desire me?"

"That's a stupid question."

Now he did break their embrace and wandered along the end of the bed dressed with a black-and-white-striped spread and one lone pillow. Always barefoot, the guy. It was sexy, his bare toes peeking out from under the slouchy hem of the leather pants. And a little sad. On the other hand, it gave him the advantage when cruising his highway of choice, the rooftops.

Domingos lifted his defiant gaze to hers. "Would you ever allow a vampire to make love to you?"

"I'd be thrown out of the Order."

He nodded. "That was a detour, not an answer. Yes or no? Would you make love with me, Lark? Answer me, and then I'll leave you alone. Promise."

The way he asked her felt as if he were asking if she preferred salami over bologna. Or a quick and impersonal contact. Make love to a vampire? Hell no.

Yet she wasn't sure she wanted him to leave her alone. It had been a long time since she'd felt so comfortable with a person. *He's not a person. He is a cold-blooded killer.* Yet he had once been mortal. The man once probably had a mortal lover, just as she once had, which made them ever more alike.

When friends and family had visited her following Todd's death, Lark had felt as if they hadn't known how to speak to a grieving widow. As if she'd magically become something different from the day before when her husband had been alive. Overnight she'd become a piece of glass or fragile porcelain. It was silly, and had only heaped upon the grief she'd already felt, smothering her and forcing her further away from the offered kindnesses.

She could breathe when Domingos was near. He did not smother her or worry about breaking her. And that frightened her.

And excited her.

"No answer?" he prompted. His resolute nod decided her answer for himself. "I had to ask. Until we meet again, hunter. I promise I'll put up a fight next time you come at me with your fancy stake. I've a good dozen or more wolves to dispatch, but the distraction of evading you will keep me on my toes. To kisses on the roof."

He winked and went out the door from which he'd entered. The stairs lay in a twisted tumble on the ground, so he jumped and landed in the grassy back courtyard crouched like a cat. Tugging the goggles down over his eyes, he wandered off, and Lark had to stop herself from calling him back.

He'd broken their connection. And now she felt cold and wanting.

Chapter 9

Time to kick this mission into gear and stop fooling around. The bargain was due to expire in an hour. Now Lark strode through the back door of the dance club, La Bouche. She never liked walking through the big red neon lips on the main street. It was far too conspicuous for a knight of the Order, and also just silly.

This club wasn't a paranormal club, but it was known to be a favorable spot for vampires on the prowl. Besides the dance floor that swayed with trance music and the exotic Indian/Electronic mix along with heavy-lidded couples that appeared half-stoned, there were the various rooms that offered illegal drugs and sex.

Todd had found more than a few of his marks here. Lark remembered him telling her how much he hated the vibe of the place. But as she strolled along the dance floor, her thighs brushed by the *shing* of a dancer's spangled skirts, and her body subtly moving to the throbbing beat, she decided she liked it. The vibe she got from it was a maharaja's harem with a gothic yet funky twist.

It wasn't necessary to scan the dance floor for her mark. She suspected dancing was the last thing that would draw Domingos to this club, if indeed, he was here at all. She'd tracked him to this neighborhood, though, and there were no other clubs in the immediate vicinity.

Shouldn't the noise drive him beyond the madness?

Maybe that was it. The noise might drown out the voices and violins he heard in his head. La Bouche could very well offer a comforting refuge for him, as ridiculous as that seemed.

After politely refusing to join a slender blond man on the dance floor, she walked right into a man who gently grabbed her by the upper arm. Gray hair gave him a distinguished aura that felt wrong in a place like this. At once Lark could feel his persuasion forcing her to stay calm. Like imperceptible fingers stroking her brain, coaxing ever so slightly. She'd been trained to recognize and fight off a vampire's persuasion, but with the music thrumming in her veins, it wasn't so easy to find that calm center in her core and tap into it.

"Will you step aside with me, please?" he asked politely, his grip directing her to the left.

He didn't seem as if he wanted to get lucky with her, and his intrusion upon her mental struggle to fight back calmed her even as she inwardly argued that she was not calm.

Lark placed a hand on the stake beneath her coat, but she wouldn't whip it out inside the club. Not unless it was necessary to protect her life, and she didn't feel danger from this vampire. Or was that the persuasion settling her? To be controlled by another so easily angered her, yet she walked beside him, reasoning that to make a scene would only draw undesired attention.

He walked her toward a hallway that glittered with red and gold spangles and tendrils of smoke that misted vanilla incense. When she thought he might be luring her toward a private room, he stopped, forcing her shoulders against the spangled wall, and leaned in close.

"I'm Vincent Lepore. I'm with the Council. I know you're with the Order. And I'll ask you to leave."

Her distinctive coat was the giveaway. The blades reflected the disco lights in intermittent flashes. And a Council member? This guy had rank within the paranormal realms. The Council was a group of various breeds who oversaw the paranormal nations. They and the Order were diametrically opposed and would never work with each other, though they had historically walked a wide circle around each other, never engaging, because the two organizations had never been given reason for such defense.

Also, Rook liked to say that the Council was a group of milksops who sat about discussing retribution and punishment, yet never actually got their fingers dirty for fear of mussing their coifs.

Lark wasn't about to change the history books by showing Lepore her aggression. It wasn't worth the embarrassment, or Rook's disappointment. And she wasn't sure she could, even if she tried. Hello, persuasion.

"I'm just looking around," she said over the music. He smelled like spice, and it annoyed her that she liked it. Must wear the same cologne her hus— She didn't want to think about him right now.

"Whatever you're looking for, we don't need that kind of trouble," he said, not raising his voice, yet she heard over the din. "Nor does the Order. You armed?"

She nodded.

"You should never have made it past security. You're out of here." Now he grabbed her forcibly by the upper arm and walked her toward the back entrance.

Fine. She wasn't about to cause trouble when her brain was feeling a bit like jelly and was sending that mushy feeling down to her arms. But the humiliation of being escorted out by a vampire would undo her.

Lark shrugged from Lepore's grasp. "I can see myself out. But I'll have you know there's a wolf slayer walking around the city. Don't you think the Council should do something about that?"

"Wolf slayer?" He laughed, and any modicum of respect his position might have granted him was lost with that callous disregard. "Since when does the Order of the Stake concern itself with werewolves?"

She'd said too much. And he'd only cemented her distrust of the Council.

But seriously? Since when had the Order given a fig what werewolves asked of them? And why had she never considered as much before?

Mushy brain, Lark. He's making you question everything and even the stuff you shouldn't.

"Sorry to have disturbed you," she said, and marched out of the club and across the narrow parking lot past a few groups of patrons either making out or getting high on the latest designer drug.

Inhaling the warm summer night air, she focused on shaking off the persuasion. Deep breaths through her nose and heavy exhales did the trick, and it was surprising how she could feel the veil lift from her brain to clear her thoughts.

The street behind the club was dark, empty of cars—most in the city traveled by Metro—and she strode down the way, close to the dark-windowed retail buildings that could never compete with the elite shops on the Champs-Élysées.

Spinning the stake through the fingers of her right hand like a majorette's baton, Lark admonished herself for allowing the vampire to piss her off. And for his easy control over her mind.

They were all alike. Among the paranormal breeds, vampires possessed a superiority complex, thinking they were better than most and putting on airs. That was the first time she'd felt overpowered by one of them, and he'd been polite and had barely touched her.

"Stupid longtooth."

"So now I'm stupid?"

Domingos joined her side, hands in his pockets, bare feet keeping time with her boots thudding upon the tarmac.

"I have a stake, vampire. Be warned."

"I see that. Up for a little clubbing tonight?"

"I've got slaying on my mind," she said curtly. "Next vampire to piss me off gets titanium through the heart."

"I'll try not to piss you off."

She stopped and swung around, walking him backward into a tight alley that fit them single file and that reeked of ripe fruit. "Why must you test me like this?"

"I'm not testing you."

"You follow me like a hungry stray."

"You were following me, hunter. I felt you on my back the whole way through the fifth quarter."

"Yeah?" The truth wasn't going to win him any points. "Well, now you're the one following me."

He shrugged. "Our deal is still in effect for another hour."

Huffing out a breath, Lark slammed her fist, clasped

about the stake, against his shoulder. "I've been given an ultimatum. If you're not dead by midnight, I'm off this job."

"Midnight is right around the end of our deal." He rubbed his palms together gleefully, ignoring the stake at his shoulder. "This could get interesting. So I assume you're not going to let me out of your sight for the next hour. Wouldn't be a very smart hunter if you did."

"You're already dead, vampire. Why prolong the agony? Just ask for it right now, and we can be done with it."

"You're very cheeky." He guided the stake away from his shoulder with a finger, and Lark relented, holstering it at her hip. "Thinking I'm some kind of creature who would ask for his own death to be free of the torments he suffers?" He chuckled and shook his head, then made a show of sniffing the air. "I can smell the lingering persuasion on you. Who was it?"

She tugged at her ponytail, adjusting it over a shoulder to hide the eerie shiver that sent goose bumps crawling up her neck. "Vincent Lepore."

"Council vamp. You're making friends in high places."

"He's not a friend. He stuck his fingers into my brain and stirred it up. I don't like being manipulated or lied to."

"I would never lie to you." He resumed following her as she strode onward. "I don't think I could manipulate you if I tried."

"You haven't persuaded me?"

"What would be the purpose? I don't want you to forget you spoke to me."

"You could make me forget I want to stake you."

"That wouldn't be fair play."

"Oh, and you're all about fairness."

"Have I given you reason to believe otherwise?"

No, he had not.

It frustrated Lark that, more and more, the vampire proved himself a worthy being, someone—were he not a creature—she could entirely see having as a friend. And he was a musician? She hadn't chattered about music with someone for years. Of course that would detract from her mission, and—hell, just being around Domingos LaRoque was proving a distraction.

The vampire nudged her gently with an elbow. "Come with me."

And he walked away without waiting to see if she cared to follow, a shadow clad in darkness that moved as if he were a ghost of mortality past.

Lark stopped in the center of the alley, feet spread and trigger hand flinching near her hip. She would not do as a vampire commanded.

But you already have.

Maybe the only reason he hadn't used persuasion on her was that he couldn't access that power since his torture? Domingos was strong physically, but perhaps his vampiric powers had been diminished. Like his inability to will up his fangs.

The shadow walking away from her turned a corner. He was right about one thing. A wise hunter would not lose sight of her prey.

Lark picked up the trail, swiftly gaining the corner and turning into an even darker, narrower pathway. Paris was a twisting labyrinth of passageways that she enjoyed navigating only so long as she didn't end up at a dead end or walking into someone's house, which happened on occasion.

Halfway down the block, Domingos strode haphazardly, swaying every now and then as if drunk. Vamps could get drunk off the blood of an alcoholic or someone who'd imbibed too much. Had he bitten someone from the club?

"Probably just the madness," she muttered. A thought that was, strangely, more appealing than knowing he might have drunken blood.

She didn't rush to catch up to him. She had time. Less than an hour, though she hadn't a watch. For some reason she wagered the vampire would announce the midnight hour to her, defying her to grant his death.

Was that it? Maybe he desired death and couldn't bring it upon himself. For the pain and mental torture he appeared to constantly suffer, it was a rational conclusion. And yet he didn't want to die until his revenge mission had been completed.

Well, if he thought to string her along until then, and then ask for the stake, she had another story line for him to read.

Surprised he didn't jump to a roof, Lark followed him at a distance through the thirteenth quarter and eventually they landed in an industrial neighborhood in the fourteenth.

Very near the ring road nestled a quiet neighborhood that looked like a scene out of a Tim Burton movie, dark and brooding, as gothic as could be. She guessed he was leading her to his home. That would put her opponent to the advantage come midnight, but she welcomed the challenge.

Had he prepared for her? Set traps to ensnare the hunter?

"Bring it," she muttered, and strode through an open wrought-iron gate set in a brick fence.

The vampire led her toward a narrow mansion tucked between other limestone mansions, which might have been built during the 1700s, and edged by high, fragrant hedgerows and a crumbling brick fence. He walked through the front door—painted black with a stained-glass inset depicting a white rose—leaving it open behind him.

Lark marveled that the overgrown vines and plants spilling across the small front courtyard could be night-shade or wolfsbane or some other wildly macabre plant. With what else would a vampire choose to landscape his dread lair of horrors? The leaves touched her boot toes, and she was cautious only until she realized how ridiculous her thoughts had become.

Crushing a white bloom into the cobblestoned walk, she strode up the crumbling steps to stand before the open doorway. She'd never been inside a vampire's home, and she paused at the threshold. No invitation was necessary for her, a mortal, unless he'd had it warded.

She tested the air before her but was not repulsed, nor did she sense an invisible barrier. She expected a trap, and had been trained to foresee the unexpected. Should a vampire claim a hunter kill, especially a knight of the Order, his fellow vampires would revere him.

Just as you are revered by the knights for your tally? Seventy-one lives destroyed in half a year's time.

Was that really something to be proud of?

Of course not. Pride was not in her lexicon. Nor could she claim heroics, such as racing into a burning building. She'd even caved and staked her own husband, for Christ's sake. That made her less than human, and closer to the creatures she stalked.

Lark swallowed and tested the threshold with a boot toe.

You go inside, and forget what the Order taught you, you break every rule Todd had and become something he was not.

"Free," she whispered, not knowing why that word came to her, but also feeling it in her heart as truth.

Domingos appeared before her and gave her a wondering look—the Mad Hatter sizing up Alice's moxie—and offered his hand. The edge of that hand was scarred with what looked like a burn patient's skin. She'd not noticed that before. Had he been out in the sun recently?

Sliding her palm over his and tracing a finger along the scarred skin, she noted that it felt fragile, almost papery. He bent to kiss her hand and then tugged her inside and slammed the door shut.

"Frightened?" he asked as he walked her down the dark hallway toward a room lit by a low-watt lamp.

Lark checked her nerves and kept her calm. "I told you I'm only frightened by falling."

"You've fallen into *la maison du vampire,*" he teased.

"I entered freely and of my own will."

Oh, Lark. Did you really just quote Dracula?

She'd read the book in high school and had identified with Renfield for reasons beyond her ken. Lucy and Mina had seemed too flighty and easily led by the menfolk.

Domingos's chuckle unhinged the first of her nerves. It was so bellowing and deep and shameless. And yet its masculine chord strummed at her innate desire for protection by someone bigger, stronger and male. And curiosity got the better of her as she followed the vampire deeper into Wonderland.

She strolled the gray shadows of the hallway, through the kitchen, where she was surprised to see it looked normal. Gray granite countertops boasted a mica gleam, and black leather bar stools queued neatly before the counter. In the living room, where one wall was completely windows shielded by heavy maroon damask draperies, she ran her fingers along the back of the leather sofa, noting the creases from wear and age.

The furniture was comfortable, the bookshelf filled with dusty hardcovers boasting gilded titles. A small television housed within a laminated vanity screamed *1950s,* and assorted rugs and pillows completed the homey look. A cushy, thick rug lay beneath her feet. Were she shoeless, she could sink her toes into it.

Dragging her gaze from the rug, Lark decided there was no sign that a musician lived here, for she'd expect sheet music, a music stand and perhaps an instrument in a case. Nor was there any sign a vampire held residence, save the drapes drawn before the windows. No coffin? A literary trope, she knew, but it felt as though something was missing.

"What's wrong?" he asked.

"It's so…"

"Normal? You expected the Mad Hatter's tea party?"

She shrugged. "Actually, yes."

"Well, then, welcome, Alice. Won't you have some tea? Sorry, I'm out of Earl Grey, but I could do with a spot of the chap's blood."

She flashed him a wary glance, and he countered with a jesting smirk.

"Sorry," she replied, "that was, just… Sorry."

"Don't do that, Lark. You never apologize. It's not in your nature to appease others. I like your honesty. If you think me mad, then say so."

"I'm not sure what I think of you. I've been told you are insane, and have seen an example of what I suspect insanity might look like, and yet you're also very clear and lucid at times."

"*At times* are the key words in that statement. I am much more lucid around you, I've noticed." He brazenly took in her attire from head to toe. "Do you wonder why that is?"

"No," she said quickly, because it felt too intimate to agree.

"Go ahead and look around. I know how women like to snoop. And a hunter in a vampire's home? You've hit the mother lode."

"I could say the same about you. A vampire who has lured an Order knight into his lair. Will your vampire buddies cheer you on when you bring them my head?"

"I don't kill mortals," he said. "That's abominable."

"Even a hunter?"

He shrugged. "Never a pretty one."

Domingos slid off the dark jacket he wore and tossed it across the back of the couch. Beneath, a black shirt was unbuttoned to reveal taut abs, and at the waist above his leather pants the shadow of dark hairs.

So normal, Lark again thought. Yet he only ever seemed to manage the one button. Weird. And...sexy.

"The woman I hire to clean is short," he noted, unaware that her eyes had fixed on his abs. "She never can dust higher than the tops of the pictures."

"Huh? Oh." Forcing her gaze from the hard landscape of his tight muscles, Lark looked about and did indeed notice the dust that sat heavily on a picture frame, but only the top part. And then she noticed the decorations on the far wall. "Seriously?"

She strolled over to inspect the wall that could only be labeled a mini arsenal. A Kalashnikov, and a few pistols, and a melting stove where she examined silver bullets.

"This is my workshop-slash-living room," he explained.

Tapping a silver bullet, she recalled her lessons on

weaponry and defense. "You know the trajectory on silver bullets is piss-poor," she commented. "They're too soft."

"You use them."

"That we do, but only to dissuade."

"I add an ash-wood core. Firms up the design."

"Impressive. So you have much slaying to do?"

"I do have more than half a pack left to dispose."

She lifted her chin to meet him directly in the eye. "I understand."

"You do." She followed his glance to a dusty clock on the wall near a machine gun: eleven forty-five. He leaned against the wall, crossed an ankle over the other and watched her survey the rest of the room. "We are more alike than you care to admit."

"We both want to destroy that which brought irrevocable damage to our lives. I can agree we are alike in that respect," she offered, gliding her fingers over a brass sculpture of a skull riddled with Celtic ribbons. Appropriately gothic, but she suspected it was more for looks than something he actually admired.

"I admire you," he said.

Letting her fingers fall from the skull, Lark bowed her head, unwilling to meet his gaze. She did not deserve his admiration, nor did she want it.

"You have it," he said, as if reading her thoughts. "Why do you punish yourself for something you could not prevent?"

"I don't understand."

"I get the need for revenge. But what I don't get is why you put yourself at the bottom, the one who must pay for everyone else's sins. Unworthy of standing your own ground, being your own person."

"You don't know me, vampire."

He sighed and nodded. "Not as much as I'd like to."

Again he glanced at the clock. "Soon enough, eh? Come with me. This is not where I feel most comfortable. If I'm to die..."

Domingos strolled out of the room and Lark mocked his parting words. He didn't expect to die tonight. Who was putting himself at the bottom now? He mocked her by toying with the bargain, their agreement to trust.

She followed him into a long, empty room framed on one end by a massive paned window that was curved along the top and fitted with a circle window, divided by six panes around the circumference. No color in the glass, but the beveled edge of each pane caught the moonlight as if lined with diamonds.

The moon was nearing fullness, and its silver shine bathed the vast floor with paned shadows. Domingos shrugged off his shirt, tossing it aside, and stood before the window, his back to it. Preparing for his death?

Nope. Just putting on an elaborate show, for reasons that she could only guess were explained through madness.

"I like to think the moonlight softens the pain," he said.

Lark walked carefully toward the window, around behind him. She gasped at the sight of his back. The skin was wrinkled and tormented, as on his hands, yet looked fragile and paper-thin, as if to touch it would flake it away.

She wanted to touch it but knew the move would be too bold, and part of her was afraid. Yes, afraid, not of the creature, but of the pain she might cause him, and of the pain she didn't want to connect with again. It would be worse than falling, because this fall would plunge her into her own pain.

"It's from UV lights," he said quietly. As he spoke the

moon flashed silver in his hematite hair. "The wolves kept them on most of the time. My little cell had six light fixtures in it. They were caged with fine mesh so I couldn't break the bulbs, though I did try. Difficult to hide from so much light."

Lark caught a swallow at the back of her throat and splayed her palm before the horrible sight, but still did not touch. To do so would connect her to all things past. "Just your back?"

"Backs of my arms, hands and legs."

Yes, she saw it on his arms now.

"I used to cower under the lights, trying to coil my body into as small a target as possible, protecting my belly and face. They'd stripped me to my skivvies, so I had to choose something to protect and the rest of me to sacrifice."

The mind concocts the worst about torture, and Lark had gone beyond worst and into chaos imagining the things her husband might have experienced during his year and a day of captivity.

And right now her mind was kicking her for passing over the vampire's threshold, and at the same time, shoving her toward the question. The question she'd always and never wanted answered.

What rabbit hole had she fallen into? This was not Lark, who ruthlessly staked vampires. This was…Lisa Cooper. The woman who had survived a year and a day in a madness of her own.

It's a ploy! He's trying to get under your skin, connect with your soft, forgiving side. A side you've buried. Don't let him do it.

Yet he'd not lied to her since she'd met him, so why suspect a trick now?

"Tell me about it?" Heavy exhales hushed quickly

from her mouth. "I need to know," Lisa said without regard for Lark's inner warnings.

"Because of your husband?" He tilted his head to look over his shoulder at her, but he did not meet her eyes. Instead he continued to bathe in the moonlight's silver glow.

She nodded, fighting desperately to contain tears. She would not cry. She could not. Tears had stained every inch of her apartment floor. Now she walked upon her pain daily, yet would she ever be able to trample it to oblivion?

Domingos stepped away, leaving her palms to cool, and her wishing she had dared touch him, to offer some solace, or maybe just feel another person's pain. He wandered to the center of the room where the moonlight barely lit the dull hardwood floor and squatted, wrapping his arms about his shoulders in a position of desolation.

"They strip away your soul," he said quietly.

Lark sucked in her breath and closed her eyes. *Stop him before he opens wide the wound on your heart.*

It's already open. Tearing it wider can't do much worse, can it?

"It seems so effortless really. To reduce a man to madness." His soft chuckle rippled across her heart, then clenched the aching muscle as if with a lasso of barbed wire. "They take away your clothes, your comforts, your means to identity. Naked. Alone. Shivering. You have nothing to anchor yourself to. No life raft.

"The pain of a weapon and the excruciating hunger for blood becomes your breath. The UV lights that burned into my skin? My air."

Lark gasped, fighting the need to run out of the room. She trembled. Her skin felt warmer, uncomfortable. His experience could be similar to Todd's. She'd never guessed they would strip him bare and humiliate him with such horrors.

"You become a child," Domingos said softly. "And all that child desires is reassurance."

He began to rock back and forth. A child who had learned to comfort himself because of the evils inflicted upon him.

She looked away. Had Todd done much the same? Had he been left alone in a small room after hours of torture, with no one to hold and comfort him?

"To be held…" His words cut through her wire-wrapped heart. "A foolish wish," he said, his voice sharpening. "You will never have it. You will be denied! But it is what keeps that small spark glowing deep within. A minute flash that prays for release. Freedom."

Freedom. That was what she'd felt when stepping across his threshold. How odd. They both wanted the same thing. And yet she hadn't identified what her freedom looked and felt like.

Lark stepped forward softly, wanting to touch him, but sensing he was not finished speaking. And for a split second he became her husband, a man she had dreamed about holding to chase away the nightmare. But truthfully, she had not the strength then, and might have let him down if she had been allowed the contact.

"My spark has gone out." He chuckled again. "Of course, you know that. Just look at my eyes. One is completely lacking in light."

"There's something in your eyes," she offered. "Don't give up, Domingos."

"Madness is not so pretty, but it is what keeps me alive. Had I not the mad revenge stalking my soul, I would have nothing to live for. Although…"

"Yes, what else? There must be more than revenge that keeps you going. Do you have hope? You can, you know."

Lifting his head, still facing away from her, he said clearly, "My hope is a pretty little hunter. She speaks to my soul. She taunts it with music and a promise of death, but in her kiss I taste desire and need, and know we are the same."

He was right. She did desire him. Against her better judgment she desired this damned creature. But the need he tasted was so much darker. Yes, they were the same; she could not argue with that.

Coiled forward into himself, Domingos rocked, his head tucked against his knees. And she wanted to have been there. For her husband. And for Domingos. To wrap his child in her arms and make it all better.

Lark dropped to her knees and wrapped her arms about Domingos's shoulders. He did not resist but continued to rock, which made it difficult for her to maintain hold. But she persisted.

He cried out. A shattering sound that reminded her of broken animals, such as birds with tattered wings. She hugged him tighter, knowing it must pain his tortured flesh, but not knowing how to release him—because she needed this connection.

He did not ask her to stop. Matching his slowing rhythm, she held on to him as she had never held on to a person before. His muscles flexed against her body and he shivered and moaned, but she did not relent. With him wrapped within her arms, she could keep him safe, above water. And he, unknowingly, lured her toward a secret dark safety she knew would never harm her.

It was what he needed. It was what she could give him. And in turn, she took.

Chapter 10

An hour after she'd coiled Domingos into an embrace, Lark realized they lay on the floor, entangled in a loose clasp. And he slept.

From where she lay, she could see into the living room and the far wall where the weapons hung. The clock hands had moved beyond midnight.

Her leg tingled with sleep, and she tried to stretch it out with a twist of her foot. Domingos startled, yet she sensed his disorientation, so she carefully disentangled her arms from his and sat up.

He shoved the hair away from his face and looked about as if in a new environment. "I haven't slept in months."

"Seriously?"

He nodded, then clasped her hand within his strong grip, which was decorated with the fragile burned skin. "Thank you."

The man had allowed her into the dark space inside him that he believed no longer burned with an ember of hope. She knew that ember still simmered, because she had touched it. Had held it sobbing and rocking in her arms. She could see it in his eyes, even the one that was completely black.

And she felt it, deep in her gut, the intense desire to connect with the spark she had sensed within him. To share her pain in the only way she believed they two could do so. She needed. Desperately.

"Let's make love," she cooed softly against his ear.

"You say so?"

She nodded.

Domingos stood and strode to the wall, not so quickly that she suspected he wanted the distance, but more a wandering pace. Confused, perhaps? No. He stopped and glanced toward the clock, then briefly back to her.

They both knew what should happen.

He turned away from her and bowed his head. Lark felt sure she'd said the wrong thing.

Making love? How dare she suggest something so simple, the easy answer to everything? Couples always crashed together in limbs and kisses when they wanted to avoid or even share. It was dramatic, and didn't require a lot of thought. It wasn't so much daring as a comfortable means to avoid talking. And they were not a couple, not even close.

And yet he'd asked the same of her earlier at her apartment.

What *should* happen was that she whip out the stake and end Domingos. Mission complete. On to number seventy-three.

Lark didn't want that. She had not felt so close to a man since, well…since. And she didn't want to lose that feeling because it was so rare. And really, she needed him right now. His touch and his regard. "I'm sorry—"

"No." He turned and put up a foot on the wall behind him. Raking his hands through his hair, he offered a surprised smile. "I'd like to make love with you."

So simple as that. Lark exhaled. She'd asked, and he had accepted. It felt freeing to her, and daring, and a little dangerous. But this danger appealed in an erotic way. It felt darkly forbidden and mysteriously alluring.

Shedding her Kevlar vest and dropping it to the floor, she approached the vampire. When he put down his foot and straightened, she pressed her palms to his shoulders and leaned in against his chest, breath to breath. She studied his eyes. The pupil of his brown eye grew large, aroused. His breathing increased and his lower lip fell slack, exposing the tips of his glinting white fangs.

"Are you sure?" he asked.

"Never," she whispered, "and always."

"Then kiss me, hunter, because you haven't yet been the one to kiss first."

"I do like challenges, but that one is easy."

And she kissed him, tenderly marking his mouth with hers. He did not kiss her back, instead allowing her to do as she pleased, which Lark liked. She expected force and control from one such as him, so the connection was refreshing and renewed her confidence in this strange and slightly frightening descent into a darkness she had vowed to vanquish.

Taking her time, she lowered her lips from his mouth, moving her fingers down his chest. The room was mostly dark; the spare moonlight glimmered in his eyes, so she was learning him by touch. The man was lean, but muscled, a sinewy sculpture of flesh and bone.

She winced as her fingertips traced over scars. Vampires should not scar but heal instantly. That could only mean he'd endured something so treacherous even his supernatural makeup could not heal the surface wounds. She wondered how deep they went and if they could ever truly be healed.

And then the anger over the injustices served Domingos forged her desire to join him on his quest to slay the wolves. Nasty dogs.

But she set aside thoughts of vengeance. This quiet moment must be honored. And her insistent desire had not gone away, but rather, had increased by standing here before him, her body snug against his, feeding off his surprising warmth. In danger's way. The risk of it upped the stakes.

The heat of Domingos's flesh burned against her palm when she pressed it to his pectoral. He slid his hand over hers, holding it there, and tilted back his head, closing his eyes. He didn't speak, but she felt his breath upon her face, his chest rising and falling more quickly.

The smoky cherry scent of him surrounded her and enticed her forward. Everything must be slow. Innately she knew it was the only way they could connect. A cautious approach to a delicate pairing. She pressed an ear to his chest, listening to his heartbeat.

"Is there a heart in there?" he asked on a throaty tone.

"Yes, and it's strong."

"Wanting," he added. "Your touch is like fire, Lark."

"I don't want to burn you."

"It's a good fire. Bold and fast."

Not like the fire he had raced into last night. He'd not brought up his heroic act, and she would honor his modesty.

Domingos skated a hand over her hair, pulling the dark strands to his mouth, so she nudged her nose above his ear, into his hair. Smoky sweet, the scent was uniquely him.

He took her hand and placed her fingers at his mouth, kissing them one by one. There, she dared to tap the pearly fang that was permanently down. Domingos moaned.

"Does that hurt?"

"Never. It's…erotic, Lark, you touching my fangs. Feels like a touch much lower."

"I see." Interesting. The Order had never taught her that. She stroked the other fang, delighting in his surrender to the pleasure she could give him, and grasping fully the control the simple motion granted her. "They're pretty and deadly."

"I can't promise I won't use them on you. Being what you are, you must know about us vampires. Blood and sex…it goes together."

She exhaled, rolling that one around in her thoughts. Training had briefly addressed the compulsion for vampires to desire sex along with blood, but hadn't focused on it, because what knight would ever get embroiled so deeply with the enemy that it would matter?

She didn't want his bite.

Or did she?

No. A knight who willingly took a vampire bite would be not only ousted from the Order, but thrown out in such a manner that his or her last breath would be witnessed by the entire Order. Live to serve. Serve until death…

You're not a knight right now, Lark. You left the knight at the threshold to the enemy's lair. Stop thinking like one.

Domingos's fingers traced along her sides, upward, slowly moving over the thin T-shirt, exploring her slight curves. The soft tickle scurried through her veins and lingered at her breasts. She leaned into him so he could feel her hard nipples against his bare skin.

A fang grazed her finger but did not break skin. Were he to steal a drink of blood, it would not kill her, and if he properly sealed the wound she would not risk transformation. The Order might never know....

But again, she let her mind race swiftly beyond that minute worry. There were better things to concentrate on.

Putting her mouth right before his, she danced within his gaze, and to the tune of his rapid breaths. Already she could imagine him thrusting his erection inside her. She longed to know that intimate surrender—and would.

Dipping her forefinger into Domingos's mouth, she wet it on his tongue and traced his lips. His moan pleased her. He stepped from foot to foot, anxious, or perhaps eager. Another dash across his tongue and then she trailed her finger over one of his nipples, a hard jewel that tightened even more.

"No music," he moaned.

She caught his hand before he could pound a fist aside his head, knowing he heard the music in his head that he so despised. "Concentrate on me, Domingos."

He twisted his head to the side and nodded. "Want to. Need to."

"Feel me," she said, and pulled off her shirt, exposing her sheer, black lace bra. She pressed her breasts to his chest and glided her leg up along his, nudging his erection with her hip. "Want me?"

He nodded, voiceless yet gasping, for she wagered he fought between madness and pleasure right now. She wasn't about to let the torture win. If she couldn't slay the vampire, then she could surely take down the madness or, at the very least, tame it.

"Touch me," she whispered, and drew back her arm to

allow him to slide his hand up her waist and to her bra. "Touch me how you please. Focus on what you desire, not what desires to end you."

His palm rubbed over the sheer fabric, bringing all sensation to her breast. Falling into the heady feeling, Lark arched her back and dug her fingernails into his shoulder, then reneged, reminding herself that she did not want him to feel any pain or madness.

His fingers moved swiftly up to her left shoulder, stroking over the raised brand that depicted four stakes in a cross form surrounded by a circle.

"Must have hurt," he whispered.

She nodded, not wanting to detail the pain of taking the red-hot brand as part of her initiation into the Order. It would only spoil the mood.

He snapped the plastic bra clasp open and she shrugged the lacy straps from her arms. "You've done that before," she murmured as the garment hit the floor.

"Just because I'm a nutcase doesn't mean I don't know my way around a woman. I am going to enjoy navigating you."

The vampire growled with pleasure and bent to glide his tongue over her breast, like a paintbrush stroking a canvas. His heat made her shudder and squirm against him. She wanted to rub herself all over him, and in turn feel every part of him. The cool sensation of sharp fang skimming her breast every so often only heightened that want. It was a danger play on her part, and she was fine with that because, even though she'd tucked away the hunter, Lark liked it a little daring.

Domingos suckled at her nipple, greedily laving and then focusing an intentness there that deepened her murmurs to moans.

Suddenly he lifted her so Lark could wrap her legs

about his hips. Holding her with his arms braced across her back, she let her head fall back, lifting her breasts to his ministrations. Her body shivered as each lash of his tongue sweetened the pleasure-pain. She ground her mons against his erection, seeking to massage her sweet spot and heighten the telling orgasmic tingle that grew stronger with every lick of his tongue.

Carrying her across the room, still tending to her breasts with his hot, wet kisses, Domingos quickly moved down the hall and into a dark, cool bedroom. The black sheers blew softly thanks to an open window. Lark couldn't make out much else in the room. It was after midnight. Darkness would be theirs for a while.

Domingos tapped the copper shade on the small lamp near the bed, and it blinked to a soft glow. He laid her on an ancient half tester bed that sported dark damask draperies overhead. Medieval gothic at its finest. The mattress was so high, her hips were level with his waist, and she hooked her heels around behind his hips and coaxed him forward to land on top of her.

He tugged at the fly hooks on her pants and then shoved down. She toed off her boots and wiggled her legs to allow him to drag the pants off and drop them onto the floor. He glided a hand aside her groin but did not touch.

Lark bit her lip at the frustration of missing a touch she craved. Already she was wet for him. She wanted him to put his fingers inside her, to stroke her and find the humming pinnacle that desired a soft yet firm touch.

He found the elastic at the top of her thigh-high stockings, which she wore because they made her feel sexy, and slid a finger under it.

"These are so hot," he muttered. "Makes it easy to concentrate."

Good. She didn't want a raging madman in bed with her. Sex would go well. It had to, or she'd never be able to look at him again without wondering if she had done something to bring on the torment.

His long, feathery hair swept her skin, and she clutched it across her breasts, stroking her nipples with the slick, cherry darkness. Tenderly, he dotted kisses below each breast, and then strolled down the center of her stomach, dashing his tongue into her belly button and declaring it "Cute," while his fingers slid one stocking down her thigh to billow at her ankle.

He lifted her leg along his shoulder and kissed her ankle, then slipped off the stocking. He did the same with the other leg.

Lark spread her arms across the bed, gripping the counterpane. Her heart raced. Her veins sang a composition she'd never learned on the violin. Her skin begged for Domingos's mouth—everywhere. She was ready to invite the vampire beyond her threshold and into her very being.

So you've gone mad, as well?

If it was insanity to crave intimate connection with another being, then bring it on.

He straddled her hips, his leather pants cool against her feverish skin, and kissed her deeply. Every move devastated and claimed. She no longer minded the tease of his fangs. It was easy enough to trust when he was the first anchor she'd been able to grasp since free-falling into the realm of the impossible and dangerous.

"Now me," he whispered. "Take off my pants."

"You don't have to tell me twice."

Lark flicked open the button and unzipped his fly. A satisfied growl rumbled in his throat as she shoved the supple leather down his hips and then claimed his heavy erection as if it were a titanium stake she had been trained to expertly manipulate.

She stroked him slowly, tenderly, taking time to trace the length of him with her fingers and learn his shape. No damage here, not that she could feel. Yet, rigid and hot, he possessed a slight curve that she traced again and again, each time her action teasing the thick rod to bounce and play against her fingers. At the head of him he was swollen and moist, hot as forged steel. She cupped her palm and it filled her hand. She couldn't wait longer.

"Inside me," she whispered. "Please?"

"Soon." Kissing her breasts, he slid a finger into her folds and slicked her wetness high against her clit. "I want to learn you first."

Lark moaned and pumped up her hips, seeking his exploration, but not wanting to be denied. Inside her with his molten hot shaft was what she wanted. The thickness of him, the—

"Ohh..." She lost her train of thought. The slick tease of his finger over her clit hummed all through her body, up and down her arms, swirling in her head and tightening at her belly.

Perhaps she could wait a bit.

Domingos moved down and traced his tongue over her, giving her pussy as much attention as he'd given her breasts. Lark gripped the fabric, pressing her shoulders into the mattress, stretching the gorgeous shimmer throughout her muscles. She put a leg up over his shoulder but stopped herself from heeling his back. The skin there was too ravaged for such pressure.

He gripped her thighs and spread her legs wider, licking her deeper, and then up to slick across her clit. He commanded her body with his expertise. She needed him, wanted his hardness inside her, but couldn't argue against the pulsing orgasm that stirred at the edge of her muscles.

"Come for me," he said. "Give me that trust, Lark."

He knew well that it required a certain trust for such a release. No woman could fly without some modicum of trust, of feeling safe with the man. He had followed her, as she had followed him. He'd fought her, and let her walk away. He'd given her the shirt off his back, and agreed to silly bargains when he could have as easily broken her neck and sucked her dry.

He had given her every ounce of trust she suspected he had. *The man had only given to her.*

Tonight she had walked over the threshold to freedom. *Take it.*

And Lark released her last thread of apprehension and soared into the bliss of release. She cried out loudly, clutching at his hair and grinding her mons up against his masterful kiss. And then her body sank into the mattress, lax and panting, her laughter spilling boldly into the room.

"Mercy, Lark, your pleasure is the most gorgeous sound I've heard," he said. "No symphony can match it."

Gasping, she pulled at his hair, directing him up along her body. "Inside me now. Feel me, Domingos. Take me."

"Yes. I have to feel your music surround me." The intrusion of his thick shaft was accompanied by his throaty growl. "You're so hot. Christ, Lark. Oh…"

Still feeling her muscles squeeze from the orgasm, she clasped her legs about his hips and followed his rapid, pistoning thrusts. And then he slammed his palm to the bed beside her head and cried out. His body tensed above her, his jaw clenching, and he shuddered, caught in the sweet, sinful darkness the two of them had alchemized.

* * *

Lark woke and sat up on the edge of the high bed. She always liked to come awake stretching out her toes and arms to greet the morning sun. The curtains were drawn, though, and she couldn't be sure it was morning. Had to be. They'd made love for hours.

Hell. She wasn't using birth control. The thought to do so hadn't occurred because she'd not used it since before her marriage. Could a vampire get a mortal woman pregnant?

Yes. And the child could be vampire or mortal. The parents never knew until that child reached puberty.

Lark squeezed her eyes tight. She would never call having sex with Domingos a mistake. And she did crave a family. Someday. With a man she loved. Could she even carry a baby to term?

She didn't want to think about the miscarriage. It had been the beginning to the end of her marriage. She'd be careful next time. She had birth control pills in her closet at home. Time to check their expiration date.

She noticed a flashing LED and jumped from the bed to grab her cell phone, which had fallen from her pants pocket and now lay under the bedside table. One text message. It was from Rook.

Time is up. You've been removed from the job. I will speak to you this afternoon at your home.

Damn. Well, it wasn't as if she hadn't expected that result.

She glanced over her shoulder to the sleeping vampire, tangled in a wrap of black sheets. So peaceful. She could stake him right now. The ash would scatter over the sheets and fall into a shapeless heap. On to number seventy-three.

Lark shook her head.

That scenario had become a mad fantasy. She no longer wanted to harm this man. He was not a danger to her or mortals. He might be dangerous to werewolves, but the dogs could go screw themselves. This was not a mission she wished to complete.

And really, when had the Order started working for werewolves? It felt…more wrong than a hunter making love with a vampire.

Sighing, she put Rook's message out of her mind. No way to start a morning. There would be plenty of time later to deal with the fallout of her decision.

Tiptoeing to the window, she pulled the heavy drapery aside. Gorgeous sunlight flooded her skin. After the rain they'd been having—

A man yelled and she heard a thud.

Lark scrambled around the foot of the bed to find Domingos crouched on the floor, the side opposite the window, shuddering. The skin on the back of his shoulder smoked and he covered his eyes with his palms.

"Oh, hell, Domingos, I'm so sorry."

She bent down by him but remembered the sunlight. Closing the curtains, she then rushed around to hug him, but he resisted her efforts and even growled when she accidentally touched his smoking shoulder.

How could she have been so cruel? "I'm sorry. I wasn't thinking. I'm…" So not equipped for this kind of relationship.

It wasn't a relationship. Couldn't be. Why? She had no idea. She'd figure that out later, as well.

Domingos tucked his head against the side of the mattress. She thought to brush away his hair and touch his skin, which had stopped smoking, but she couldn't bring herself to cause him more pain. After they had shared such tenderness last night, this must truly be a slap in the face to him.

"Can I get you a cool towel? Will that make it better? You should have some ointment, something for the burn?"

"Nothing stops the hurt."

Biting her lip, she looked aside. They had spent an amazing night together. And a wrong night together. A knight of the Order sleeping with a vampire? If any knight learned about this and went to Rook with the information, she'd be ostracized, if not terminated in the most final way possible.

You weren't going to think about it, remember?

"I'll get some cool water." She stood, but he clasped her hand and pulled her down beside him.

"I don't need anything but you. It was good," he said wincingly. In so much pain, yet trying to be strong for her. "Last night?"

He needed reassurance.

"Making love with you was amazing, Domingos." She kissed his forehead, then touched her lips to each of his eyelids. Finding his mouth, she burnished a slow and lazy kiss there, tasting his tongue and quickly dashing each fang. "The curtains—forgive me?"

"You didn't know. The pain has already subsided. Just—" He pounded his head against the mattress, and that horrible laughter burst out.

"The noises in your head?"

He nodded, squeezing his eyelids shut, and pounded again. Fingers clutching the sheets, he growled and shook his head.

"I wish I could take away whatever it is that torments

you. I mean that. I'd do anything to make life better for you, Domingos. You deserve better."

"I have better." He slid his hand into hers and, even as he fought against the voices, held her tenderly.

It was difficult to watch. Helpless, without a means to stop his interior foe, Lark stood and swept his hair into her hands. Like molten hematite it flowed over her fingers, too dark, beyond blackness, but so soft and comforting when splayed across her skin.

"You got a phone call?" he asked.

"A text message from my superior." She stood and plucked one of her stockings from the end of the bed. "He wants to see me."

"And then it's back to slaying?"

She smirked as she pulled up her hose, followed by the leather pants, then sought her abandoned shoes. "I'm not sure anymore. I received an ultimatum yesterday. If you weren't dead by midnight, then I would be taken off the job. It's close to noon now, so you can guess what that means."

"You are no longer my death?"

"I don't think I ever was."

A wistful glance to her lover confirmed what she'd guessed—that she could never have harmed him. The man had gotten inside her, perhaps brushed her soul. She liked the feeling, and didn't want it to end.

But she couldn't ignore the real world or the vows she had made to the Order.

"I should probably head home." To find those birth control pills. "And please, don't follow me today, Domingos. My superior is meeting me at my apartment. The last thing either of us needs is for him to discover our liaison. Such information could prove deadly to us both."

He nodded and smiled up at her. "You made me whole

again last night. For a few blissful hours the madness receded."

She stroked the side of his face and he rubbed into her palm as if he were a purring cat. "You helped me forget the bad things, too. Thank you for sharing you with me. All of you, even this stuff that haunts you now."

"It's not bad when I'm in your arms. It's become background noise again. Your voice wins against the screaming cats."

Lark managed a chuffing smile, then tapped his skull. "I'd like to know how cats got in there."

"Me, too. Why couldn't it have been owls? I like to listen to owls hooting in the night."

"Now, that would be plain spooky. I'll be in touch."

He made a reluctant, silent nod, which she felt wasn't so much agreeing as accepting. They stood on opposite sides, yet last night the line between them had been peeled away, only to be placed back on the ground in a circle that encompassed them. It felt right.

And yet Lark had betrayed not only her husband's memory, but Rook, pack Levallois and the entire order of men who had vowed to protect the world from evil.

Domingos wasn't evil, but she would have a tough time convincing any in the Order of that.

"I do like a challenge," she whispered as she tugged on her shirt and left her lover sitting beside the bed.

As the hunter walked out of the bedroom, Domingos listened to her boot heels sound with dull thuds across the wood floor, stop at the front door, then exit. The door closed with a click, and the mansion was so silent he thought to hear the falling dust particles in the vicious sunbeam that entered in a thin slice down the center where Lark had not drawn the draperies tightly closed.

He stared up at the tin-tiled ceiling, painted black because he preferred the dark—needed it. For a few blissful hours while he was wrapped in Lark's embrace, the madness had retreated. He had felt whole. Lost in a place in which he never wanted to get found.

And now she was gone. The wholeness shimmered away into the shadows that controlled his life.

And the torturous music began.

Chapter 11

Rook arrived at Lark's apartment ten minutes after she had showered. Flipping her loose wet hair over a shoulder, she directed him into the living room and asked if he'd like tea or coffee, neither of which she had, but it was polite, and she suspected he'd refuse.

"I'm not here for a chat," the Frenchman said. "You've been taken off the job."

Nothing new to her. She was surprised he'd even repeat himself like that.

"I got the text message. Gunnar replaced me, then?"

"He's promised to make Domingos LaRoque dust before midnight."

Doubtful, Lark thought to herself. And then she prayed Domingos kept a low profile, and knew he would not, for pack Levallois was not yet extinct.

"Since when has the Order set time limits on its marks?" Lark dared to ask. Rook deserved respect, but she'd always toed the line between his authority and her subservience.

"Since when does one of our best knights completely botch the job assigned her?"

He strolled before the window, eyeing her sharply. He had a certain look that crossed propriety and touched lecherousness. He'd never made a move toward her, but Lark suspected he moved all over her in his mind. The little she knew of him outside the office walls told that the man indulged dark, dangerous passions best exercised in the privacy of his own home.

"I'm disappointed in you, Lark. Your husband would be, too."

He knew exactly how to plunge the stake deep into her heart. A heart that had been shattered the moment she'd had to jam the stake into Todd's chest.

Yet recently, something had occurred to rearrange those pieces of her heart, just a bit.

"I always give the Order one hundred percent," she tossed out, yet cringed inwardly. She wasn't sure she had this time. Well, she knew she had not. "The mark was elusive."

"But you said you had him in sight once."

"And then was distracted by werewolves." *Poor excuse, Lark.* Would she allow the exhaustion of emotion to drag her into lies? "Doesn't matter now, does it?"

"Not at all. I have much faith in Gunnar."

The rumor Lark had heard about that knight was that his wife had once had an affair with a vampire. Gunnar had slain the vampire, and then his wife.

"So, you know you must pay penance for letting down the Order?"

She nodded. This again? How many times had she

done the same when in training? Too many times to count. Because of that, she was an old pro.

"Bring it on," she said. "Just let me get my shoes."

"I have a car waiting below to bring you to the chapel."

The chapel. Which really was an old chapel in a cathedral the Order had retrofitted to serve as headquarters. An appropriate place for penance.

It wasn't difficult to track Lark through the city. Domingos used the rooftops as a highway to follow the black limo, dashing from roof to roof, navigating the slippery tiles with ease. Yet the sun threatened to pop out from behind the thinning clouds.

It was midafternoon. He wore the goggles and gloves and had tied a scarf about his neck and pulled the jacket hood over his head. A smart vampire would have a special suit made up for traveling during the day to keep the UVs in check.

He knew Truvin Stone had designed DragonSkin armor years ago for vampires to wear as protection when witch's blood had proven poisonous to them. Yet he hadn't traversed the roofs during the day so often until he'd met Lark. If his rooftop excursions were to become a habit, he'd have to give Stone a call.

He suspected the place the man—who he guessed was the Order supervisor—took Lark to served as base for the Order of the Stake.

"Interesting," he muttered, knowing such information would be valuable to other vampires. If he were a shady sort, and had a need for money, he could sell the information to the highest bidder.

He'd keep it under consideration.

Half an hour later, Domingos lay on the roof of an old cathedral, palms flat to the ceramic roof tiles. From his initial reconnaissance through a stained-glass window, he'd determined Lark had been brought into the chapel. She'd entered, had prostrated herself stomach-down on the cold slate floor and now lay still, arms out and cheek to the hard surface as if a monk.

Must be some kind of punishment. For not killing him?

He smirked. Such a wily creature he'd become, and not even in full grasp of his faculties. What a coup to give the infamous Order of the Stake the slip! And if they knew he'd fucked one of them? Ha!

Yet another juicy piece of information to keep tucked close to his vest.

The triumph was brief. Domingos kicked the damned phoenix coursing through his veins in the ass. It wasn't like him to take joy in the suffering of others. And to know it was Lark, the one woman in this world he...

Breathing out, Domingos closed his eyes behind the goggles.

The one woman he what? Loved? He wasn't sure what love was. The one woman he trusted? Part of him trusted her, but an even bigger part, a part that liked to rage and claw at his insides, would never again trust another living being, and especially not one who had been trained to slay his breed.

He pressed his palms flat to the tiles, which were cool thanks to the overcast sky. It wasn't difficult to pick up her heartbeat many stories below. Though his body was damaged and broken, his senses were still sharp. He wanted to be in the room with her, lying alongside her, sharing her discomfort. Could his presence spare her some pain?

You're not capable of such selflessness. You were only following the hunter, getting close to her, because you've put it into your brain a woman would never be able to kill you if she spent a small amount of time with you.

No one could kill someone he knew without regret. And she had emotions. Women were always compassionate.

Maybe. Though he found it hard to believe he'd be so callous. Again, was it the phoenix? It didn't own a part of him as if it were another entity or some kind of demonic possession. Or was it becoming more whole, claiming yet another section of his brain with each tirade, each fight against the noise and the madness?

Domingos did not care. Just as he didn't care when he plunged his fist through a werewolf's chest to rip out the beating heart. They all deserved to die for the heinous crimes against him and his fellow breed.

So now you're including the rest of the vampires? Since when did you become so magnanimous? Doesn't that sound similar to Lark's blind quest for revenge? Thought this was a personal crusade.

He could not have walked by the burning warehouse. It would have been unconscionable.

Only five years he'd been vampire. Changed against his will one night by a woman he'd not known, and had never seen after. Zara Destry had been her name. She'd come to him, frilled in pink with pouting red lips, praising his artistry after a local concert at the Opéra. He'd taken her home and slept with her, but had decided he'd not been interested in a second liaison. One-night stands were fine, but a relationship had always seemed like too much work when music had demanded his attention.

Zara had retaliated against his dismissal of her by biting him. And then she had stormed out of his life, laughing much like his maniacal phoenix. And he'd not known then what he knew now, that he could possibly have stopped the transformation to vampire if only he'd found his blood master and killed her, or had not taken mortal blood before the next full moon.

After being taken in by Truvin Stone and later, tribe Zmaj, Domingos had learned that when a mortal was bitten by a vampire, he could fight the transformation by not drinking blood before the full moon. If that was possible, the vampiric taint would pass through the mortal, and he would not change. Of course, fighting the full moon was literally impossible, and was rumored to drive the mortal insane.

One way or another, Domingos had gotten the wrong end of the crazy stick.

It was a powerful pull, the blood hunger. Admittedly, he liked the taste of blood. It was his comfort, or had been. Yet now, since he'd escaped from the pack and daren't return to Zmaj—for he didn't wish to inflict his crazy upon them—every time Domingos drank from a mortal the images filled his brain. Images of the heinous blood games. Of being shoved into the circular cage, pitted against another blood-starved vampire, and of struggling to survive. He'd been so animalistic as he sought the sustenance he'd been denied. When in captivity, he had drunk many times from a fellow vampire—to the death.

When a vampire drank a mortal to death, he experienced the *danse macabre,* a vicious replay of the mortal's nightmares, over and over. Now, having drunk his own kind to death, he experienced the nightmare daily.

Swallowing, Domingos tucked his forehead against his elbow and beat a fist against the roof.

Lark stirred minutely at the sound overhead. Too loud for a bird. Had someone thrown a rock onto the roof?

Instinctually, she knew it was neither. Her body stiff

and cold, and her muscles aching after countless hours of immobility, her sense of sound and smell had surged to the fore, and she had known the moment he had stepped onto the roof with his bare feet. The landing had been more graceful than a bird's.

He must have a homing instinct toward her. She only prayed the clouds did not move away from the sun.

Hours later, her thoughts had not reverted from the one focus that made this punishment bearable. Domingos should be hunting werewolves. Yes, she now advocated his revenge, only because she was angry at herself and at the Order. Why must every vampire be marked for death?

Okay, she knew not every one was marked and in the Order's crosshairs. They only went after those vamps who presented a threat to mortals, which could be construed as all of them. She suspected each knight possessed his own gauge of threat level when it came to vampires and very likely had varying scales of moral compass. Herself, she had never blinked an eye if the vamp had been female. If she'd encountered a woman vampire gnawing on the throat of an unfortunate victim, the stake had come out and she'd dusted the bitch.

Yet Lark had her limits. What of a child vampire? If inborn—meaning the child had been born of a mortal female and vampire male, or even bloodborn, which meant born of two vampire parents—the child only came into fangs and bloodlust at puberty. Lark reasoned that the child knew nothing else and had learned to reason in favor of its survival, and so was thankful she'd never come face-to-face with one so young.

Yet an even younger vampire could be created if a vampire bit a child and left it to transform. Any vampire capable of biting a child landed lowest of low on Lark's scale of humanity. What a bittersweet cruelty to have to stake that child to save both it and innocent mortals from its blood thirst.

Again, Lark was thankful such an encounter had not occurred.

Rarely did the Order take on a job from outside sources, though Lark had only been with them for a year, and couldn't know all their dealings. Rook kept details close to his vest. If a knight was dispatched to hunt a vampire, the intel provided was on a need-to-know basis.

Pack Levallois had hired the Order to dispose of a threat, yet it was the pack that had manufactured that threat through their vicious torture of vampires. As far as Lark was concerned, Levallois deserved what Domingos served them, and the Order should not have agreed to liaison as server of justice to one side when both were equally to blame.

Only now, alone with her thoughts, could she finally begin to reason that out. Why was she working for the werewolves? She should have questioned this assignment.

On the other hand, had she not received the job, she might never have met *him*.

"Domingos," she mouthed, not putting the name out in sound, but feeling every syllable form a tune with her heartbeat. Gorgeous night music, that.

Sensitive Domingos LaRoque, with the scarred skin and blown-out pupil and a mad frenzy screaming in his brain. Skull clatter, as he called it. Their lovemaking had pushed all that torture aside for the moment. When they had been entwined, naked limbs seeking, holding and exploring, he'd seemed sane, whole. And if the noises had started to torment, he'd gotten them under control simply by focusing on her.

Lark imagined lying beside him in bed now, her body warm against his. The damaged skin on his back had been sensitive to her touch, so she'd carefully hugged up to him, her hand clasped to his chest, feeling his heartbeat thunder against her breasts. So strong. Always he smelled of sweet smoke, like a peat fire burning low in the countryside on a lazy summer evening. It brought back memories of her childhood, a good time when the only nighttime frights the world had offered were spooks under the bed and rattling branches against the windowpanes.

It didn't matter to Domingos that she was mortal and hated his kind; he'd given of himself freely and without fear. She didn't hate him. Couldn't hate a man who had touched her soul as if with an inexplicable hush of his breath. The little he'd told her about his torture had drawn her up from the wondering and stalled fears regarding Todd, and now perhaps she could open her tightly grasped fist and let her husband's memory move on, peacefully.

Maybe?

She believed Todd now resided with the tiny soul they'd lost early in their marriage. Together she would hold them both in her heart, but not so tightly they could not comfort each other where they were now. Heaven. She had to believe in that place, if only to know her family had made it there.

Release them. Give them the freedom you are just beginning to claim.

She wanted to. She needed to give them freedom so she could finally know her own freedom.

Opening her palm now, Lark did just that. She closed her eyes and pictured her husband's loving smile in her thoughts. He'd had his own path, and while he'd loved her, at the time, she hadn't been fully prepared for where that path had led the two of them—into a horrifying darkness. But she loved him for pursuing his passion, and for being kind to so many homeless strangers, and for making her laugh and yes, even for those few occasions his absence because of his job had made her cry.

Despite the need to form lies to protect his family and hers from learning about what he really did for a living, Todd Cooper had given her the best love he'd known how to give, even after the death of their child. And Lark had reciprocated.

"Goodbye, Todd," she whispered. "I will always hold you in my heart. Keep our child safe in your arms. I send blessings to you both."

Pressing her palm to the cold stone floor, she sent thanks three stories above to the man who risked his life merely by putting himself outside, above her, close and always there.

A new anchor in her life that she clung to fervently.

The midnight bells rang and Lark took long minutes to turn over and sit up, allowing the blood to move through the parts of her body that needed it and tingling as sensation returned. A few yoga stretches were necessary. She bent forward, gripping the soles of her feet and bowing her forehead to her knees. That felt freakin' outstanding.

She'd been lying in the chapel all day. She needed a bathroom, stat. But more important, she prayed her vampire lover, who still lay above her, would not follow her escort home and risk being seen by the Order.

Lark unobtrusively lifted her head skyward as she got out of the escort limo before her building. The moon sat like a gorgeous disk in the starless night. She couldn't see the rooftop from her position on the street, and so hoped that he was not above.

For his own safety.

Though she had no reason to believe Rook suspected her involvement with Domingos, she couldn't take the chance he wouldn't look into all reasons for her failure to complete the mission. Surely, a knight would be assigned to tail her for the next few days. See if she led him anywhere particular. Like a vampire's lair?

She wouldn't make anything easy for the Order. Strolling through the building lobby and taking the stairs two at a time because she needed exercise after her long day spent inert, she entered her apartment and closed the door. Leaning over, she placed her palms on the floor and stretched out her spine and back again. A long session of yoga felt appropriate to work out the kinks, but she wasn't about to linger in an asana.

She couldn't. A soul-deep compulsion moved her quickly through the apartment. She showered in less than five minutes, not washing her hair because she didn't want it wet. Afterward, she combed her hair into a queue, then twisted it into a chignon and stuck a silver poniard through it. Stylish, yet functional as a weapon, if needed.

Shuffling through the shampoos and body creams in her closet, she found the birth control pills. Not expired. She took one and placed the rest in the medicine cabinet, close at hand.

Looking over her Order clothing, she shook her head. Didn't need the protective Kevlar tonight. But the little black dress hanging from thin spaghetti straps on the velvet hanger had not been designed for the adventure she had in mind. Slender black leggings and a simple black T-shirt would serve. No underthings, because it was hot tonight and the humidity curled up tendrils of her hair against her neck.

Slipping her feet into flat sneakers with good treads,

she then opened the back door and scanned below. The iron stairs still lay below in the courtyard. Building maintenance would probably call it a loss and leave it as it lay until someone coughed up the euros to have it removed to a junkyard. Across the street, the rooftops were clear.

The Order knights were like ninjas. You never saw them until the stake was aimed for your heart. But one ninja could always outsmart another if she was determined.

Closing the door and balancing on the narrow wood threshold, Lark muttered thanks this side of the building was shrouded in darkness. Gripping the lip of the roof easement, with some difficulty, and more thanks for the workouts that had given her impressive biceps, she levered herself up and onto the roof. Admittedly, it had been much simpler when she'd had a vampire to hoist her up.

Crouching low, she walked along the shingled surface, leaped to the next roof, which featured a border about two feet high at roof's edge, and then looked out over and down to the main street below.

Paris never slept, though her neighborhood was quiet and just far enough away from the main touristy areas to offer a peaceful lifestyle. So spotting someone moving about would raise concern, if not alarm, since it was after midnight.

As suspected, she located the knight lurking in an alley across the street and two buildings down from hers. What caught her eye was the glowing embers at the end of a cigarette. That surprised her. Most knights took better care of their health. Wonder which one that was. Couldn't be Gunnar; he was a physical specimen of health, spending most of his free time in the gym the Order maintained for training.

"One of Rook's lackeys," she decided.

With a smirk, she took off across the rooftops, knowing he'd never think to look for her above, rather than on his level.

She hadn't gone farther than two buildings south when a hand reached out from behind a stairway entry door and grabbed her, clasping over her mouth to keep her from screaming. She had no intention of screaming because his smoky scent curled about her, softening her reactive muscles and melting her against his hard, lean frame.

"What are you doing?" Domingos whispered.

"I knew you'd follow me home, and I wanted to see you again."

"You did?"

She nodded. He released his tight hold on her and she turned in his embrace, fitting her body against his seductive darkness. Lark kissed him in the shadows of the entryway, leaning into his body and finally, perhaps for the first time all day, releasing her tensions completely to the only one with whom she felt safe.

"I knew you were up on the chapel roof all day," she said. Another kiss. A stroke of her finger down his fang stirred up a wanting moan from her lover. "Good thing it was a cloudy day."

"I can't stay away from you, Lark. I need you in ways even I don't understand."

"It's because I keep your crazy away. But I don't want to question this attraction. I just want to have it for as long as possible."

"You don't know how that makes me feel."

"I do, because I feel the same way. We belong together. I don't know how or why, but we do."

"Mercy, Lark, you are too good for me." He buried his face against her neck, his breath warm upon her skin.

The press of his fangs to her skin didn't make her cringe because it was not done with intention to bite; he just couldn't help it. "Please, don't ever change your mind. But I know if you do, and you have to stake me, I'd take the stake willingly, knowing it's by your hand."

"Don't say that, lover." She lifted his chin and stroked the hair from his eyes. "I won't harm you. Ever. And I'll do whatever I can to keep anyone else from going after you with a stake. It's not right. You present no danger to mortals."

He tilted his head. "I do need to drink their blood to survive. But I don't kill. Never. I couldn't do that to an innocent."

"I know that. And the Order understands that is how vampires must survive, and we normally only go after the ones who present serious danger to mortals. That's why I'm so angry they accepted this assignment from pack Levallois."

"Let's not talk about the dogs now. Come home with me? Let me make love to you until the sun comes up, and then we'll close all the curtains and continue to make love until we fall asleep in each other's arms."

"I'm right behind you, lover. Lead the way. But be watchful. There's a knight on the street below, keeping an eye on my movement."

"I think you've given him the slip."

"There could be others."

"Then we'll take my highway home, yes?"

She slipped her hand into his and let him lead. With this man, she had no fear of falling.

Chapter 12

Domingos poured Lark a goblet of dark red wine, kissed her mouth, wet with wine, then whispered for her to go wait for him in the bedroom. She pulled the silver poniard from her hair, letting the soft darkness spill over her shoulders, and winked at him as she strolled down the dark hallway toward a glimmer of moonlight that drifted through a window.

"Don't be long," she called back on a sexy chime. "Or maybe…yeah, take your time. I'll be waiting, thinking of you."

She turned a corner, and he squeezed the neck of the wine bottle so hard, it cracked. He barely managed to get it to the sink before the bottle fell and he dropped the thick, shattered glass into the stainless steel basin. Gripping his head, he tugged his hair and clamped his jaw tight.

"Go away!"

The clattering in his brain rattled right back at him, defying him to expect that he could have another night of sanity with the sexy woman who had teasingly walked away from him.

He scented blood, and his phoenix growled, slapping his cut hand to his mouth. The taste of his blood did not satisfy, but it reminded that it had been too long since he'd fed. He'd spent the entire day on the cathedral rooftop and had tracked Lark home, ignoring the insistent blood hunger.

Normal vampires had but to feed once or twice a month. Since Domingos had escaped the pack? He needed blood daily. The madness demanded it—or perhaps it was the phoenix—and when he thought he could starve it, the world only went darker and his bones began to shake within his skin.

He should have fed before bringing Lark to his home tonight. Slithery whispers coiled inside his brain in wicked agreement. Could he slip out and quickly find a donor? It was well after midnight, and he lived in a quiet neighborhood. Unlikely to stumble upon someone taking a stroll this late. Most of his neighbors were elderly and hit the mattress as soon as the sun set.

Squeezing his fist forced out blood from the cuts that then dripped onto the crimson wine stains in the sink. He risked letting his hunger loose should he venture into the bedroom in search of the sensual pleasures Lark's body teased him to enjoy.

Go get her! We want!

"If you keep quiet," he muttered, "then I will give you what you want. But give me sanity this night. That is all I ask."

No reply clanged about inside his skull, so Domingos took that as an agreement. He washed the blood from his hand under the faucet, then claimed a new bottle of wine from the rack beside the fridge and padded down the long dark hallway.

He could smell her, the sweet, dark richness of her blood mingling with the citrus scent that must be shampoo or body wash. It was a deliriously gorgeous flavor he could already taste on his tongue. And he knew her skin tasted salty-sweet, clean and warm. And bright, so bright. And there, between her legs, he liked to lick her until she moaned and grasped his hair, pleading with him to never stop, never stop—oh, he never would.

Pausing outside the bedroom door, Domingos put a palm on the wall and bowed his head. Tendrils of discordant violin notes prodded the edges of his thoughts. He would not bite her. He must not, for he risked losing her trust, and that was all he had in his life. One woman who trusted him.

Heh, echoed the repulsive nightmares in his head. *Heh, heh.*

Blocking the intrusive madness, Domingos swung around the doorway and leaned against the frame, presenting a forced smile that he quickly erased for fear she would see the lie in it.

Sitting on the bed, her back to the gothic, carved wood headboard and wine goblet lifted near her chin, sat the sexiest bit of flesh and blood he had ever known. A finger toying with her lower lip, she cast him a glance from under a fall of lush, thick hair as black as his own. Drawing out her tongue along her upper lip, she teased up the jittering desire that fizzed through his veins. Now it melted throughout his system, relaxing him, chasing the madness to the depths, and stirring his greedy wants to the surface.

"Too perfect," he said, thinking he was undeserving,

and then not caring, because he wanted to take all of her while he was able and worry about the consequences of right and wrong later. "Mine."

She tilted her head. "Yes, yours. Come to me, my dark lover."

She stretched out a leg and drew the other to the side, opening herself to him. She'd taken off her pants and wore only the long T-shirt, but the move revealed the soft darkness between her legs. Her eyes sparkled teasingly.

Domingos set the wine bottle on the dresser and, taking off his shirt, approached the bed and glided forward like a cat, coming up between her legs. He kissed her there, upon her mons, a worshipful morsel for her beautiful design. Drawing his kisses down into the crease where her thigh met her torso, he then worked upward, pushing the soft cotton T-shirt higher with a hand.

She sipped the wine and, with a sigh, imbued the air with the heady grapes from the Rhône valley. "You want to know what I was thinking before you got here, lover?"

Had to be better than his struggle with the broken wine bottle in the kitchen and the resulting hunger pangs. Domingos moved onto his knees, straddling her. He tugged up her shirt, lifting it to reveal breasts unhampered by lacy things. "Yes."

"I was thinking about how much I love this wrong. The *we* wrong."

That label hurt him, but he didn't lose his composure, and instead bowed to kiss her breasts, one, then the other. Small yet round, they sat upon his palms lightly and beckoned a good squeeze, which he gave each of them.

"I am wrong," he had to agree, "but *we* are not."

"We are, lover. Don't deny it. But I'm okay with that. In fact, I think I need this wrong. Everything right hasn't been working so swell for me lately." She strolled her fingers through his hair, which always made his scalp tingle and tighten. "Will you be my wrong?"

He didn't want to be that for her, but he knew it was the only truth they could have. A hunter and a vampire defined wrong. And so Domingos nodded but couldn't force himself to audibly agree.

He dashed his tongue around her nipple, losing himself in the luxury of Lark's lithe, toned body instead of dwelling on her wine-induced theory of their relationship. When he suckled her she responded with her entire body, arching her back, spreading her legs wider and moaning sweetly. Her stomach brushed his chest. One foot hooked about his ankle, and she drew her fingers through his hair and down the back of his neck, where her fingernails grazed, yet did not worry the tender skin on his back.

Undone, this woman literally unfurled beneath him, changing from a controlled, bladed and vengeance-seeking hunter into a soft and supple vixen receptive to pleasure.

Beautiful danger, she.

He lifted his head from her breast and she tilted the goblet to his mouth. The wine was not sweeter than she, but it was just tart enough to ward off the growing desire for something else he wanted to drink from her. Yet the blood hunger pangs poked at his nerve endings, unwilling to let him forget the one thing necessary to his survival.

And when she stroked his fang—he never should have told her how that action aroused him—he had to grip the sheets tightly not to lunge to her neck and sink them into sublime heaven.

"You torture me, Lark," he said on a tight moan.

"Don't say that. I don't ever want to hurt you."

He took her fingers from his mouth and kissed them.

"It is a torture I could endure ever after. Lost in you, falling deep into your skin, your breasts, your mouth." He glided his fingers down between her legs. "Your wetness."

Setting the goblet aside on the nightstand, he moved up to kiss her mouth, and she pulled him in for a greedy devouring, wrapping her legs about his hips and crushing her breasts to his bare chest.

"Give me your madness," she whispered. Her eyes sought his. "Take me beyond the strange darkness that haunts you and show me how you want me. Kiss me. Bruise me. Kill me with your need."

Her words frenzied his want, and Domingos followed her commands, kissing down her jaw—avoiding her neck—and moving to her breasts, where he suckled roughly and brought up the color of a bruise to her skin. Pretty, his mark. And there, below the gorgeous mound of bosom, he licked along her ribs, snaking his fangs over skin, teasing at making a cut, but knowing he must not.

He could, but he mustn't.

You can. We need her.

Lark's body responded to the tease, nudging against his mouth, begging for a roughness he was willing to give. Sucking hard at her skin, he tasted the salt and sweet of her, and when he pulled away, he admired the love mark coloring her pale flesh.

Gliding a hand down between her legs, he pushed one leg aside and pinned it down with a knee. With his other hand, he gripped her wrist and pressed it high against the headboard.

Lark sucked in a gasp, her lips parted as her gaze locked to his. Pleading? Yes, she was his now, and he could do as he wished, and while she squirmed, she didn't utilize anywhere near the strength he knew she possessed.

Hooking a hand up under her knee, he drew up her leg and she pressed the heel of her foot against his shoulder, her toes curled against the skin that wasn't damaged. Domingos bent to worship her with his tongue. No roughness here, only the soft yet insistent lashes that he knew would bring her to the edge. She clutched his hair, which he liked because he could gauge her needs with each tug or push against his head. *Yes, more, like that.* Or maybe, *no, not so hard.* Or even, *linger, do that longer.*

"Domingos." She thrust back her head, releasing her grasp on him and stretching her arms out across the pillows. "Find me, find my core and burn it. Mark me."

Mercy, he wanted to do just that. Mark her with his fangs.

Not yet.

Soon.

Keeping his tongue on her clit, he slid his fingers inside her, moaning at the heat of her, the slippery entrance and clutching muscles that greedily begged for all that he could give. Unrestrained gasps, short cries of "Yes!" assured him she liked it all. And when her hips bucked and her voice let loose loudly, he did not stop until she pushed away his head and rolled to her side, drawing up her legs to her stomach briefly, then rolling again to her back and letting out a laughing sigh.

He loved that orgasmic laughter.

"Fuck, that was good," she said breathlessly. "You are a master."

He licked a fang and offered a wink. "I could listen to you come all day. Much better than the noises in my head."

"You're okay?" She pushed up onto her elbows, sweat

pearling on her breasts and belly, and lush hair spilling into her lashes.

"Yes." He lied only a little. The insistent nudge to bite her tingled at the roots of his fangs, but the voices only whispered for him to take her and did not yowl like a skinned cat. One small, yet odd, blessing. He could manage for now. Stroking aside the hair from her lashes, he asked, "Again?"

"Mmm…" She reached for the goblet and finished the last of the fragrant wine. "It's my turn to make you come, lover. But first more wine."

He claimed the bottle and instead of pouring another goblet, offered her the bottle, which she took and tilted back to those lush red lips. Quickly sliding her legs over the side of the bed, she handed him the bottle, which he indulged, while she unzipped him and hastily drew out his cock.

Domingos groaned at the contact of her hot fingers to his shaft. Wine dribbled down his chest. Lark bent to lick it away, teasing her tongue to his nipples, all while squeezing his rod and drawing him closer, onto the bed again.

He tilted up her head and tapped her mouth. She lashed his fingers with her tongue and she drew them into her mouth as she would his cock. The intimacy of their hold, her hand on his cock and his fingers in her mouth, floored him. A man should be thankful for such trust, and he was.

Her pretty little moans composed a melody, and in that moment, Domingos decided he needed more music in his life. He'd denied himself that precious song too long. Be it a woman's voice, or perhaps the mournful bellow of a cello, he would seek it more often from here on out. Be damned that he was a vampire. He would not taint the music any more than the madness could kill him.

The fingers about his cock tickled across the head of him, a delicious touch that flashed sensation from his shaft and throughout his body. So sensitive there, he felt each stroke as it tightened his muscles, then released them in anticipatory awakening. Every nerve alight with brightness that set him to an ultra-aware state.

"Suck me," he said, daring his tousled sex kitten. He'd learned she favored a good challenge.

Eyebrow arching, and mouth kissing his wet fingers, she gave him that look he'd seen the first night they'd stood defiantly facing each other in the alleyway—bring it.

Lark bowed to his erection and enveloped him in her hot mouth. On all fours, and kneeling at his side, she wiggled her gorgeous derriere and he smoothed a palm over the soft curve of it. He cried out at the intense pull at his root and almost came were it not for her tight grasp just under the head of his cock. Her tongue stroked him up and down, alternating with suckles and squeezes that put his mind in another universe, one that could never house screaming cats or screeching violins or any other dark diversion that threatened to destroy him.

Lark renewed and saved him. She gave him the desire to continue, to move beyond...

To be better?

Only if you stop the killing.

Pushing the dread thought away in favor of ecstasy, Domingos wove his fingers into her dark veil of hair that spilled across his stomach and, when he could no longer hold back, released it all. The anger, the pain, the fear and the torture. He slammed his hands to the sheets beside him and shouted for the freedom he had gained and would forever have.

And then the phoenix laughed and the cacophony raged anew inside his brain.

Morning brightened the room, and Lark rushed to pull the curtains shut before the sunbeam could breech the bed and her lover's bare skin. But as she turned away from the heavy curtains, she felt Domingos's hands slide up her waist and cup her breasts. His mouth landed on her shoulder, whispering soft kisses along her skin. And he turned her abruptly away from him, her palms catching the high wood dresser that she knew was empty, for he owned very little clothing, save a few things in his closet.

Facing away from him, she cooed as he tilted her hips back and toward his hard cock and pressed his steely length between her buttocks. With one hand at her breast, squeezing, kneading, hurting so sweetly, the other guided his hardness inside her pussy. Slow, so slowly, achingly teasing, until she insisted, "Harder."

Taking her demand to heart, Domingos slammed into her repeatedly. Gripping her hair, he pulled none too gently, holding her pinned against the dresser to suit his needs.

She loved the possession, the utter surrender to a man's needs. Arching her back and thrusting her hips up higher, she ensured that he could hilt himself completely. He muttered things like "need you," "want you," "fuck you," "so hot" and "blood."

She couldn't ignore that last hissed word—*blood*— nor did she expect the intrusion of his fangs at the side of her neck.

Chapter 13

It hurt. Twin fangs pierced her skin and sank in deeply. Lark's blood oozed out from her vein. Domingos's mouth began to suck as he withdrew his fangs. She shoved at him as best she could, but he'd come at her from behind, and his cock was still embedded deep within her.

She wanted him to stop. This was not the wrong she had asked for.

Or maybe it was.

Fingers clinging to the edge of the dresser, she tilted back her head and shouted, "No!"

He clutched her tighter, his hands greedy at her breasts, his cock now slipping from her and his hips jamming hers against the furniture.

"You said you were mine," he growled against the puncture wounds.

"Not like…"

A piercing shock of sweetness permeated the stunning

intrusion and Lark gasped, finding the orgasm that had been imminent when he'd been inside her only with his cock had not subsided. It raged at her need to push him away, while at the same time, protested the abrupt disconnect, begging for it to continue. It was because of his sucking at her neck, drawing out her life, sneakily mining the roots of her pleasure.

It hurt and she wanted it to stop.

And it felt like nothing she had ever known before—and she wanted it to never end.

"Fuck yes." Lark reached back and grasped for his head, pulling him down into her, inviting his feast upon her, allowing it, surrendering to what was impossible to fight. "Yes, Domingos."

Spreading her legs and supporting herself against the dresser with both palms, she fed the enemy what he needed, giving him strength and depleting hers. And it was all good because she had wanted this wrong, even though she wasn't sure what all that entailed. And now she had it completely.

Don't regret, her conscience whispered.

I don't think I will, she silently answered, as Domingos's mouth slipped away from her neck and he sank to his knees on the floor behind her, his hand trailing down the back of her leg until he turned away to crouch forward, facing the bed.

"I'm so sorry," he said softly, covering his face and bowing into his hands.

A drop of her blood spattered the floor near her toe. Lark breathed in. She felt woozy, as if no longer in her body, and the orgasm was fluttering away. Panting, her muscles stretched, her core worn to a luxurious exhaustion. At her neck, her skin burned and she felt her blood seep from the wounds. It spilled down her collarbone, dripping onto the floor again.

But she wouldn't change what had just happened. Not at this moment. Later, when her head was clear and she stood outfitted in Order gear and wielding a stake, her mind-set might pull a one-eighty.

Until then?

Raking her fingers through her lover's hair, she pulled his head back and against her stomach and held him there, feeling minute shudders rack his body and wondering if he was sobbing.

"You needed blood," she said, stroking his hair, weaving in her fingers and clinging. "I'm glad it was mine and not someone else's."

He looked up, eyes frantically searching hers.

"I mean it," she said. "I really do. But I don't want to transform to a vampire."

"You won't," he rushed out. "I licked the wound. It should heal before nightfall. Lark, you're too good to me. And your blood—so sweet and rich. I needed it. I couldn't stop myself."

She squatted, bringing herself eye level to him. Teasing her finger along his neck, she stroked it over his shoulder to where the burned skin just peeked up from the back. Her damaged vampire lover. How strange was that to think? Yet she needed him as much as he needed her, because walking through this wrong had become so right to her.

"If the Order learns you've bitten me, I'm dead."

"But you won't change," he protested. "I made sure of it."

"Doesn't matter. I've been tainted by the enemy."

"I'm sorry."

"Stop saying that." She kissed him fiercely, bruising

her mouth against his. He tasted like blood, but it didn't offend her. "I could have kicked you across the room to stop you. You know that."

He dashed his tongue out to taste the lingering pressure from her kiss. "I do know that. We're a match to each other in the physical fight."

"You just keep believing that, vampire." She gave him a small smile. "I wanted you inside me like that. When your cock is inside me…" She traced a finger down his semihard staff. "It meshes us together intimately and without words. It's a beautiful thing. And when your teeth were inside me…" She touched his mouth, and he allowed her to tap a fang. "It gave you the power I want you to know again. You owned me in those moments, Domingos. And I like how that made me feel. Controlled, yet never dominated. Did you feel that power?"

He nodded. Grabbing her across the back, he crushed her against him, nuzzling his face against her neck. "Don't ever want to lose you. You put the music back in my life."

If only that were true. Beyond the pain of being bitten, Lark could hope for Domingos to someday have back the piece of his missing soul.

"Will you ever play the cello again? I'd like to hear you."

He shook his head against her body.

"Maybe someday," she whispered. "No need to rush it. We've enough to deal with as it is. I'm not sure what I'm going to do about the Order now."

"What is there to do? They'll never know. The wounds will heal to smooth skin. Not like my back."

"Doesn't matter if they scar. What I wonder now is, do I even need the Order of the Stake anymore?"

She stood and strode to the window, almost parting

the curtains to look outside, but at the last moment, re-membered and turned to admire her long, lean vampire wandering across the room to claim the half-empty wine bottle.

"You joined the Order for vengeance, yes?" he asked.

"Yes." She slid a knee onto the bed and sat, one foot toeing the floor.

When he offered her the bottle, she tilted back a swallow, then wished for something more substantial, like eggs and bacon. He might have just quenched his hunger, but hers yet needed abating.

Stroking the bite wound carefully, she winced at the violence to her skin. She'd let him do it. No regrets.

"I vowed to stake one vampire for every day they made my husband suffer."

"And how many days was that?"

"Three hundred and sixty-six. A year and a day."

She spoke with surprising lack of emotion. Since she'd said goodbye to Todd while lying prostrate in the chapel, it was as if she could now stand beside all that had happened in her life over the past two years and look at it more analytically. With reason and acceptance.

And realizing that straightened her shoulders and made her smile. Not because she was glad to have put it behind her—what she'd shared with Todd would always be a part of her—but because she'd stepped into the ineffable idea of freedom she desired. Though the idea was not yet completely formed in her mind, she felt she was drawing nearer to it all the time.

"You would have been number seventy-two," she commented.

Standing before her, Domingos lifted her chin and pressed the wine bottle to her lips. She drank from it as he fed her.

"I could still become a number to you," he suggested.

"No. Never."

"So, find a new seventy-two and move on."

"It's not that easy anymore. I…" Falling back across the rumpled sheets and flinging her arms high and above her head, she closed her eyes. "Do I need it anymore? Really? Like you said, I'm punishing vampires who weren't even involved in his torture. When will it be enough? Can it ever be enough?"

"It's enough when you decide that it is."

"Right. And maybe enough is now. No, I know enough is now. It has to be."

Curling to her side, she patted the bed and he snuggled up beside her, knees to knees, wrists to wrists, face-to-face. The man was beautiful in his darkness. He touched the bite wound, and the stroke of his finger sent tiny tingles of orgasmic bliss shivering through her system.

"Maybe," she said on a gasp, "we were supposed to get entangled in this wrong to teach me a lesson."

"If that's the way you want to look at it."

"How do you look at it?"

He touched the ends of her hair, twisting them between his fingers. "I see a gorgeous woman who tried to kill me but decided sex was more fun, and despite my manic moods—and having just bitten her—she still wishes to remain in my life. I don't know why you've chosen to do so, but I'm glad you have."

He kissed her nose, and then her mouth, and she tasted a faint hint of blood twirled within the wine.

"I've become a vampire's lover," she whispered. "There are many women who would find that sexy."

"Yes, well, you've become the crazy vampire's lover. I'm not sure how sexy that is."

"It's beyond sexy. It's intoxicating." She nuzzled up

against his body, twining her legs with his. The smoky wine smell of him lured her to lick his biceps, and the muscles flexed beneath her touch. "And I don't want it to stop. I can honestly say I don't need the revenge anymore, and I have you to thank for that."

"Learning to forgive is very sexy to me," he said.

"Then when will you learn? I don't argue with your need to slay the Levallois pack, but now I can only worry whenever you're away from me. Where is Domingos? Will he get staked, or worse, have his head ripped off by a werewolf?"

"I'm smarter than that."

"Really? Even when the voices are raging in your head?"

"The voices make me stealthier, sneakier and swifter."

Lark closed her eyes. He thought the voices did that for him, but she suspected it was a figment of power and confidence summoned by true madness. He was not safe so long as he continued to pursue the pack. But she didn't want to be the one to stop him. Her tattered lover deserved that retribution.

"Maybe I could help you?" she suggested.

"It's not your fight, Lark, nor is it the Order's."

"I would never get the Order involved. I'm not stupid."

"You're not. But this is my fight. The only thing I want from you is this." He kissed her mouth, her breast, her shoulder where the brand raised the skin in a circle and then her neck where the bite wound tingled, yet no longer pained.

"Will you need my blood every time we make love?" she wondered quietly.

"Unlike normal vampires, I need blood every day. The UV sickness demands it or else I get loopy and you don't even want to see me starving, Lark."

"How long before you'll drink me dry?"

"I won't do that."

"*Can* you do that? I mean, the human body only has so much blood. It takes a while to regenerate. I used to give blood in college. They made me wait eight weeks between donations for the red blood cells to rebuild. If you bite me every day…"

"I won't. I swear it to you. You mean more than life to me, and I value you more than myself."

"Don't say that. I need you to value yourself, to want to live, Domingos."

He nodded and nuzzled his cheek against her breast, and she cuddled him there until he drifted into a peaceful sleep.

Lark peered into the fridge in Domingos's kitchen. Inside, a bottle of Bordeaux lay on its side, and next to that sat a box of batteries.

"Right. Like I expected to find food in a vampire's home?"

At least there were no bags of blood. Vampires required warm, living blood for sustenance and couldn't survive on blood that had been removed from the human body for long. To think about it? Ugh.

But to have experienced the bite? Mmm…now, that had been a new kind of crazy-sexy-goodness. And to think she'd never wanted it?

"What do they call those mortals who chase after vampires in hopes of being bitten?" She searched her memory of the Order's lessons. "Fang junkies."

Closing the fridge door, she turned to lean against the cool stainless steel surface and rubbed her neck where she determined the bite wound had already begun to heal and scab over. No, not a fang junkie, but she couldn't let any in the Order see her until the puncture wounds were completely gone. And then she chastised herself for the lie.

She hated lying to anyone. And to be lied to? That burned her hide. But right now she realized she'd been lying to herself ever since she had walked through the doors of the Order's headquarters and defied Rook to take a chance on her. Seeking vengeance for her husband? Who had she been fooling but herself?

She would not argue that she hadn't been cut out for the physically taxing job. Yet with hard work she had gained strength and was now damned proud of her martial arts and defensive skills.

But mentally fortified for the challenge was another question. She'd taken on the brand of the knight at a time when she'd been most vulnerable. Grief had clouded her judgment. More than ever she had needed a hand to offer help, to console. Her mother had lived back in the States. They'd never been close. When she'd told her mother about the wedding, she hadn't the money to make the flight and had been satisfied with the wedding photos. And the funeral? The bouquet of red roses her mother had sent for the service had died that same day.

And when the Order hadn't willingly offered that consoling hand, Lisa Cooper had reached out and grabbed it herself, by means of vengeance. Rook had tried to convince her she wasn't capable. She had proven him wrong only through blind, stupid determination.

But now?

"Rook may have been right."

Clasping her arms across her chest, she wandered through the kitchen and into the bare room where the sun beamed across the hardwood floor. This was the room in which she had first witnessed Domingos crouch in on himself as he'd confessed the horrors committed against his very soul.

Standing in that spot now, she lifted her head, inhaling through her nose.

"I will fight for you," she promised her lover who slept in the bedroom. "Because I have given Todd the revenge he deserved. As best I could. Now it's your turn, Domingos."

It didn't occur to her that perhaps it was her turn to take the solace and peace she needed. No, she preferred to look outward. Because that was easiest and required the least amount of soul-searching.

Helping strays, don't you know?

Wandering back into the kitchen, she found paper and a pen and left Domingos a note that she had to run home because food was a necessity in her life. She'd return in a few hours.

As she strolled down the hallway, she trailed fingers along the wall, and arrived at a spot close to the front door where the paint was peeling and the plaster dented in. Without doubt, she knew Domingos had beat a fist here many times as he'd fought against the pain of racing the sunlight, or even battled the ineffable voices from within.

Before turning to open the door, she glanced down the hallway. Images of Domingos kissing down her stomach, her mons, her thighs, scurried a delicious shiver through her veins and tightened her scalp.

And those gorgeous fangs sinking into her skin…

"Miss you already."

As she closed the door and assured herself it was locked, she scanned the neighborhood for anyone lurking who shouldn't be. An ingrained habit. A habit that could save her and Domingos's lives.

She hated walking away from him without a word, but

if she didn't eat soon she'd get a headache and her whole system would protest, leaving her off her game. If she intended to make this relationship with a vampire work, they both had to come to terms with the fact that they might be alike in some ways, but in others, they were vastly different. Especially when it came to eating habits.

"Relationship?" she muttered as she strode swiftly down the street, knowing a Metro station was not far. "I think his crazy has rubbed off on you, Lark."

If so, she liked it. And with a broad smile curving her mouth, she quickened her steps toward the main street.

Rook inserted the laser-cut key card into the reader and the LED light blinked green before the lock clicked open and the door to the basement level beneath the cathedral opened to allow admittance.

He descended the stairs, lit by fluorescent lights and inhaled the dry air from the limestone walls. Above, an actual historical cathedral held daily tours through the majority of the nave, led by an Order employee. A perfect front for the Order of the Stake. No one had been the wiser in the two centuries they had used this facility.

Strolling down the hallway to his office, he could only lament that his office did not have windows. There were days he entered before sunrise and left after sunset. Hell, he could practically be a vampire. But he was not.

He tossed his car keys onto the marble-topped desk and then flopped onto the leather office chair and faced the dark screen of his computer monitor. For reasons beyond his figuring, this morning he couldn't get the image of Lark's determined gaze out of his thoughts. The woman had surprised him at every turn of her training. Never once had she backed down from all the rigorous exercises, drills and assignments he'd given her. Truly, she was a match to any male knight they employed.

And yet he could not help wondering if he had failed her in some manner he wasn't capable of understanding because she was a woman.

Could it be so simple as male/female differences? Or perhaps he should claim it complicated, never simple. Not once had she failed to make a kill. Never. And always she completed a mission within twenty-four hours. When on the hunt, the woman was relentless. While training her, he'd used her grief to fortify her willpower, and he would never apologize for that.

So what had made tracking one insane vampire so difficult for her? Had some tendril of compassion invaded the hardened hunter's mien to make her question the inevitable death punch?

Rook sighed out through his nose and beat a fist on the desktop. He could simply ask her. That would require… talking. Getting into a conversation that went beyond delving into her mind for weaknesses and strengths in the physical fight. It would require a certain degree of emotional understanding that he was incapable of employing. He was not without emotion. He just found it difficult to relate to the knights on any level other than that of leader to the flock.

And King would insist he not get emotionally involved with any particular knight. Made things messy, a lesson both had learned over the centuries of heading this organization.

He need only place a hand over her heart, though, to see her truths.

Still, he worried about Lark. And with good reason. He'd molded her into what she was at a time when conditioning had been easy because of her weakened emotional state and grief. Touch her in the wrong spot, and she could snap. Which was why he'd tried to keep her on regular missions and always busy so she would never have a chance to snap. To think. To wonder if what she had done was right.

She had done the right thing.

And he had done the right thing by taking her off the LaRoque job. But in order to continue to do the right thing, he'd keep an eye on her. Make sure she didn't stumble off the path and fall apart. Or worse yet, stumble onto things better kept secret.

Chapter 14

Hearing a knock at her back door, Lark shoved up from the kitchen table, her runny eggs and crunchy bacon finished, and rushed through the bedroom. Quickly she opened the door and, though she wanted to beat her fists against the idiot vampire's chest for putting them both in danger, instead she received Domingos's hug and they stood inside the threshold, silently holding each other. He folded her into his shadow with an ease that made her feel as if she were a natural edge to his darkness, and their bodies melded as if the earth's magnetic forces demanded nothing but.

Was this love? Not so quickly. And certainly she did not have room in her bruised heart to love another so soon after…

Maybe? It felt different this time around, this relationship with a man. Not forced, though certainly strange.

Who could know if she'd find love a second time? Or if perhaps she'd already stumbled into it.

"I told you not to come here," she finally said. "The Order is watching me. Stupid vampire. I would have returned to your home. And the sun is out!"

He tapped the goggles around his neck. And he did have a hood pulled down low over his forehead.

"You can't cover all your skin. And there aren't enough shadows on the rooftops during the day."

He revealed the back of his hand. The skin had burned red and blistered. "Worth it to be close to you."

"Don't say things like that, Domingos. My God, you are a masochist." She pressed her head to his shoulder, just glad he was in one piece and close enough to hold. He was moving far too fast in the emotional arena. Or was she? "You're not falling in love with me, are you?"

"I don't think I know what love is."

"What?" She studied his eyes but found no tease or coyness in them. "You must have been in love. At least once?"

He shook his head. "Yes, once, as a mortal. It was a yearlong thing. She dumped me for a guitar player. It's always the rock stars who get the girls. But nothing like the love you had for your husband. Such a love must have been very strong for you to commit so many acts of murder."

She didn't like hearing it put that way. She had slayed vampires. That was not murder, but rather, removing a dangerous force from society. Someone had to do it.

"Everything I have done has been for him."

Except when it came to getting her own needs met. Which she had indulged all day and last night. When had she decided to stop doing the right thing? It felt... not wrong.

Could the wrong she and Domingos had created possibly be right?

"You know he's gone, Lark?"

"My husband? Of course I do. I told you I'd said goodbye to him while in the chapel. What are you implying?"

"Only that he doesn't know what you've done for him. Vengeance doesn't matter to anyone but you."

"I can't believe you said that. You can't possibly know what I'm feeling. How my heart feels as though it was torn from my chest. How I'll never, ever find the happiness I once had."

"How if you speak the impossible sadness you felt, then it becomes ingrained in your being. You are making yourself unhappy, Lark."

"Don't give me psychological bullshit. I can't believe this. An insane vampire is telling me how to think."

He grabbed her by the arm. "Stop using your loss as a shield, Lark. Just let me inside you."

She stepped back from him, defensive now, and eyeing the titanium stake she kept at her bedside. Yet the need for protection was a lie she immediately recognized. "I've done that already. Let you in. In more ways than one."

"He's still there, though."

She nodded. "He—Todd—will always reside in my heart. We were married. I was going to have his child. Can you understand that? But I've started to let him go."

"I'm sorry, I don't understand. It helps that you're telling me these things, though. But you said you were going to have his child?"

Hell, she'd let that slip. Lark sighed. Hadn't been a slip. She needed Domingos to know her truths, all of them.

"I need to tell you why I married Todd, even knowing he was a hunter."

"You knew that about him?"

"Yes, he never hid his job from me. Though, it was difficult not to think him a wacko, initially. I mean, vampires?"

Domingos raised a brow.

"Come on, you've always been myth, legend. But I eventually believed Todd. How could I not when he'd come home with bruises and injuries and shown me the stake? Anyway, we'd been dating four months when I found out I was pregnant. I was on the Pill."

"Ah."

"He did the right thing and asked me to marry him. I didn't want to marry because of that, but when you're only twenty-four and pregnant, and the father of the baby asks you to marry him, it's…a relief."

He met her eyes, and she could sense his question.

"That's an awful way to put it, but truthfully, that was my first reaction. Relief that I wouldn't have to do the single mother thing. I did love him."

Domingos leaned against the bed and bowed his head. "But you have no child?"

Lark breathed in deeply through her nose and forced out what she'd not spoken about. Ever. "I miscarried two months later."

She couldn't cry about it now. All her tears had been ransomed during Todd's captivity. And that sweet little baby that she never got to hold was now with Todd in heaven, she felt sure of that.

"I was never prepared to be a mother, but I'd accepted it, and was looking forward to it. Had even bought a little green outfit with puppy prints on the toes and ears on the hood. I gave it to charity afterward. Had to get it out of the house."

She sighed, remembering the pain that had made her shiver while standing in line to drop off the bag of baby clothes at the charity thrift store. Nothing like a kick from a vampire to the gut. That pain had been marrow-deep. It had scarred her, surely.

"It was easier for Todd," she said, forcing the doors closed on that memory. "We never talked about it. And he immersed himself in the Order."

"You two *never* discussed it?"

She shook her head. She'd never been good at feelings, and sitting down and looking Todd in the eye and discussing things that made her sad, or even happy, had been set aside. And he'd mirrored her reluctance, which had probably made it easy for him to push away his grief, or at least, not share it with her.

"I'm sorry," Domingos offered quietly. "That child's soul was not ready for this world."

She'd not heard it put in such a manner, and for some reason, his simple explanation lightened her heavy heart. "You think so?"

"I believe in a higher power, Lark, that grants life and takes it away. The universe has a plan for us all. Doesn't mean the plan isn't sometimes going to suck, but, well, there you go."

"Like you being turned to vampire?"

"I would never compare my misfortune with your loss, Lark."

"Thank you."

And that was all she needed. Buoyed by her confession, Lark stroked the bite mark on her neck. The scab was gone and the skin almost smooth. "Our lovemaking has become more than sharing torments, yes?"

"I had hoped so. I make love to you for pleasure, Lark. Nothing but."

"Me, too. But you need to know, I…wasn't using birth control that first night we had sex. I am now. But, uh…"

He nodded and shrugged. "Vamps can get mortal women pregnant."

"I'm sorry. I wasn't even thinking."

"It's all right, Lark. Really. If it happens…" He smiled, almost too big for a man who should be pissed at her reckless sexual slip. "We'll deal with it then."

"I want to have a family someday. But the right way. You know?"

"I understand. Me, too. I'd love a family."

She took his hand, grateful for his understanding. "I'm just— It freaks me that you'd risk so much by coming here. I don't want to lose you—" *Too* was the word she couldn't say.

So much she had lost.

He nodded. "But I can't promise it won't happen again. If I could keep you with me all the time, then there would be no need to go looking for you. You left me a *note*."

"I'm sorry, but I was hungry."

"I'll buy food to keep in the fridge for you."

"I would appreciate that." She gathered her hair with her hands and, pulling it into a ponytail, then released it over her shoulders. "So, we're going to do the couple thing, eh?"

"Can we?"

"I'd like that. Does that mean you'll allow me to accompany you when you track the rest of pack Levallois? I could be your sidekick. I pack a mean left hook, and there's not a werewolf alive who can stand up straight after my kidney kick."

"No." He strolled toward the bed and with a jump landed on it, sitting. The vampire splayed out his hands before him in surrender. "I'm done."

Lark lifted an eyebrow, her heartbeat thundering in anticipation. "You mean it?"

"You've shown me that there is no need to continue such a destructive path. I have so much to live for now. That is…" He winced and bowed his head, looking aside. "If you could commit to the two of us."

Lark rushed to him before her training could stop her from doing something stupid with the perceived enemy. "I commit. I want us. I need us."

"For more than what we get from each other," he tried. "You know? We both feed a sort of twisted need for what you call is wrong. Right?"

She relented to agree with a nod. No way to put it in kinder terms. They were both damaged. The means they sought to soothe that damage were greedy and selfish. Yet beneath their quest for something better, something right, lay the roots of true need and trust.

"So let's move beyond," he suggested. "We've both been through a lot. We understand each other's need for trust and acceptance. We also know to dwell in the past, and its horrors will never allow us to step forward. Can we stay in the pleasure we seek, and not stray back to the pitiful helping-each-other-ignore-their-torments stuff?"

"I like the sound of that."

"We've put everything out there, yes?"

"Yes. You know all my truths now." She pressed a palm over his heart.

"You know I can feel you touch my soul? I want to go soul-deep with you, Lark. Beyond the idiot revenge and surface labels of hunter and vampire."

"Can you? Will the crazies in your head allow that to happen?" She tapped the goggles he wore about his neck. The sheers before her window let in subdued light, but she suspected the UVs couldn't permeate as strongly and not to the distance where he sat on the bed. "Because if you can, I'm there for you."

"That makes me happy. I need a happy."

"We both do."

"Then let's figure out a new kind of happy that includes the two of us being right and not wrong."

"Agreed."

She kissed him soundly, lashing her tongue out to dance with his. Who would have thought this dark soul could lighten hers? She wasn't going to question it anymore.

"And now we seal that agreement with some sex, yes?" Domingos's eyes glittered expectantly.

"You're wily, vampire, but I can't think of an argument against some sheet twisting."

Lying back on the bed, he pulled her down onto him. "You want to do this with the goggles, or can the curtains be pulled tight enough to give me darkness?"

"The goggles are kind of kinky."

"You like kinky?"

She teased her tongue along her lower teeth, tilting her head in a wondering gesture. "I think I could do the kinky, but not so much if it brings up a screaming vampire. I'll pull the curtains. But don't toss the goggles, lover."

After a delicious session of licks, tickles and moans on the bed, Lark preceded Domingos to the shower to warm up the water. She stood before the stream, the tepid water beating down upon her breasts, head tilted back and eyes closed.

She slicked her fingers between her thighs, soaping up the achy sweet folds that her lover took pleasure in worshipping. He'd grazed his fangs along the sensitive skin there and it had brought her to some kind of crazy, screaming orgasm. Because the fear that he'd hurt her had mingled with the trust that he would not, and once again, she had easily released, falling into his arms. The sanctity of Domingos's darkness.

He'd bitten her once, and promised not to do it so often. The man was good on his word. But for the same reasons she still wasn't clear on what freedom meant to her, she also felt being bitten wasn't so awful as a knight should believe.

Suddenly over the drum of water she heard the thumping sound of a familiar melody. Domingos was humming something—the theme from *Psycho?*

He tore back the shower curtain and at the sight of the naked man standing there with goggles over his eyes, Lark let out a nervous scream, then punched him on the shoulder as her fear gave over to relief and laughter mingled the two of them together beneath the warm water.

"Scared you." He tossed the goggles out onto the bathroom rug, then encircled her around the waist.

"I do not like horror movies," she said. "They scare the crap out of me."

"Yet being this close to a man with fangs does not?"

"I can deal with the movies about vampires and werewolves. They are—used to be—fiction. Something I know could never hurt me. It's the serial killers and knife-wielding clowns that can show up on a girl's doorstep any night and take her out that frighten me."

"That is some amazing rationality." He spread his mouth wide to give her a corny vampire snarl. "Not even a little scared?"

"No fear."

"Right, only falling and apparently serial killers and clowns. I'll protect you from the serial killers, but the clowns—eh—they freak me out, too."

"Guess we'll never go on a date to the circus."

"Absolutely not."

"Mmm…" She gripped his thick cock, which was hard as a fighting baton and no less a weapon when she considered how having it inside her utterly devastated her need to stay strong and not surrender. "I'm not afraid of this."

"I should hope not."

"It's big and hungry. I like it when you shove it inside me and pump your hips fast. Let me show you how much I love this guy."

She slid down to her knees before him and pressed his hardness aside her cheek, looking up at him with a sweet smile.

The vampire shivered. "Lark, you know how to make a man happy to be alive."

Taking him into her mouth, she quickly brought him to orgasm, and then he sank onto his knees and pulled her to him. Beneath the rain, the vampire and the hunter cast all their fears aside because they knew that as long as they were together, nothing could harm them more than the damage they had already incurred.

"You didn't find LaRoque?" Rook beat a fist against the desktop.

Gunnar Svedson did not flinch. That he'd been given this assignment because the Order's best had failed had been an incredible coup. After a pitiful month of no kills, he needed to prove himself. And he would.

"He'll come out tonight, I'm sure of it. I will not fail where the female knight did."

Rook eyed him out the corner of his eye. The man had a way of looking at him that made Gunnar wonder if he could see things even he wasn't aware of about himself. "You don't like women much, do you, Gunnar?"

He wasn't sure what Rook implied, but he wasn't

willing to provide too much information about the way he viewed the world. Women were meant to cook and clean, not slay. Never again would he make the mistake of trusting one enough to call his wife. He'd heard the rumors among the knights about his former relationship. He couldn't deny them.

"I will show you who is the best," he said. "I've got Pavel keeping an eye on Lark, as you requested. She'll slip up."

"Slip up? You suspect her of…?" Rook left the question hanging.

"I have to wonder why the Order's best wasn't able to kill one miserable vampire who is supposed to be crazy and certainly should not be able to hold his own against a skilled fighter."

"She's not involved with LaRoque," Rook offered as if he knew it for certain. Yet the man looked aside, the muscle in his jaw pulsing tensely.

Never thought about that one until now, eh? Gunnar thought.

Well, he never missed an angle, and until this one had been proven wrong, he was going to stay on the female hunter's ass. In fact, he was headed to her place right now. She would speak to him, whether or not she liked it, and he would get the truth from her, by fist or by blade.

"I like this," Domingos said as he weighed the brass knuckles with the blade in his palm, then slipped them over his fingers. "I have to get something like this."

"They're actually made from silver, not brass. Excellent werewolf deterrent. You can have it. A gift to my lover."

His eyes twinkled. Lark giggled. "And here I thought men preferred ties or sporting equipment."

"I've always sucked at sports." He pulled up his leather pants and threaded his arms through his shirt.

The knock at the front door hastened Lark as she pulled up her pants and tugged on her shirt. She shoved Domingos's goggles into his hands as he was dressing, and pushed him toward the back door.

"Leave! Get out of here, quick!"

"You have no idea who is at the door. It could be a neighbor—"

"I don't know my neighbors and I don't have any friends." She didn't blanch at his pouting "that's so sad" look. "It could be Rook returned, or even that bastard Pavel who's been tailing me. If you care about us, then go!"

With a decisive nod, Domingos opened the back door. Evening had fallen and he didn't need the goggles, which he strung around his neck. He grabbed her by the wrist and tugged her in for a quick but searing kiss. Lark slid a leg up his, holding him to her even as she wanted to push him away. His dangerous allure pushed her to risk everything.

And if not everything, then what was life worth?

"Don't go to the roof," she said. "I don't want to risk a chase. Get out of here while you have a chance."

She shoved him outside and closed the door.

The knock came again, pounding this time. Lark rushed to it, wiping her mouth with the back of her hand as she did. Removing all evidence of the vampire. Never could she erase him from her soul. They'd revealed all to each other and had accepted without judgment.

"He is my freedom," she whispered with sudden clarity.

But she didn't have time to linger on the revelation. When Lark opened the door, she saw the hand sweep forward with a dark cloth that landed on her face. She gasped in a strong chemical scent. Her brain dizzied and her eyelids fluttered.

Domingos tracked over the roof of Lark's apartment building from the back to the street side. She should know better that he would not take the streets home. She should also know better that he wouldn't leave until he could be assured things were well with his girl.

Something didn't feel right. As he'd sensed her heartbeat while lying on top of the chapel, he sensed it now. It pounded too rapidly.

Scampering across the roof to the street side of the building, he crouched at the edge. A werewolf in human form emerged from the lobby of the building, carrying an unconscious hunter over one shoulder.

The wolf's mangy scent curdled his gut. "Levallois," he growled.

Leaping, Domingos landed on the ground solidly on both bare feet. Without pause, he swung his fist, clutched about the bladed silver knuckles Lark had given him, and put it deep into the werewolf's neck. Hot blood sprayed his face.

The wolf dropped Lark onto the sidewalk and grasped his bleeding throat.

Domingos figured the limo they stood next to had been waiting to drive off with the wolf and his captive. He opened the back door, spied Principal Caufield's horrified face, and shoved the dying wolf into the backseat.

"Next time I'm coming for you," he said, and slammed the door. He didn't need to attack Caufield. He'd just delivered the pack principal a nice juicy bit of horror.

Picking up Lark, Domingos ran down the street and made a running leap to land on a one-story rooftop. Behind him the echo of a werewolf's howl punctuated the moon he ran toward. The silver had entered the wounded wolf's bloodstream and had quickly rushed through, resulting in an exploded moon-dog. That was going to be hell to get out of the interior, not to mention all those little crannies like air vents and speakers.

Drawing Lark up to his chest, he scented the strange chemical odor on her breath. They'd chloroformed her.

Why would the wolves go after a hunter? They'd hired her. Had they intention to punish her for a job gone bad? That wasn't their place; it should fall to the Order of the Stake to discipline their own.

Whatever was going on, one thing was clear: she wasn't safe in the city. The wolves would not drop her scent until they were satisfied she'd been punished properly.

Sensing he was being followed, Domingos jumped to another rooftop and sought a dark neighborhood to lose the tail in.

Chapter 15

Gunnar stood before the principal's office desk, within the ancient confines of the eighteenth-century mansion the pack had relocated to after the idiot LaRoque's crazy escape had taken out a well-fortified compound. That the vampire was still running free boiled Gunnar's blood.

Or course, it had occurred because someone had trusted a woman enough to hand her the job. He respected Rook as far as running the Order and training the knights went, but now? The Order required some serious restructuring.

Gunnar had charged into the pack house after learning that Caufield had attempted to kidnap the female knight, and had failed. Supposedly he'd lost a perfectly good Mercedes in the process when one of his wolves had died within. Sometimes wolves could be so stupid.

"Why did you do that?" Gunnar asked now, after he'd refused the whiskey the principal had offered. "I was going to speak to her, see what information I could wring out of her. Now it's too late. She'll be suspicious of anyone and everyone."

"We want that hunter out of the picture," Caufield snapped.

"Then you must have a reason to believe she's a danger to the pack."

"A feeble woman? Not at all." The leader tilted back a finger of whiskey. "Just don't like to leave loose threads."

Gunnar looked down his nose at the pack leader. The man was half a foot shorter than him, but he knew he was no match to him should he shift and unleash his talons and beastly strength. Yet he'd dealt with Remy for too long and knew he could talk to the man in this manner and not fear retaliation. They each offered something the other wanted.

"I don't understand why you didn't come straight to me when you wanted LaRoque dead." Gunnar paced to the window and, not turning his back on the principal, lifted his chin. "Had you left the task to me, it would have been taken care of immediately, and more discreetly."

"Yes, and how then to explain that one? I needed the Order to take out the vampire, so I used a contact of my own instead of going through Rook? Don't be foolish, Gunnar. I had to make the request through official channels, then sit back and hope it was you they assigned to the task. Most unfortunate they put an idiot woman on the job. I can't believe your organization actually admits women."

"She is an anomaly. And now that she's proven her lacking worth, I expect King will have her banished."

"Yes, the King. That enigma who pulls the strings yet remains an anonymous force behind the Order." Caufield crossed his arms and leaned against the desk. "Have you ever met the fellow?"

"When I was knighted."

Caufield chuckled. "Knighted. Ha! You know only legitimate royalty can bestow knighthood."

"How do you know he's not?"

The wolf took that one into consideration. Gunnar believed the rumors that King was a king, or had ruled somewhere at some time. There were many countries still ruled by a monarchy. But he'd never buy into the insipid rumors his leader was a vampire. How ironic would that be?

No, he trusted King and Rook implicitly. Though that didn't mean he didn't have his own side business going. An Order knight was not rich by any means, and while the Order's salary provided a bit more than the average working stiff's, Gunnar preferred a grander lifestyle. Thus, his partnership with pack Levallois.

"You may be right," Gunnar conceded. "The woman needs to be taken out. But she may have information that will lead me to LaRoque, so keep your men away from her and let me do my job."

"Fine. But if one more of my pack dies at that madman's hands, I will hold you accountable. And you won't walk out of my sight alive next time I see you."

"Fair enough." Gunnar saluted the man, and strode out of the office, cursing the idiot wolf's superiority.

He'd show him who would do the walking soon enough.

A brilliant flash of lightning woke Lark from the forced state of unconsciousness. Sitting up, she realized she wasn't in her own bed.

"Domingos," she murmured as she ran a hand over the rumpled black sheets. The room was dark, the curtains drawn, save for the thin crack that had emitted the lightning flash.

Her brain buzzed and an awful chemical taste lingered in her throat. She couldn't recall much after sending Domingos from her bedroom, other than opening the door and not liking who she'd seen.

Glancing to the clock by the bed, she sighed when seeing the flashing LED lights. The electricity must have gone out. That explained the intermittent flashes of lightning through a crack in the draperies. The black sky made it impossible to tell what time of day it was, or how long she'd been out. It had been early evening when she and Domingos had gotten out of the shower and had decided to get dressed after a day of making love in all places, positions and speeds.

"Chloroform," she guessed, assessing the icky chemical aftertaste in her mouth. "But who did this to me?"

She couldn't be sure. The image of the man who'd stood in her doorway was fuzzy at best, but she knew she'd never seen him before. She was thankful Domingos had brought her to safety. He must have been watching from the roof. Her own private guardian gargoyle. Thank God, the man had not listened to her pleads to leave. She loved him for that strange stalkerish tendency.

"Do you?" she whispered in the quiet darkness.

Love was a word she had thought would never again come easily to her tongue. She had thought it only in reference to the act of Domingos rescuing her. She wasn't so swept up in the fantasy of falling into the arms of a bloodsucker that she couldn't be rational.

Not that love was ever rational. A girl did all kinds of crazy things when she thought she was in love. Like saying yes to secure a family for her and her unborn child.

Standing and checking around the room for a sleeping vampire before parting the drapes, Lark pulled aside the damask curtains and inspected the heavy downpour through the water-streaked window. She loved the rain. It smelled fresh and in this tight, compact city, it was very welcome.

But what was that out back in the little courtyard overgrown with honeysuckle vines? Flashes of lightning flickered on a form. Domingos stood outside, shirtless, his arms spread out to the sides and his head tilted back as if worshipping the rain. Or rather, he looked a god who had summoned the rain.

"Perhaps he did," she mused, thinking if anything were going to soothe the vampire's tormented skin, it would be rain. He'd once used standing out in the rain as a pitiful excuse to be granted invitation into the Order safe house.

"Such a schemer," she muttered, but would not hold it against him.

Already barefoot, she opened the glass patio door. Above, the roof overhang protected her from getting too wet, though mist of rain tickled her skin and she couldn't argue against the cold sensation that chased away the last tendrils of brain fog. Without calling out, she waited for him to notice her presence because to walk up behind him seemed intrusive. He was lost in a ritual that must touch his soul.

This was the soul-deep he'd asked her to give him, and it was easy enough to simply stand there and give it to him. Her admiration and trust. A quiet reverence. Something she'd never imagined doing while training to slay his breed. Now her anger and vengeance seemed best directed toward the werewolves.

What in the hell was the Order doing involving themselves with werewolves?

As well, she needed answers to why and who had tried to kidnap her. The only way to do that was to go into Order headquarters and start asking questions. That wouldn't jibe with her shaky status right now. Dare she call Rook and ask him? If she let on about the attempted kidnapping he'd wonder what reasons anyone could have to take her, and she wasn't ready to spill those bloody beans yet.

Domingos turned and smiled widely, gesturing her to join him under the downpour. Tentative at first, Lark made a dash across the small patch of grass, bare feet squishing through the lush lawn, and he received her in a surprisingly warm, yet wet hug that reminded her of their shower antics earlier. His kiss tasted like sky and summer. Raindrops splattered their noses and plinked Lark's lashes until she laughed.

"You like the rain?" she asked.

"It soothes me," he said. "Feels good on my back."

"Maybe it has healing powers?"

"I like to think so. I've been told faery magic could heal me."

"Really? Then why don't you try it?"

"The downside of such a cure is that faery dust is addictive."

Indeed, faery dust to a vampire was like meth to a mortal: instant addiction, and not a pleasant habit to take on. "You don't want that."

"Never. I've enough to deal with without adding addiction to the list." He brushed aside the hair that clung to her cheek. "You feeling okay? That damned wolf dropped you on the ground. I didn't see any bruises on you."

He'd inspected her for bruises? To imagine her lover looking over her body while she was passed out wasn't so much worrying as tantalizing, and Lark's body instinctually pressed along his, seeking his heat.

What was more worrying? "It was a wolf? You're sure?"

"One of the Levallois pack. Principal Caufield was parked at the curb, waiting to whisk you away."

"Hell. I don't understand that one. Thank you for saving me." She kissed him again. "Why are the wolves after me? I mean, there's a new hunter on the job—and a very good one at that."

"I have no idea why the moon-dogs think they've a right to mete punishment upon you, if indeed, a new hunter is on the job. What I do know is you're not safe at your home anymore."

"I get that. But I'm going to have to return for some stuff. Weapons and—"

"Stakes?"

"They work well against wolves to fend them off while I can get the silver bullets loaded in my pistol. And I would like to retrieve my violin. It's about the only thing I worry about getting damaged if another gang of crazed wolves breaks in."

"You're not going home. I'll go there for the violin, and if you really think you need your stakes."

"You don't think I can protect myself?"

"Not against wolves that have a vendetta against you. Have you ever fought wolves? Trained to fight them?"

"No, but you saw me handle myself just fine in the alley."

"And who swooped in to rescue you?"

"You helped," she conceded, "but I could have held my own."

"If that's what the pretty little hunter wants to believe."

"Fine. The big bad vampire saved my ass."

"And a gorgeous ass it is." He gave her backside a squeeze. "It's settled, then. You'll stay here with me. My estate is warded against wolves."

"Yes, but supposedly my place was, as well. The ward master put up new wards after the first werewolf invasion."

"Did the one who took you cross the threshold?"

"No. I don't know. As soon as the door opened I was out like a broken lightbulb. I guess I could have leaned forward across the wards."

"A properly enacted ward should have repulsed the werewolf. Unless you invited him in?"

"Never! You know, something doesn't feel right. I've been asking myself the same question over and over. Why is the Order involved with wolves?"

"Who ordered the wards?"

Lark shrugged and almost said Rook's name, but stopped herself. Just because she was sleeping with the enemy didn't mean she had to endanger any in the Order. "My supervisor. Nothing in the Order of the Stake is done without his approval."

"Is that the infamous King?"

"No. King's liaison."

"Ah. Rook."

She shouldn't be surprised at his intel, but she was. "I'm not even going to ask."

"I heard the name mentioned while in captivity. Which now makes me wonder as much as you do. Why would the wolves be involved with the Order of the Stake?"

"If they even are. It's just conjecture."

"And yet I heard both the names of King and Rook while caged at the Levallois compound. The pack is involved, Lark."

"Yes, it seems so. I'll have to check with Rook. Perhaps a ward was missed. But I'm not sure it's safe to stay here at your home, either. Once Gunnar gets your scent, you're in danger, Domingos."

"I like danger. It is more interesting than mindless pain, yes?"

"That knight would deliver you focused and excruciating pain. Trust me on that one. You do not want to stand against Gunnar. He killed his wife for having an affair with a vampire. The man has no emotion, no remorse."

"Sounds like the wolves." He kissed her forehead and bracketed her face with his palms. "All right, you check with your Order and learn what you can, but you do it from my place for now, yes?"

She nodded. "I'll stay safe. I know how to do that. And I accept your offer to protect me from the wolves. I know I can hold my own against vampires, but wolves, I'm not so sure. Besides, we make a great wolf-fighting team."

"That we do. Come here, I want to show you something."

He took her hand and led her across the yard to a small arc of vines that formed a shelter from most of the rain. Once beneath it, Domingos brushed vines heavy with flowers from Lark's shoulder, and she felt only a mist from the rain.

"It's kind of romantic under here," she said, sliding her hands up his chest. "Who would have thought you'd have a cozy little love nest?"

"I like that I can surprise you. Kiss me once more," he said. "I want to check something."

"What?"

He bent to kiss her and dashed his tongue against hers. Gripping her tightly against his body, he deepened the kiss, as if he required her breath to survive. "Still taste the chloroform."

"Yuck. And here I thought you were all about eating me up."

"Oh, I don't mind the taste." He kissed her again deeply, roughly. "It's fading."

"Let me try a rain gargle."

Lark leaned out of the grotto and stuck out her tongue to collect rain and wash away the awful taste. She felt Domingos hook a finger in her belt loop, and dared to lean forward even more, at an angle that would see her falling, but he held her securely. She spread out her arms and, for the moment, got lost in the joy of it all, raindrops splashing her skin and lashes.

He would never let her fall.

It had been a while since she'd forgotten to be angry. And a small voice inside her whispered that she should ride the joy while it was within grasp.

"Pull me back!" she called.

She stumbled against Domingos's chest with bubbling laughter tickling up her throat. The vampire put back his head and laughed, too, then stopped abruptly and asked, "Why are we laughing?"

"Because the rain tickles."

"Better than laughing because something wicked is scratching inside your skull."

"You're lucid right now."

"Again, it's the rain, combined with the powerful elixir known as Lark, The Vampire Healer."

"I like that title. But don't ever let my superior hear that one."

"Promise. I don't even want to meet the guy, let alone worry about saying the wrong thing to his face."

"Just so."

"It tickles even more if you can feel it on your skin."

He tugged up her shirt and she let him take it off.

His fingers played over the wet black lace bra, teasing her nipples to hard peaks. Lark let out a humming sigh. Something about musicians and their fingers; they certainly had skill. Toying with her bra clip, he waggled his brows suggestively at her.

"Go for it," she offered. "I've never made out in the rain before."

"Different than the shower. No serial killers."

"And we can be fairly certain there are no clowns in the vicinity."

A flick of his fingers sent her bra spilling from her shoulders to land on the soggy ground. Domingos's skin slicked over her wet skin, his hands gliding across territory he'd marked as his own as he suckled her nipple. Holding her across the back, he possessed her, claimed her. Just like that. She was his. Lark didn't want to be anywhere else.

This wrong had become right.

Suddenly he spun her around and she landed against the wall of vines and flowers, upsetting thick droplets to splatter her face and breasts. He unfastened her pants and slid them down, helping her step out of them. Her panties followed. And the vampire fell to his knees, gripping her hips and kissing her belly. He moaned, and muttered something about how soft she was, but remained intent on giving her pleasure.

Lark threaded her fingers through his hair, weaving the wet strands into twists. His tongue entered her, piercing her with the sweetest fire. As he directed, she arched her back and put up one leg over his shoulder.

The scent of honeysuckle toyed with what might still be dizzy remnants from the chloroform. All Lark knew was that this was a bliss she wanted to indulge. He licked her until her insides jittered and she balanced on the verge of orgasm.

"Yes, please," she murmured. One hand clutched his hair, the other grasped at the fragrant vines twisting across the wall beside them. "Set me free," she said.

And with an exacting rub of his thumb, he set her off to a soar. Crying out loudly, she did not care that neighbors might hear because the rain beat down steadily, disguising their lovemaking with a rhythmic patter matched by her steadfast heartbeat.

Domingos glided up to hug her, his taut muscles flexing against her panting softness. He tucked a kiss to her ear, her forehead and then her eyelids. "My sweet hunter. You think I can give you freedom?"

"You already have," she said, and followed with a tug at his jeans. "Put yourself inside me, lover. Here." She squeezed his erection through the wet material as he shimmied down the pants. "And here." She tapped his fang.

The man met her gaze with a wondrous smile. "Yes, oh yes, my love."

And he lifted her to wrap her hips about his, and as his long, hot shaft glided beyond her folds, the cold, hardness of his fangs pierced her throat. Lightning flashed in the sky, and Lark cried out in ecstasy.

Chapter 16

Lark stepped inside the house through the patio door and leaned against the wall. Her body deliciously racked through with pleasure and the pain of her lover's bite, she breathed evenly, luxuriously.

From behind her, Domingos slid his hand along her neck, then followed with his tongue, dashing away the last tendrils of blood she assumed the rain trickled down her skin.

"You are inside me always," he said, and wandered past her, naked, dropping the heap of his wet clothing on the floor near an old unused hearth she had not before noticed for the darkness.

"Always," she whispered, clasping her arms across her bare breasts. The sound of her agreement was romantic, epic even. But it disturbed her.

She'd wanted his bite out in the rain. But had that been her? Or had that been Lisa Cooper grabbing for solace, for a place to hide her fears? Lark had protected Lisa from those emotions over this year. Lisa was the obedient one who married for safety. Lisa had always tried to please. Lark flipped off the need to be liked, or to have love in favor of reckless bliss.

Had Domingos set Lisa free?

Yes, please.

She caught a loose black shirt he tossed to her and slipped it over her moist arms, then strode into the bathroom and closed the door behind her so he wouldn't follow her inside. The illumination from the constant lightning streaks outside the small paned diamond window provided enough light so she didn't need to flick on the switch. Funny how she'd become more accustomed to the muted light since she'd met Domingos.

She went to the bathroom, wondering briefly if vampires needed to do the same. They didn't eat, but they did drink. Was the blood absorbed into their bloodstream? The Order had never taught her things like the bodily functions of vampires. Funny to think about.

Flushing, she then stood before the mirror, stunned to see the ghostly flashes of a woman drowned by more than the rain. The skin around her eyes was growing darker, and her cheekbones seemed more defined. Had she lost weight? After Todd's death she'd dropped fifteen pounds from her already lean frame. Training had put back on ten. She just looked paler, for some reason. Pulled down into the depths by things that had occurred in her life, and now she was sinking deeper—but not flailing.

Lifting her chin, she defied the woman who resembled Lisa too much. Lark took what she wanted and made no excuses for it. She had wanted Domingos's bite. This was not a fall that would wound her further; she wouldn't allow it to be. Lark was strong, and this step into the wrong was making her stronger because she had chosen it, and she was making her way through the darkness and shadows, navigating it with a simple goal—connection.

And if that freed Lisa in the process, then so be it. It was time she returned to herself.

The smiling face in the mirror suddenly quirked an eyebrow. Why did he have a mirror in here? "Must have been here when he moved in."

She wondered if it made him sad not to see his reflection. And then she couldn't help wondering how the female vampires managed makeup and hairstyles.

As she shook her head at such silly thoughts, something startled her to quiet. Far off, not in the bedroom, she heard the deep bellow of an instrument. Had he put on some music—no.

"He's playing?" Her reflection beamed.

Rushing out of the bathroom and down the hallway, she followed the luscious cello notes, which started slowly, testing, pausing after a few notes. Reluctant, or rather reticent? A few plucked notes. Testing the tuning of each string. Adjusting the tone by ear.

She proceeded slowly, one palm tracing the dark wall, her bare feet making no sound on the hardwood floor. Buttoning a center button on the shirt, she tossed her wet hair over a shoulder. Arriving at the open doorway to the vast, unfurnished living room, she waited outside, not wanting to barge in and scare the man from what she suspected must be the first time he had picked up an instrument in possibly years.

There were no chairs in the room, so he must be standing with the cello. Lark loved the deep, resonant tones of the instrument. She'd taken up the violin because at the time, in school, the orchestra had needed more violins, and the cello quota had been filled. Good ole public school system, assigning the creative what they need instead of what they desire. Despite being fitted with her number two choice of instrument, she had excelled and had made first violin chair halfway through the school year, and hadn't been knocked out of that seat for her entire high school career.

Now, music was a hobby. She had almost lost touch with it while married to Todd. Almost. On weekends when he'd been gone the most, out slaying, she'd sneak her violin out of the closet and play. He hadn't liked her music. That was something she'd tried to overlook. Lisa had shoved that annoyance aside rather neatly, ignoring her husband's disinterest to her detriment.

The music inside the room stopped.

Lark's heartbeats filled in for the missing notes. She closed her eyes, willing the gorgeous sound to resume, wanting Domingos to alchemize the precious pieces of his soul together through music.

"Come in," he called to her.

She turned around the corner, shyly drawing a foot up the back of her opposite leg. "I didn't mean to interrupt. You're playing? It must make you so happy."

He shrugged, dropping his bow hand at his side. Indeed, he'd lengthened the tail spike at the base of the cello so he could play while standing. Just when he made to set the wood instrument down on its side, Lark rushed to him.

"No! I want to hear more!"

He cringed from her sudden outburst, and dropped the instrument with a dull echo, moving away from them both, the bow still clutched, his head shaking miserably. Smacks of his palm against his skull clued her she'd done more than just startle him.

She'd done what she hadn't wanted to do—frighten up the voices.

With a glance to the instrument to ensure that it was safe, no cracks or apparent damage from the drop, she stepped around it, approaching her cringing lover.

He sank into the shadows near the curtained window, drawing up his bow hand before him protectively, head bowed against his wrist as he shook it and shouted for her to get out. Or was he pleading for the voices to get out of his head?

The cello had seduced him toward touching his past normal. And she had stopped it. Hell, he'd been so relaxed around her lately, the voices had been distant, infrequent. Must have been why he'd dared to take out the cello.

Well, she was not going to let the madness win. Not this time.

"I'm not leaving until you play me something," Lark said evenly.

She wouldn't step closer. His reaction to her could turn volatile, and he would hate himself for his inability to control it.

Domingos banged the side of his head against the wall and hit his fist, clenched about the bow, in time to the beats knocking inside his skull. It hurt Lark to watch the pain he self-inflicted, but it wasn't because he wanted to.

"It's not right," he managed through clenched teeth.

"Your playing? It was beautiful. Just give it some time, Domingos."

"Out of my head!" He sneered at her, revealing the fangs she had grown to crave at her throat, yet now they presented a violent facade that nudged at the hunter inside her. "Destroy them all!"

He swiped the bow before him, but Lark dodged it deftly. Without second-guessing the move, she lunged for him, gripping his wrist to direct the bow downward, safely out of range from poking her—or him. He was strong, but she was determined.

"Don't let this become the enemy, too," she said, still holding him, but moving her other hand to stroke across his forehead. He tried to bang his head backward against the wall, and she held firm, keeping his inner demons from harming him.

She remembered he'd told her he'd stopped playing after he'd been transformed, not after his captivity with the pack. So long he had denied himself. Music was a piece of a musician's soul. It wasn't meant to be ignored or closeted away.

"Take back the music this creature stole from you," she said. "You may not have asked for vampirism, but don't punish your soul for it. You deserve some beauty in your life."

Gently, he clutched the hand she held about his wrist, and she felt the tension at his head release and knew he would not resist her touch any longer.

"You are my beauty," he declared on a whisper.

"This." She drew the bow from his hand and held it properly in her right fingers as if posed to stroke across the strings. "This is true beauty."

"It is just music."

"*Just* music? Domingos, this is your soul! And I want you to share that part of you with me. I think your music can defeat this—" She pressed her palm against his forehead, signaling the madness within. "You know it can."

He twisted into her, tucking his head against her shoulder and drawing her into a clinging embrace. A child's desperate clutch. *Wrap him up tightly and rock him, keep him safe.*

"I'll never let you go," she cooed.

"Never?"

"Promise. But neither will I ever stop wanting you to have your music back. You need it, Domingos."

A different tack was required to coax out the musician trapped within the vampire's chains.

"Will you allow me to play?" she asked. "I saw you have a violin in the cabinet, as well. You must play all stringed instruments."

He lifted his head, and though the room was dark, in that moment Lark saw into his soul. She didn't need light, she could feel the lightness of Domingos LaRoque rise to the surface and brush her softly. The musician. The man who once was. He wanted. He needed.

With but a nod, he granted her permission.

Lark took his hand and placed the cello bow in it, then tiptoed to the cabinet to take out the violin case. Gorgeous inlaid arabesques danced about the body of the pale wood instrument. Reminded her of the henna designs Indian women wore on their hands and feet. She almost dared not touch it. It was glossy and well cared for. A jewel nestled within soft black velvet.

Kneeling before the case, she put her hands on her knees, now unsure she could do this. After a two-year hiatus from daily practice, she was no professional. Yet she could play a few pieces well enough.

"Play," he whispered softly from the darkness by the curtains. "Play louder than the demons rapping against my skull."

Swallowing back a gasp, Lark wiped away a raindrop that had fallen from her hair to her cheek. She could not cure his madness, but perhaps, stroke it softly to submission?

With a decisive nod, she lifted the instrument and unhooked the bow from its soft, clasping hooks. Experimentally, she tested each string, not surprised to find that each one sounded in tune, crisp, vibrant. The instrument had a voice that wanted free.

As did its owner.

With a glance over her shoulder—Domingos's legs, clothed in tattered leather, were visible, yet shadows concealed his upper body—she began a simple piece. The one she had played most often when she had been alone and wanted to soften the space around her, an allegro in A minor. It was a sad yet buoyant piece, and she played it slowly, walking across the room toward the curtains where a slim stitch of lightning intermittently flashed. The piece was designed for two violins, and she had once been able to play the majority of both parts at the same time, but having not practiced in a long time, she stuck to the melody.

"L'Estro Armonico," Domingos stated from his dark corner.

"Yes." She paused, seeking the voice. In the darkness, she'd lost track of his position.

"Continue," the ghostly voice said.

"If you'll join me? It's for two. The cello would be a lovely—"

He suddenly scrambled to his feet and strode out of the dark and toward the doorway.

Lark rushed after him, beating him there and blocking his exit. The hunter wasn't about to let the vampire sneak away this time.

He still held the bow, and she rapped it gently with her bow. "Play with me. You know the piece."

"Lark, you press me."

"Yes."

Jaw tense, he looked down his nose at her. Fangs were revealed as he opened his mouth. Ready to lunge? A scare

tactic? Nothing about him scared her anymore. Except the
idea of him forever trapped within the madness.

"I'm not moving," she said, and held the violin beside
her as a defiant shield should he think to lunge at her.

He straightened and looked aside, avoiding her eyes.

"Domingos," she whispered. "The music wants you.
It lured you here today. You're stronger than you think
you are. Will you let those crazy cats in your head win?"

She caught his smirk, and figured that was a good sign
if he could find the humor in her question.

The man pointed the tip of the bow onto the floor
and stood there, hand at his hip as if contemplating the
deep question. And she saw the minute change in his
body, the relaxing of his neck muscles, a subtle shift of
his shoulders.

With a sigh, he wandered over to the cello. Standing
over it, he waited so long she wondered if he'd retreated
into the madness again, but he was too still.

Please, she thought, *give me this part of you. And win
it back for yourself.*

"Something quieter," he finally said. "A funeral
march. Adagio molto."

He hadn't named a piece, but rather the slow tempo
with which it should be played. Not knowing what he
would play, Lark could not accompany him. But it didn't
matter.

He was going to play.

Domingos lifted the cello and carefully, his back to
her, placed his fingers and the bow on the strings. Pensive
in his stature, he began to bow a few notes. After a few
bars, Lark recognized the piece, which could be echoed
by violin, but she felt no desire to intrude on his rendition.

And as the notes grew fluid and more emotive, she
closed her eyes to the exquisite sound this tormented soul

produced. The empty room grasped the notes and ampli-
fied them, spreading them out and swelling the gorgeous
tones beautifully. No wonder there was no furniture in
here; he must have once used this room for practice because of the acoustics.

And now as the lightning flashes ceased and the rain
pummeling the roof quieted, a master commanded her
sensory world, bringing Lark down, sliding along the
wall to crouch there. Her lover's soft shirt spilled over
her bare legs, and her still-moist hair soaked the shoulders of the fabric. She set the violin bow on the floor,
dropped her arms to her sides and tilted her head back
against the wall.

Drowning in his music, and so happy for that death.

Suddenly silence.

Lark glanced up from where she crouched. The vampire held her gaze. He stood in a beam of illumination
cast by the moon, newly revealed by parted clouds. Not
knowing what to say, she simply looked at him. There
was nothing she could say because she was out of her
ken and didn't want to risk touching the darkness that
loitered along his edges, waiting for the chance to en-
velop and pull him down.

With a tilt of his head, he nodded and placed the bow
on the strings, turning completely to face her. "My own
composition," he said, and began a different tune, more
modern, like none of the classical pieces Lark could recognize.

A deep mournful tone was lulled by a higher melody that was not too quick or fluttery. A dark winged
insect soaring through a mist in search of brightness.
Lark closed her eyes and allowed Domingos's song to
soar into her, permeating her skin, her muscles that had
been used to slay creatures, the blood she had given to

a hungry vampire and the bones that held her together after so much struggle and pain.

And there, deep in her core, the music opened her wide and up spilled tears that glistened silently over her cheeks and down her jaw. She'd not cried in so long. It felt…renewing.

Bending forward, she went onto her hands and crawled forward, seeking the lure of her savior, wanting to touch the sound and embed it into her heart. She touched the masculine curve of the cello body, feeling the vibrations of Domingos's song against her palm. And when the melody slowly landed with a final beat of wings, she pressed her face to the body of the instrument, reverent and lost.

His fingers stroked through her moist hair, tickling sensation down her neck and spine and finding her humming core to clasp it gently yet firmly. Holding the cello aside, he opened himself to her.

Lark knelt up and reached for him, resting her hand on his bare chest. "I love you," she whispered.

He bent to draw her up into a kiss, one hand wrapped about the back of her head, the other holding the cello. His fangs grazed her lips, and his tongue softened the minute sting of his teeth. Breaths shared, and heartbeats mingling, her lover gasped out a sigh as he moved high to kiss her nose, her brows, her eyelids; then finally, he knelt before her.

"You are mine," he said, "and so is this." He clasped the neck of the cello firmly.

"You've taken your music back. That was the most beautiful song I've heard. I felt it here." She pressed a palm over her stomach.

"I've never played it for anyone, had only composed it in my mind."

"Really?" That was an amazing feat, for any musician.

He nodded. "It just came out. I think I made it for you before I knew you would need it. We both needed it. I really have taken my music back."

"You have, lover, you have."

Heads bowed to each other, they knelt there in the bright darkness. Lark ran her fingers along the body of the instrument, dipping down into the sexy C-shaped curves and tracing the F-holes that arabesqued nearby.

"Make love to me as if you were playing this," she whispered. "I want to be your instrument."

He dipped her backward across the floor, cradling her with one arm while he stroked her hair aside with the other hand. Fixed to his shadowed gaze, she gasped as the bow moved across her stomach, ever so lightly, and only the edge of the strings where the rosin was not so thick, and did not catch against her skin. The elegant wood bow tilted against her body, and he lifted the shirt with the tip of it. Domingos bit open the single button placed between her breasts, and then laid the shirt aside with deft strokes of the bow.

The narrow wood glanced along the undercurve of both her breasts. Lark inhaled as anticipation giddied her to instant desire. When the fine bowstrings tickled across her areolae, she gasped.

Domingos pressed a kiss to her open mouth, tonguing her teeth, and then he retreated. Back to exploratory strokes across her nipples with the bow. He touched her lightly, carefully, because to draw out a long note would probably irritate more than excite her, and he seemed to be aware of that.

Spreading her legs, she wrapped them up and around his hips. On all fours above her, her vampire lover composed a symphony of silence punctuated by her wanting moans. She drew her fingertips carefully along his torso, ever cautious of his tormented skin, but wanting to touch him, to play harmony to his melody.

Dipping his head to her nipple, he swept his tongue over her slowly as he moved the bow aside. Heat and fire at his mouth. Lark arched up her back, taking it all, pleading for more, more and more.

"Thank you," he murmured at her breast. "For trying to slay me."

"No problem, lover. But you actually have the wolves to thank for that."

He hissed and bit playfully on the mound of her breast.

"It's true," she said.

"No talk of puppies. I'm going to make more music." He slid his fingers down between her legs. "You will sing the solo, yes?"

"Oh yes."

Chapter 17

Lark took a phone call in the bedroom while Domingos lingered in the kitchen. He should see to stocking some food in here if she was going to stay over more often. Which he hoped would happen.

They could create music together, both in and out of bed.

He'd been compelled to pick up the cello earlier, to play a few notes. Testing. To see if it irritated him. It had not, until he'd realized Lark was listening. Then the forces inside him, that angry phoenix, had protested and had wanted to smash the instrument, not allowing him to share that part of him with anyone.

But she had been insistent and firm with him, and while he had relented the moment she'd walked into his life, only when she'd held his bow hand down, away from slashing out at her, had the noise inside him coalesced and taken pause.

Someone who cares, he'd thought. All of him had come together in that moment and had only wanted to please her.

By playing the composition he'd designed in his head for the first time, he'd cemented his need for music in his life once again. And Lark's approval, her loving acceptance of his art, had only burnished that deeper into his soul.

She'd said she loved him. Had it been a reaction spurred on by the emotional moment?

Probably. He wouldn't ask her about it. If she'd meant it, she would bring it up again.

"I have to run home," she said, pausing in the kitchen doorway. Her hair was pulled back into the sleek ponytail he associated with her hunter persona, and the dark, fitted clothing further detailed that kick-ass mode.

"I thought we agreed you wouldn't return home."

"I know, but I need to claim a few things."

"Let me go. I'll get your violin and stakes and—"

"No, I, uh…" She waved her cell phone as a means of explanation, before shoving it into her pants pocket. "It's not something you can pick up for me. Just a, uh… project I need to deal with concerning the Order. I'll be back soon. Promise."

She blew him a kiss and left him waiting for a real kiss, that connection they seemed to achieve so easily. But no, she'd been reserved, closed off for some reason.

And Domingos wanted to know why, so he grabbed his goggles, pulled on his coat and gloves and set out after the hunter.

What he witnessed half an hour later brought the bile to his throat.

Crouched upon a rooftop, the sky still gray after all the rain they'd had, yet the ceramic tiles dry in most spots,

Domingos watched as the bald vampire, sporting a centipede of silver hoops along the outer cartilage of both ears, shoved a mortal woman behind a garbage bin and slapped her face, demanding her silence.

This had been the real reason for Lark's sudden need to leave, and not allow him to come along to protect her. The project? She'd gotten a call from the Order to dispatch a vampire.

The urge to leap down and take out the vampire for his cruelty toward the mortal woman stung in Domingos's veins, but to do so would put him next to Lark and he didn't want to reveal that he'd followed her.

Quickly, she approached the vampire, titanium stake ready to plunge into his back. She grabbed the vampire, spun him about and landed a high knee kick in the gut, setting him back against the wall. Without pause, she slammed the stake against his chest.

The vampire grunted at the painful intrusion. The mortal woman screamed and ran off. And Domingos clutched his chest, feeling as if the stake had just cut through flesh, bone and muscle.

A murky plume of vampire ash dusted the air about Lark as if hell had just coughed up darkness. She shook off the ash from her arms, holstered the stake and, without a glance skyward, took off down the alleyway. Tugging out her cell phone, she must be calling in the kill.

"Number seventy-two," he muttered.

Domingos lay back on the roof, eyes closed behind the goggle glass. He winced at the tightening in his chest. She had been clean, efficient, like a machine.

Would she be so when she ultimately staked him?

The knock on her front door was followed by Domingos announcing, "It's me, Lark."

Surprised he hadn't come up the back way, and curious as to why he was here, Lark opened the door, and her stalker vampire wandered inside.

He walked right past her.

Not even a kiss? A curious beginning to his house call.

He strolled through her living room, hands in his pockets, and veered away from the windows, which were shielded by sheer white fabric and only allowed muted sunlight inside.

"I told you I'd be back after I took care of some—"

"You staked him without a care," Domingos said.

Staked—ah. So he'd followed her. She hadn't been as careful as she'd thought. Hadn't expected him to follow her. Her mind hadn't been in the right place, seeking only to secure a kill to prove to the Order she was still a damn good hunter.

"It's my job," she said, not wanting to get into an argument about it when she was already feeling conflicted over the staking. Truly, had she gone after the kill just to prove herself to an organization she was now questioning having joined in the first place? That dug at her morals, but only until she got to the part where she had saved a life. "He would have killed that woman."

"You can't know that."

"I received a report from my supervisor."

"Rook?"

"Yes. That vampire had been noted twice in the area. Both times he left behind victims, one near death, the other with her throat torn so horribly she's now on life support at the Hôtel-Dieu. You still think I should have given him a Hail Mary pass?"

Domingos lifted his head, and his lean frame was silhouetted before the window, an imposing figure of darkness haloed by the pale illumination. "Will you be so quick with me when the time comes?"

"How dare you ask such a thing? Domingos, you know I would never—"

"I know, I know. But what if you receive an order from your supervisor?"

"I've been taken off your case. It would never happen."

"But if it did? Don't answer that." He gripped his fingers back through his hair, then thrust out his hands before him. "Just know, when the time comes that the stake is for me, I hope your hands wield it. It will be the sweetest death."

She plunged into his arms, and held him so tightly she knew it must hurt the damaged skin on his back, but she didn't care, she needed him to understand. "Never, Domingos. I…" Breaths coming lightly, she remembered saying it to him earlier, when she'd been enraptured by his music. And now it felt even more important to say it—and mean it. "I love you."

He found her mouth with a wanting, greedy kiss, and she answered with abandon. Wrapping a leg high about his hip, he lifted her and carried her across the room toward the dark side and pressed her against the wall. They tangled within each other, arms, legs, lips and tongues.

"I love you, too," he said. "Wasn't sure if you realized you had said it earlier."

"Oh, I knew. Love is not something I take lightly."

"I am undeserving."

"Don't say that. And I don't want you to think I could ever stake you. It is what I am. But you are fast becoming what I am also."

"Not anymore. You've changed, Lark. You're not the hunter you were trained to be. You know that."

She nodded, wanting to surrender to that easy abandonment of what she had been branded to accomplish, but feeling as if the task she had been given was too immense. Could she ever give up slaying? If she did not protect innocent, unknowing mortals from vampires, then who would?

Could Lisa have freedom while Lark continued to exist?

"I don't know what to do, Domingos. Someone has to keep them safe."

"Keeping innocents safe is a noble thing. So long as it's no longer for revenge."

"It isn't. I swear it to you. I wasn't even thinking of… *him,* when I went after that bastard. I think I need this still. The stake. For a while, anyway."

She glanced to the couch, where she'd dropped her coat and the stake. Domingos pressed his head to her chest, his hands at her waist, and her legs were wrapped about his hips. He nodded.

"I can't ask you to change for me," he said. "I wouldn't dream of it. And I agree that innocent mortals need protection from those of my breed who think they've the right to take lives. We don't need that. We can take blood without killing."

"I know. But some vampires are wilder than others. Undomesticated."

She winced to use that word. It was an awful way to describe those vampires who killed. They were not animals; they were intelligent beings who surrendered to their hunger, and the more they took, the darker and more violent they became. It was called the *danse macabre,* and it infected those who killed. Eventually they lost almost all their control. Almost.

Domingos took blood daily to survive. Would he grow as dark and evil as those she sought to destroy?

Not if he never killed. But would the madness someday push him to kill a mortal? He was capable, as she'd witnessed with the werewolf outside the burning building.

"Don't ever follow me again," she said. "Please? Or tell me if you feel the need to keep close. I don't mind you wanting to be close, to protect me. Makes me feel safe. But when I'm on a job, I need distance from the one good thing in my life."

He nodded again against her chest.

"Can we be okay with that?" she wondered. "Because of what this world has made us, we'll never completely stand on the same side, but I believe we can honor each other's very reason for being."

"That sounds fair. You've given me so much, Lark. I will respect your request not to follow you on a job. Just...tell me when that happens, yes?"

"Deal." She sighed. This was some strange and new territory she trod, but she was willing and ready to plunge in. "I need to report the kill to Rook."

"Do you want me to leave?"

"No. Just give me a minute, will you? I'm going to shower, too. There's wine in the fridge. Why don't you open it while you're waiting?"

"I don't think we should linger here for long, do you? It could be dangerous—"

A loud, demanding knock sounded on the door. Lark exchanged glances with Domingos, who mouthed, "Like that," and stepped aside to allow her to answer.

She opened the door to reveal a tall blond man spinning a titanium stake about his fingers.

Domingos hung back as Lark immediately took to action. He guessed the guy with the stake was another knight, and while he wanted to lunge forward and sink his fangs into his carotid, he'd let Lark handle this one. One, because he didn't care to put himself in the way of two stakes, and two, because she'd just asked him for that trust.

The knight didn't flinch when Lark lunged toward him, and only when she bent to deliver a roundhouse kick did the man dodge. Lark caught him aside the head with a palm and shoved, sending him staggering toward the sofa.

Lark grabbed a steel baton that had been tucked behind the television and went after the hunter with such boldness and measured skill that Domingos could only be impressed. She fought one of her own. And the match was incredible. Yet it tugged at his conscience to observe the tussle. Hadn't he committed the same crimes against his own to save his life while trapped in the cage?

He banged his head against the wall and clasped his arms across his chest. Something wanted out.

While the blond had height and bulk over Lark, she possessed smooth efficiency and her petite frame allowed her to dodge punches and kicks as if they were a nuisance. Domingos had been on the receiving end of her skill and wondered how soon before the man would fall.

Kill them all!

Domingos grasped his head, wincing as the horrible noise clattered into his skull, this time screaming like the last victim he'd slain while the wolves had looked on. Trapped within the rusted steel cage, the phoenix had bled tears. As they fought for their very lives, their skin had slicked off each other, so coated in each other's blood they'd been.

"What the fuck is that?" The hunter slanted a look at

Domingos. "Vampire? That's the insane one! You bitch, you've betrayed the Order!"

"Yes, I suppose." Lark glanced to Domingos, who gritted his jaw to keep from crying out. "But since when is the Order concerned about werewolves? All of a sudden the wolves tell us to jump, and we do? Something isn't right. And I need to find out what that something is."

"What isn't right is a knight from the Order of the Stake hanging around with a vampire. Is he fucking you?"

"Since when are you concerned about my love life, Gunnar?"

Gunnar. The one she'd said had been assigned to replace her as his killer. Domingos fisted his hands at his sides. The cacophony exploded in his head, and he twisted it down sharply, bending and crouching against the wall to fend it off.

The hunter, noting his inner struggle, marched to the window and drew open the curtains. Brilliant sunlight hit Domingos squarely in the eyes. The whiteness was instantaneous and piercing. He screamed and dropped to his knees, clutching for his goggles, though it was too late. The light had blinded him, chasing away the noise. Instead of dark, only white filled his vision, a white so painful it felt like blades piercing his pupils.

He heard Lark swear at the man and a fist connected with flesh and bone. "You're not going to take him out in my home," she said. "Get out of here, Gunnar."

"Not until the vampire is dust. You think you can use that stake on me? You are a stupid little girl. I never understood why they let you in the Order. And now look how you represent us, by screwing the enemy!"

The hollow echo of a steel bar connecting hard with jawbone ended the hunter's tirade. Domingos's body took the brunt as the man fell onto him and rolled onto the floor.

"Come on." Lark grabbed Domingos's hand. "Let's get out of here before he comes to."

"I can't see."

"Put your goggles on. It'll get better, yes?"

"Yes, but not for a while." His fingers coiled against his chest. "The pain is excruciating. You go without me."

"Don't be stupid. Come on. I'll be your eyes for you."

Sensing she was in some sort of hunter action mode, Domingos followed her insistent tugs and stumbled after her, using a hand splayed out before him as she led him toward the stairs and directed him to step down.

"That steel bar to the side of his head should have taken him out," he said as they landed on the main floor and he could feel the cool darkness of the afternoon shade in the marble exterior. "What, does he have a steel plate in his head?"

"Worse. Scandinavian stubbornness. We'll go out through the car park below the building. It's dark, and there's an exit to the Metro."

She kissed him, and it was an unexpected moment. Blind to the world, Domingos slid his hands about her back, melting into the sanctity of this hard, dangerous woman who protected him as much as he wished he could protect her. And the pain slipped away, screaming for a hold even as her softness chased it to oblivion.

"Love you," he whispered into her mouth.

"Love you back."

They emerged from the Metro after the sun had set. Domingos could see again, though his eyes were sore and itchy, as if he'd swum in a highly chlorinated pool for hours. He still wore the goggles, and had felt like a freak sitting next to Lark on the bench on the Metro platform, but he figured he fit right in with the rest of the freaks he saw walking around.

She held his hand, his knuckles pressed to her mouth, both hands clasped about his as if to let go would send him reeling and she'd never get him back.

"We need to avoid Gunnar and find out exactly how pack Levallois is involved with the Order," she said. "This doesn't feel right. Something is off, and I suspect Rook isn't at all aware of it. How are you feeling, lover? Eyes better?"

She hugged up alongside him, imbuing his senses with her brightness and lemon scent.

"I can see now. That damned sun will never take me out completely."

"Why is that? Most vamps can endure the daylight for long periods of time. And yet some vamps can't walk in the sun at all. It'll burn them to a crisp and reduce them to ash. How are you able to keep coming back injury after injury?"

"I think it's the phoenix blood in me. Takes a licking and keeps me ticking, burn after burn after bloody painful burn."

"How did you get phoenix blood in you? Isn't that a vampire who has consumed witch's blood? Something about a protection spell, but I can't recall the whole history of it."

"Witches once conjured a great protection spell against vampires, because supposedly back in medieval times vamps were all about enslaving witches and stealing their magic. So the spell was enacted that made all witches' blood poisonous to vampires. The rare vampire was able to consume witch's blood and survive, yet not without literally dying first and coming back from the ashes. Thus, he became a phoenix vampire."

"I think I heard about one who exists in the States. Can't recall his name, though."

"Nikolaus Drake," Domingos said. Truvin Stone had mentioned him. "It wasn't until recently the protection spell was dropped, and vampires had no longer to fear witch's blood. The last vampire I was forced to fight in the cage was a phoenix."

"I'm so sorry." She kissed his knuckles and then pressed his hand to her heart. "But how could you defeat a phoenix? If they are unkillable?"

"Apparently you can kill one if you rip out his veins, and— I don't want to detail this, Lark."

"You don't have to. I understand you were forced to fight for your life. And the madness, it must have pushed you to desperate measures."

Domingos sighed heavily. That she accepted him, even knowing the horrible things he had done, was amazing. So it was easy for him to forgive the fact that she had to do horrible things to other vampires to protect those in need of protection.

"I think I might know someone who could get us some answers about pack Levallois," he said. "Danni Weber was in tribe Zmaj along with me. She's a good kid. Was transformed against her will by an asshole in the tribe who thought she could do things for him."

"How would she have info about the pack?"

"She's dating Christian Hart. He used to be in pack Levallois. In fact, he was the wolf who tossed me in the cage for my first death match."

Chapter 18

"You sure you want to do this?"

Lark squeezed his hand and snuggled up beside him as they strode the street toward the boat docks on the Seine. It was cool this evening, and she'd worn only a thin silk shirt that showed her hard nipples. Domingos had admired them only until he'd noticed her shiver, and then he had given her his coat. He liked seeing her wear his things. She was comfortable in them, and that strung a note of pride through him.

Because if a hunter—whose husband had been tortured by vampires—could accept him—a vampire—then he must be doing something right. And he didn't want to upset that right.

"I'm sure." He led her down the stairs toward the docks where the Bateaux-Mouche parked, tourists' boats that sailed from the launch dock, right in front of the Eiffel Tower and down and around the Île Saint-Louis for half-hour cruises. "Hart is no longer in Levallois."

"Yeah, but if the guy was the one responsible for putting you in the cage…?"

"He was following orders. Though I admit a certain amount of disdain for him, any wolf."

"Disdain must surely be putting it lightly. Am I going to have to referee a fight?"

"That's why we're meeting on public grounds. Danni thought it best. We need to talk to her boyfriend if we're to learn information about the pack that can help us both."

"Fine. But tell me about Danni. Is she an old girlfriend?"

"No. She's too young for me."

"Is that so? I'm barely twenty-eight. How old are you?"

"Mid-thirties for the rest of my life. And you wear twenty-eight gorgeously." He stopped in the middle of the wide stone staircase leading toward the docks and pulled her to him for a kiss. The breeze swept her loose hair across his face and mingled it with his. "But I'm going to age much more gracefully than you."

"Thanks," she said with a teasing edge. "Do you really want to have a relationship with a woman who will age while you remain the same? Do I?"

"I don't know. Never tried it before. Have you?"

"No, but I can't imagine in a few decades how strange it will be."

He kissed her again. "I love that you think of our relationship in decades. But let's take it a day at a time, eh?"

"You're right. The now is perfect just as it is. God, I love you. And I sure hope when I'm seventy you'll be saying the same thing."

He swept her off her feet to a spill of giggles that settled his nerves. Because he was nervous about standing face-to-face with a werewolf. But with Lark by his side, he could accomplish anything.

Decades with this woman? Yes, please.

The boat was set to take off on the last tour for the evening, and was about a quarter full with tourists scattered randomly throughout the dozens of rows of metal benches. Domingos sighted Danni's bright red hair at the back of the boat—she waved at him—and he paid for their tickets and boarded behind Lark.

Tall, fit and always wearing some kind of military T-shirt and camo pants because she'd once served in the armed forces, Danni greeted them, shaking Lark's hand and saying how nice it was to meet her. Then she put her arms around Domingos's neck and hugged him. "It's good to see you, Domingos. I'm glad they didn't beat you."

"You can't put a good vampire down. Not for long, anyway," he added.

Looking behind Danni, he nodded to the stoic man with broad shoulders and a stern demeanor. The side of his face and neck revealed long slash scars. From talons? Interesting.

Danni slipped an arm around the wolf's back and stepped beside him. "Lark and Domingos, this is Christian Hart."

The wolf offered his hand to Lark, who shook it, and then to Domingos.

Domingos could but stare at the offering. His throat closed off and he was suddenly hot, then cold. The tingling in his fangs warned that he was hungry—for revenge.

"I, uh—" Danni looked to the werewolf "—didn't explain completely to Hart who you were, Domingos."

"You don't remember me?" he hastily asked the wolf, who showed no sign of recognition. "Danni didn't tell you about my adventure with pack Levallois?"

"No, I—" He looked to the redhead, who still held him, and then back to Domingos. Memory moved behind the wolf's pale gaze, and as the boat shifted into motion, swaying the foursome briefly, Hart shook his head. "Oh, man, I'm so sorry. You. The pet."

Domingos winced at the label. Remy Caufield had taken malicious joy in calling him that. His idiot leech of a pet who wouldn't die, no matter the tortures he was served. He'd been reduced to an animal, and had been labeled one, as well.

"Oh, dude, I shouldn't have said that," Hart hastened to say. "I had no idea. Danni, you should have told me. I didn't remain in the pack long after they took you in." He stroked the scars self-consciously. "I know that's no excuse."

"Doesn't matter anymore," Domingos said, shaking if off. "What's done is done."

He could do this, and without screeching cats playing harmony. Lark clasped his hand, and he fought not to clench her fingers. For now, she anchored him.

"I heard you've taken out half the pack."

"Close to that."

"Deserving," Hart said. "Are you…okay?"

"Does okay mean I have UV sickness that blinds me in sunlight and burns my flesh instantly, and puts crazed voices in my head and forces me to feed daily? Then… sure. Okay." He grimaced at Lark. She offered him a comforting smile and a squeeze of his hand. "But we came to get information, not discuss my health."

"Sure." Hart moved to the railing, now avoiding Domingos's eyes. The wolf didn't smell like the mangy pack wolves, but that didn't mean Domingos was going to embrace him. "You're a friend of Danni's, and that makes you a friend of mine. I'll tell you anything I can. I've been out of the pack for months, though. I don't have current intel."

"Have you ever known the pack to have an association with the Order of the Stake?" Lark asked.

Hart's eyebrows rose. He looked to Danni, who nodded that he should speak.

"Uh, yeah. Why do you ask?"

"I'm a knight," Lark said.

"A woman?" Hart put up a placating hand. "Sorry, I'm saying all the wrong things, guys. The two of you have knocked me a little off-kilter. The Order of the Stake and pack Levallois? Yes. Well, not officially. One specific knight, to be exact. He and the pack leader, Remy Caufield, have been associates for a while."

"Associates?" Domingos said, while at the same time Lark asked, "How long?"

Hart shrugged. "Few years? Let's see. The pack started taking in a lot more vamps for the blood games, hmm...about two years ago."

"What does that mean?" Domingos insisted. "How are the blood games associated with the Order?"

"This is information I shouldn't even have—"

"Tell them," Danni insisted. "You have no alliance to the pack now. They were going to kill me, remember?"

Hart lifted his girlfriend's hand and kissed it, displaying a tenderness that Domingos could relate to, yet he wasn't going to give the wolf any slack.

Hart nodded. "Right. One of your knights has been providing the pack with vampires for the blood games for years."

"Gunnar," Domingos guessed.

The werewolf met his gaze, his pupils growing wider. "You know him?"

"He's the knight currently assigned to stake me," Domingos said. "And I suspect he'll take Lark out, too, if given the chance."

"A knight going after another knight?" Danni asked.

"I was the one who was originally assigned to stake Domingos," Lark said. "I failed." She planted a kiss on Domingos's cheek, which made Danni smile and hug her wolf closer.

"So, what does Gunnar do?" Domingos asked. "Bring the vampires he's supposed to slay to the pack?"

"I think so," Hart said. "I was never in on it, not allowed access to that inner knowledge. But I saw him talking to Caufield a few times. And I did see him enter the compound with an unconscious vamp over his shoulder once. Had to unlock the cage to let him drop the bloodsucker inside."

That slur tipped him over the edge. Domingos lunged for the werewolf, yet was stopped not by Lark, but by Danni's hands to his chest. Lark's hand he felt smooth down his back, reassuring, but not stopping.

The werewolf had not moved, nor did he show fear. "Let him have a go at me," Hart said. "He's owed that much."

"Not with a bunch of mortals on the boat," Danni cautioned. "Though, if we were someplace private, I'd let him loose on you."

Danni pushed Domingos away, and he came to a stand, but his ire fluttered high now and the irritant inner wailing spun. The whispers were so loud they grated against the curves of his skull. He gripped his head, and Lark shuffled him back a few steps, putting herself between him and the other two, gentling him with her presence.

"Don't let it win," she whispered. Her sweet scent threatened to still the madness. "You're better than that."

"You don't know what it was like being caged," he

said, tucking his head against hers, not willing to let the wolf see his pain and anger, but unable to push it completely away.

"I know, lover. I don't ever want to physically know. The boat has turned and is heading back. Another fifteen minutes. Can you make it?"

"Of course I can. I'm not an imbecile." He gave his head a good shake and pounded it once. That seemed to joggle the whispers to background noise, and the mangy cats fled.

Cats. *Heh.* Fighting the wolf with a screaming invisible cat. Yep. He was a certified nutcase.

"Gunnar Svedson," Hart offered. "That's the knight you want."

"Thank you," Lark said, and stayed beside Domingos as the lights from the buildings onshore reflected across their faces in haunting flashes. "Give us a minute, will you?"

And she wrapped him in her arms, her hair falling over his face and her body crushing against his, surrounding him with her brightness and sweetness, and forcing him to think only of her. His luscious lover, his beautiful hunter, the woman who spoke to his soul.

His beautiful danger.

"What are we going to do now," he asked, "about this information?"

"Nothing tonight. I'm going to take you home and make love to you and not think about anything like hunters or werewolves or nasty cages. Just you and me, lover. Then in the morning we'll face reality."

"I thought you were my reality."

"Yes, and all that other stuff is my new wrong. You're my right, Domingos. Do you understand that?"

Those words whispered over the noises inside his head and conquered them. "Yes."

Domingos held Lark until the boat docked, and while Hart disembarked right away, Danni remained to give him one more hug.

"He feels bad," she said about the hulking wolf who waited for her on the landing, his hands stuffed in his front jean pockets.

"I hold nothing against him," Domingos offered. "The wounds are still sore, though. Give me some time before you invite us over for cocktails."

"I will, but I will also consider that a date. We gotta stick together, we, the few vampires unaligned with a tribe. We can protect one another, yes?"

"As best I can, I will always be there for you, Danni."

"I know you will. You're a good man, Domingos. Goodbye, Lark. It was great to meet you. Take care of him."

They watched Danni and Hart wander off, hand in hand, a vampire and a werewolf, and both agreed that if those two could manage a relationship, then they could, as well.

Instead of returning to Domingos's home, he led her to the right bank and through the busy streets that glittered with lights and tourists still lingered, gazing into the windows of closed high-scale clothing and jewelry shops.

"Where are you taking me?" she asked.

"My home is too dark and broody for us tonight. I want to treat you. Make love to you in style on fancy sheets."

"I don't need fancy, lover. I just want you."

"Yes, but I want to see you in fancy. Indulge me?"

She shrugged. "Lead on. The glaring headlights don't bother your eyes?"

"Nope, only UV light. I have definitely become a night creature, eh?"

"That was a surprise to me when I was learning about your breed, that vampires can walk in the day. Though I know there are a few strains of vampire who can't do the rays. So you're not a member of tribe Zmaj anymore?"

"No. I didn't return after escaping from the Levallois compound. I didn't want to inflict my crazy on them. And their new leader, Slater, is not exactly friendly. I'm thankful Danni is still my friend. She's right, we need to stick together."

"Maybe form your own tribe?"

"Maybe. There is something to be said for strength in numbers."

"When you're feeling more like your old self, perhaps," she agreed.

They walked toward the Place des Vosges, an elite shopping area in which Lark had once loved to spend the entire day. High-heeled shoes had been her crack, and with Todd's small trust fund she had indulged. After her miscarriage, she'd cut down on the spending, but not the window-shopping. A girl had to have some dreams to take her mind away from the real world on occasions.

As a knight she made a moderate salary, but she'd been sticking that money away for the future, which, in her new dreams, involved a cozy little cottage out in the country and maybe a studio in which to practice.

"Will you ever tell me about your mortal life?" she wondered as they strolled hand in hand down the street. "Intel reports you were a studio musician."

"I was, and I played with a few local orchestras. Was getting into some alternative rock 'n' roll stuff, as well.

I'll tell you all about it sometime. If you'll tell me how a pretty girl ended up married to a vampire hunter, and then became one herself."

"You know the part about me saying yes because I was pregnant. There's not much else to tell. But whatever you want to know about my life, I'm an open book. But I warn you it's boring."

"Boring sounds pretty damn good to me."

"I bet it does." They turned down the Champs-Élysées. The street was always lit as if for a grand celebration. "Danni is pretty, and her boyfriend seems like he could be a nice guy. For a werewolf, that is. He was nervous around you, and very apologetic."

"Yeah, but those scars on his face and neck. They should have healed. Something wrong with that."

"No doubt."

"No more talk about wolves, eh?"

"Right. Wait." Larked recognized the elegant black wrought-iron *porte-cochère* before the hotel foyer. The doorman in regal forest-green livery nodded to them. "Are we staying at the Shangri-La?"

"You like?"

"Like? I've always wanted to stay here. It's supposed to be ultraluxurious." She rushed ahead toward the tall white, paned doors that led into the hotel. "Can we order room service? Something decadent that you can watch me eat?"

"Whatever you want."

"Oh, my God, I love this!"

They checked in and Domingos secured them a suite overlooking the Tuileries Gardens, which were currently lit with decorative lighting strung through the chestnut trees in celebration of Bastille Day. The view from the patio was amazing. Across the river the Eiffel Tower twinkled, lit up like a Christmas tree. And on the Seine the boats cast golden waves in their wake across the darkened waters.

Right away, Lark called up room service and ordered champagne, caviar and rice pudding with rum-soaked currants. Sounded decadent, and she had a craving for something sweet.

Domingos stood on the threshold of the opened patio door, shirt unbuttoned and hands slack at his sides, watching the bustle in the royal gardens below while Lark pulled back the soft Egyptian cotton sheets and fluffed the pillows. She then wandered into the bathroom to inspect the soaps and shampoo and the soft, plush guest robes. Something about staying away from home was such a treat that she couldn't contain her joy. Made her forget all the dire things that she probably should be thinking about.

"In the morning," she decided with a wink to her reflection in the bathroom mirror. "Tonight is for us."

Shrugging off Domingos's coat and her shoes, and following with her clothes, she slipped on the thick terry robe, then tiptoed up behind her lover and ran her hands down his chest. He smelled like the air outside, mingled with smoke and a tint of the river. She sensed his arousal and then felt it as she glided her hand lower and gave his erection a firm squeeze.

"I want you now, lover," she said.

He turned from the sights and stepped into the room. "What about room service?"

"Threesomes are not my thing." Tugging him toward the bed, she shoved him hard and he landed splayed across the emerald comforter. "Unless you want to invite the delivery guy in when he arrives?"

"No way, just the two of us." With a tug of her hand,

he pulled her onto him, and the hard crush of their bodies was an exquisite pain.

Domingos let out a harsh chuckle that he noticeably fought to control.

Lark bracketed his head with both hands and stared into his eyes. "No, not now," she said to the intruders that inhabited his thoughts, perhaps his very soul. "He's mine, and I will take him away from you."

Such a Cheshire smile appeared on Domingos's mouth she thought surely it wasn't him, but instead the cats or violins, or those mysterious whispers. But he gripped her hips and flipped her onto her back, straddling her and planting a hard kiss at the side of her neck.

"I love you," he said. "And I'm not going to ask why you can stand to be near me, but instead just take it for what it is."

"What it is is love." She pulled him down for a long, deep kiss. He ground his hips against hers, and she rocked against him because he'd pinned her wrists and she couldn't use her hands to get him off. "Wait a second."

He paused from the kiss, and followed her gaze out the window.

"It's just so beautiful," she said of the twinkling iron lady. "I've never really looked at it. You know, to admire the craftsmanship. And the view is perfect from here. It's kind of phallic, isn't it?"

"You just went from a pretty landmark to a penis reference, Lark. I like the way your brain works. It's almost as twisted as mine."

"I like twisty."

He dived against her neck, his tongue lashing across her vein. When he traced the spot where he'd bitten her twice she felt an incredible erotic surge trace her skin. He'd marked her, and her body knew his touch.

She wanted to feel his fangs penetrate her again, and squirmed within his tight grasp to free herself.

"You don't need to touch right now," he muttered against her neck. "You're mine."

"I want to touch your fangs."

The sharp prick of his ivory tooth against her vein made her suck in a breath, and her body rose against his in anticipation.

"Mercy, you're so wanting," he growled. "Every touch, no matter how soft, speaks to you."

"Yes, it makes me want your bite. I know it's wrong but—"

"But we made our wrong a right, yes?"

"Yes," she said on a gasp. "Please, Domingos?"

Two pinpricks pressed against her skin, the tip of his tongue teasing the heat of her as he did not sink them in but merely lingered there. Heart pounding, she anticipated the sweet pain of his intrusion.

A knock at the door brought her down from the tightened stretch of want in a gushing exhale.

"Sorry," he whispered.

"Room service. It's my fault. Blame it on a need to indulge."

Domingos rolled off her, arms outstretched and tonguing his fangs. Lark lingered as she crawled over him, teasing her finger across the tips of his fangs, until a second knock hurried her to answer the door. It was all on the room tab, so she had to merely sign.

"Open this." She handed him the champagne after the bellboy had left, then dipped her finger into the caviar and tasted the tiny, salty black pearls that rolled across her tongue. "So good. You ever try?"

"Doesn't look appealing." He plopped onto the chair beside the food cart.

"Vampires can eat a little, yes?" She crawled onto his lap and fingered another wodge of caviar into her mouth. Then she kissed him, rolling her tongue across his, chasing the black jewels. "What do you think?"

"The kiss was great. The fish eggs?" He made a face. The cork popped out of the bottle and spilled onto the floor. Domingos made the save by putting the neck to his mouth and drinking the bubbling contents. "Ah... Much better. What about that other stuff? What did you order? Looks mushy."

"It was on the dessert menu." Lark leaned over from the chair and dipped her finger into the rice pudding. It smelled strongly of rum and cinnamon. A wodge sat warm on her tongue. "Mmm, I love this even more."

She kissed him again, mixing the taste of champagne with the decadent treat.

"That is good. Another taste." He scooped up a glob on his finger and she opened her mouth, but half the pudding landed on her cleavage. "Messy. But I couldn't have planned that one better."

He bent to her chest, his tongue seeking the sweet dessert. He pulled aside the robe and sucked her skin clean.

Lark dipped her fingers into the rice pudding and this time managed a mouthful of the dessert, but he pulled her head down for another kiss and they mingled and tasted each other. She crushed her breasts up against his chest, and the sticky trail of food smeared into his skin.

Taking the champagne bottle from him, she tilted back a swallow. It was so bubbly that she choked a little, then laughed, and almost spat it out. "It went up my nose! This stuff is crazy."

"Better the drink than me, eh?"

"Apparently I like my men a little crazy."

"Do you? All that hair pulling and screaming at nothing turns you on?"

"It's the never knowing what you'll do next, and the surprises, that I adore."

"And my bite?"

"Yes." She stroked one of his fangs and he moaned deeply. "Your lovely fangs. I will have them inside me before the night is over."

"You will. Promise."

"But what I love most about you?" she said. "Is simply you. You're unique, and different, and, well, I love you this way. Promise me you'll never be normal?"

"Normal sounds good sometimes. Kind of like boring. But if you prefer me crazy, I have a feeling I won't have to try too hard to achieve that goal. More sweet stuff, please." He stuck out his tongue and waggled it at her.

Lark stepped back from his lap and stood before him, parting the robe and letting it fall to the floor. She glided her hand down from her shoulder, slowly over her breast and along her stomach to rest on her mons. "How about this sweet stuff?"

Her vampire lover lunged forward onto his knees and looked up to her as he strolled his fingers down her stomach and to her hips. Lark felt certain she had never seen a more adoring gaze from a man. It was a look she could get used to.

Sliding her fingers through his hair she then directed his head toward her mons, and when his tongue lashed out to taste the dessert she offered him, she bent forward, drawing her palms across his damaged back. The scarred and papery skin displayed a map of his pain, and she navigated it tenderly with a feather touch. And he did the same at the junction of her thighs. Until he did not, and his touch grew deeper, harder, more intense, and she gripped hanks of his hair and supported herself upon his shoulders as he deftly brought her to orgasm.

As her body shuddered and her breath gasped out, he rose before her and pushed her into the bed. She landed, face forward, in the midst of orgasm, hands catching the sheets. He grabbed her hips and plunged deep inside her from behind to take advantage of her pulsing muscles.

The vampire cried out in pleasure as he rammed inside her. And Lark met his vigorous thrusts with rhythmic shifts of her hips against his. Hard and hurried, he was not gentle, pressing a hand to her back and gripping her hip. And when he came, she felt as though he surrendered all he had to her, and the trust was so implicit that no one could ever part them no matter what tactics they used.

Chapter 19

"Bite me," the hunter whispered in the vampire's ear.

As aroused as he still was after making love to Lark for hours nestled within the soft sheets, Domingos's cock stood up at attention at the sound of those two words. He slid down Lark's lithe body, kissing every inch of her skin in his path, until he landed the spot he ranked as one of his five favorite places on her body.

"Right here," he said, and licked the curvy underside of her breast. "You'll taste so good here."

The graze of her fingernails across his scalp sent good shivers down his neck, and the inner whispers took a little thrill from that, too. But when he nudged his nose against her breast, the whispers receded as his focus and desire increased. Her breast filled his hand, and the nipple hardened against his palm. She spread her legs, and he moved his hips so he lay between them and on her stomach. He loved when she hooked a leg up over his back and it didn't hurt his damaged skin so much because, well, because all he could think about was tasting her blood again.

Poking his fangs against her skin, he nudged gently as if testing a balloon that might pop, and then slowly, taking his time because the sweet first droplets of blood hitting his palate were always the best, he pierced her.

Lark's nails dug into his scalp, and her hips rocked. She rubbed her mons against his chest, working at the sensitive nub that would get her off, while he sank his fangs as deep as they would go. His lips pressed hard to her hot flesh, his tongue teasing at the wodge of skin his teeth dug up into his mouth. Normal vamps would now retract their fangs, but he had to physically lift them from her body.

As he exited her skin, Lark's moan grew orgasmic, and the hot blood spilled into his mouth. It swirled over his tongue like wine, and satisfied his needs like ice water on a hot summer day.

"Fuck yes," she said on a shuddering tone.

He sucked roughly, taking what he could from the area that was not rich in veins, but did serve him a taste. What he really needed was the vein, a nice thick one, like that on the inside of her thigh.

Biting into that one could kill her, the whispers cackled. *But she's a hunter, so...*

"Domingos..." Just his name, as she reached orgasm and her body shuddered beneath his command.

Blood quenched his desires. Sweat meshed his body to her skin. The smells of spice and champagne and her brightness dizzied his senses as he, too, fell into the swoon. A delirious place of rightness and dark, courtesy of taking blood. And he free-fell, high-fiving the whispers, giving the finger to the yowling cats and manic violins and soaring into a sweet oblivion that no one could take away from him.

Blood on his tongue, metallic and bittersweet, Domingos swallowed and sighed against Lark's breast.

More. You need more.

He closed his eyes to the irritating whispers and glided on the swoon, reaching to curl his fingers about the ends of her silky hair.

Don't deny the hunger! Fight for survival. Without blood, you die, vampire. Do you want to die in a cage? Surrounded by idiot dogs?

He curled his fingers tightly.

Lark tugged at her hair. "That hurts, lover. Be careful."

Careful? Careful is for the dead. And dead vampires are tossed in the Seine, a pile of ashes!

Gliding down Lark's belly, Domingos licked her skin, already missing the taste of blood, and seeking a pulsing vein to renew the delicious swoon. An abrupt draw of the bow across the violin string screeched through his nervous system. His fingers twitched against Lark's hip.

She reached for his hand, still panting and sighing from the tremendous orgasm she'd experienced. He pulled away from her seeking touch.

There, over her mons, which smelled of sex, champagne and heat, he then moved to her thigh, where the scent of blood racing through an artery drew him like a heat-seeking missile.

Without a second thought, Domingos jammed his fangs into the artery and swallowed the gush of hot blood.

"No!"

Lark's other leg slammed against his skull, but the hit did not silence the insistent whispers. He growled, pulling out his teeth and lapping at the spurting artery. "Mine. I will not be defeated."

"Oh, hell, it's the madness. Domingos!" Her fist crashed against his temple. The hunter struggled for freedom. "Focus. Don't let the blood—hell, it's the blood. He can't see beyond that."

The woman suddenly slammed her thighs together, crushing his head between them, and with a deft shift of her hips managed to flip him to his back and kick away to freedom.

Domingos, empowered by the blood, scrambled after her across the bed, grabbing her by the leg. He swiped his fingers across his tongue.

"Not going to get away from me, hunter."

Her heel landed on his shoulder, and she pushed away, which sent her reeling off the bed, to land in a catlike roll that ended in her pounced upon her feet and hands.

She studied her thigh. "Shit, I have to bandage this, or it'll bleed out. Or if you could lick it to seal the wound—"

"I'm going to suck you dry."

Domingos jumped from the bed and landed beside her, using an elbow to put her down and rolling on top of her. He struggled to get her hands in his, to pin her, but she was strong.

They'd danced this dance before, and they'd called it a draw. *No one defeats you, idiot vampire pet.*

"No one," he growled.

A kick to his stomach hurt, and he hadn't been prepared for such force. Domingos's back and shoulders hit the bed. Lark managed to get up on her feet and raced into the bathroom, slamming and locking the door behind her.

Licking the blood from his lips, Domingos reveled in the sweet treat. A violent rage of noise clattered within him, begging for more. He banged his head against the mattress and gripped his fingers through his hair, tugging.

"Can't let you win!" he shouted at the madness inside him. He shouldn't have bitten her.

It's what you do! You are vampire!

"Yes," he mumbled in response to the demanding whispers.

Heaving, he felt his energy wane and he collapsed into a weary acceptance. *No. Don't give up.*

With an agreeing nod, he crept up to his feet and made a run for the bathroom door. It was solid and did not give.

"I'm not coming out until you settle down," she called. "Don't let it win, Domingos!"

"Come out and play with me, hunter. What happened to your desire to stake me?"

"I love you, Domingos."

"So she says." *She loves to tease you and tempt you with her blood. But she won't give it all?* "I won't hurt you, I just want to make it all better."

"Bullshit."

He banged a fist against the door, clawing his nails down the wood. "Come out here!"

Silence pounded in his heartbeat. The air, heavy with blood and sex, taunted him, prodding up the voices, the maniacal screams and clatter and music. Why had he let back in the music?

Domingos slammed his head against the door. It hurt, so he did it again.

And the third time he aimed for the door, it suddenly opened to reveal a shivering woman. She stood there before him, arms crossed over her bare stomach and breasts. Tousled hair hung over one side of her face, and the other side revealed a wide, frightened eye.

Frightened? His mighty hunter feared nothing but falling.

You just pushed her over the edge. She's fallen into your madness.

Heh.

And there, at her leg, she'd tied a white towel, yet already it bloomed with crimson. It would continue to bleed if he did not seal the wound. She would die.

"No, you can't— Not you," he gasped. "Not Lark. I... Lark?"

A tilt of her head and her lips, plumped from his kisses, parted.

"No, I didn't want to do this." He gripped his hands before him, unsure how to touch her, to make it better. The whispers had ceased. The cold reality of seeing his lover standing defeated before him shoved back the insanity. "No."

He pulled her to him and wrapped his arms about her body. She hung lax in his embrace, her head falling to his shoulder, her body so warm and trusting against his.

"I'm so sorry. I—the voices—they wanted more. Oh, hell, Lark."

He pushed her away and strode to the other side of the bed, where her blood spattered the thick white carpet. Falling to his knees, he bent to the blood droplets and let out an agonizing moan that scraped from his insides and forced up all the pain he'd felt since that first night of captivity.

The first time the cage bars had clanked behind him had stiffened his spine. The first fight, another blood-starved vampire stalking toward him had opened his veins and carved up his soul. Many fights to follow. So much blood. And the agonizing death screams. Until finally he had felt nothing. And each time the cage bars clanked he'd moved as if a machine, going for the veins to survive.

Domingos pressed his face against the carpet and clawed with his fingers as yowls of agony birthed from his core. And the music shattered the frail cage about his soul. Falling, falling away from sanity, and landing...

A bare foot appeared near his head. The touch of soft fingers upon his scarred back. She fell, more than knelt, beside him. Weak from blood loss, Lark leaned over his back and wrapped herself upon him.

"I'm here, lover. I'm ever here."

Domingos sniffed away tears and turned to catch her limbs in his arms. Her eyelids fluttered. Her head fell heavily upon his shoulder.

"Screw my damaged soul," he said. "If you die, I'll never rise above this insanity."

He tugged the towel free from her leg and bent to lick away the blood that had slowed to an ooze. And he licked the wound to seal it and stop the bleeding. It was different than his tongue pressing to the skin while he drank blood; this was a purposeful act that delivered his saliva over the wound until the blood stopped flowing. And he took no pleasure in the taste of it; he could not.

Lark's fingers fell upon his hair and he moved with them to lie down beside her on the floor. Tears stained his lover's pinkened cheeks.

"Thank you," she whispered. "That was close."

"Sorry."

He nuzzled up against her chest, seeking the comfort that only she had offered him. A hunter had seen that he possessed light within a vast darkness. And he'd just punished her for that blind trust.

She would accept his apology and tell him she loved him. But was it so easy as that? Could he trust himself around her to never again go into a manic rage in quest for her blood? Next time he might kill her.

He couldn't conceive of hurting the one good thing he had in his life.

Must he walk away from her to keep her safe?

"Never leave me," she whispered, as if reading his mind. "We'll survive this."

He nodded against her body but couldn't bring himself to speak the truth he knew without doubt—the vampire must leave the hunter.

When Lark woke on the bed, she spied Domingos sitting in the easy chair near the patio door, naked but for a pillow clutched on his lap. The curtains were pulled against the rising sun, yet his goggles sat on the glass-topped table, within reach.

Yawning and stretching, she inspected the wound on the inside of her thigh. It was ugly and ragged, but it would heal. Probably scar, but that mattered little to her.

He'd almost killed her. Yet she could summon no reason to run away from him in fear. She'd feared him for moments last night when she'd struggled to stanch the bleeding behind the closed bathroom door. And then when she'd opened the door, and she had looked into his tormented gaze, she'd seen *him,* the man who had promised never to hurt her.

He might fight the madness forever. She was strangely okay with standing alongside him for that fight. Because she had seen into his soul, and knew it was good.

Sliding off the bed, she tiptoed into the bathroom and turned on the shower. He'd didn't join her, and she was sad about that. Space was probably what he needed. Because she suspected he was fighting his inner voices and his own morals right now. She twisted off the water.

Forgoing a shower for now, she answered the urge for distance and food. Dressing in the same clothes she'd worn yesterday, and wishing she had something different, she pulled her hair back into a ponytail, then padded out into the room and tucked her feet into her shoes.

"I need a decent breakfast, maybe something savory," she said as Domingos strolled past her into the bathroom. "I'm going to head out and find a pastry shop. I know there's a fancy one in the shopping center not too far away."

"Yes, good. I'm going to shower."

"I love you," she tried, but the vampire closed the bathroom door without responding. "I really do."

Closing the room door behind her, she headed out, wishing he'd answered with *I love you back*.

Exhaling deeply, she took a moment to get her bearings. Her body ached in that sweet way it did after a night of lovemaking, yet her thigh pulsed with real pain. She looked a mess. This would be a quick run for sustenance, a few breaths of fresh air, then back to face her lover.

They had plenty to talk about.

Lark didn't get farther than ten steps from the hotel entrance when a sleek black limo swerved before her, blocking her from walking forward. From out of the backseat swung two knights outfitted in Order gear. They worked efficiently. One wrangled her arm behind her back while the other injected her with what she knew was a tranquilizer at the side of her neck.

Her eyelids fluttered, and she caught a glimpse of Rook sitting in the backseat before blacking out.

Chapter 20

Domingos stepped out of the shower and dried off, afterward using the towel to wipe away the fog from the mirror. It was a habitual action that he couldn't seem to drop. Wasn't as though he could actually see himself in the mirror.

Tossing the towel aside and staring at his clothes piled on the floor, he wished he had something clean to change into. Lark's blood had spattered his shirt when he'd attacked her last night.

What kind of animal had he become? He'd violently attacked the woman he loved. And she could have bled to death had he not settled and gotten the insanity under control.

Had she not touched you and called you back to sanity. She always does that for you. She is your savior.

And he had to protect her now by walking away from her. It was the right thing to do.

He didn't hear her out in the room, so she must still be out eating breakfast. It had been a while since he'd gone into the bathroom. Maybe she needed some time away from him? But she would return eventually. And he thought it best if he was not here when she did.

"Really?"

He stared hard at the mirror, thinking if he looked long enough he might see a glimmer of a reflection. Yet he was no longer worthy of a reflection.

"Can I leave her?" he wondered. "I love her."

And what kind of man told a woman he loved her and then took a hike? If she loved him as much as he believed, then returning to an empty hotel room could devastate her. He didn't want to hurt her that way.

"Much better than killing her."

And that was it. He must choose the lesser of two evils to save Lark.

He strode out into the room and tugged on his shirt and pants. He'd guessed at the time wrong. It had been an hour since Lark had gone out. Where was she? It was closer to noon than breakfast time. Had she decided to do a little shopping? Linger over some food?

Maybe she'd decided to take the same hike he was contemplating?

Domingos landed on the end of the bed and sat there, staring out through the pale sheers at the blurred image of the Eiffel Tower.

"She left me?" His heart thudded and his throat went dry. Something in his brain tittered and cackled that laughter he hated so much.

It made a hell of a lot of sense. And, since meeting each other, neither of them had been using much common sense. Had the hunter won over the woman who had fallen in love with the vampire? Perhaps she had returned home for a stake.

In which case, Domingos should get the hell out of here.

Yet it was daylight, and the sun was high. He fingered the goggles. They would only protect for so long. He couldn't navigate the streets back to his home, clear across the city. Not unless he took the Metro. Still, he risked burns to his skin because he had no gloves or a hood.

He was stuck here. And maybe that was for the best. If Lark returned, they'd face each other with the truth. And if not, then he would know for certain that he'd lost her.

Lark stood before the marble-topped desk that mastered Rook's office. The office was located beneath the chapel in the lower level of the cathedral. All the Order rooms were situated underground. The main floor was a front for tourists.

Beneath her feet stretched an Aubusson carpet that hailed from the seventeenth century. The walls were hung with weapons ranging from medieval-era maces and halberds to modern-day throwing stars and blades. The Mac—the only thing on the desk—flashed a screen saver that featured a Zen sand garden raked into a circle.

Rook was a yoga master, and had tried to instill in her the peaceful yet mind- and muscle-taxing practice of yoga. Who would have thought yoga could be so challenging? She'd never been able to concentrate beyond her busy thoughts to hold a pose for very long.

Woozy yet, she managed to hold her own and stand upright. She figured she must have been kept in the holding cell for three hours, because that was the usual wear-off time for the drug they'd injected into her vein.

Rook, clad in steel-gray Armani, stood but three feet from her, yet he leaned back on the edge of the desk, his legs crossed casually at the ankle and his arms resting over his chest. It wasn't a defensive pose, nor was it chastising. He often let long minutes pass without speaking. Allowing her to think about what she had done, as if she were a child who'd misbehaved. And always, his all-seeing gaze bored into her very soul. His still disposition freaked her sometimes.

But the jig was up; she knew that. Somehow, someone in the Order had learned about her involvement with Domingos. Hell, she knew who it was: Gunnar. After she'd knocked him out at her apartment, he'd likely returned to the fold and tattled on her. Which she had expected, but she'd thought to start figuring things out this morning, not to be whisked away from her lover's arms before she even had a decent breakfast. And a shower.

Hell, she could guess what Rook was thinking about her appearance.

Her thigh ached. She should have been walking, exercising the muscle, but lying still for hours while sedated had allowed the muscles around the wound to swell.

"You know why you're here," Rook offered, standing now, approaching her and closing their distance to but a foot. He smelled like cloves, which reminded her of the rum pudding she and Domingos had shared so intimately last night. "I'm ashamed for you, Lark."

"Don't be. I'm a big girl. I can get in and out of trouble all by myself."

The slap to her jaw would have been expected if she'd been all there, completely clear of the tranquilizer. Instead Lark lost her footing and stepped quickly not to fall over. She resumed calm, wincing at the sting of the strike. The man never held back his strength against her.

"You were my best knight," he said, now standing so close she could head-butt him, but she thought better about doing that. "It was a simple assignment. How difficult can it be to take out one deranged vampire?"

"You don't really want my answer, do you?"

Another slap, this one equally as hard. So, she would speak only when prompted.

"He's infected you."

No, she wanted to protest. Domingos might have bitten her, but he had been careful, sealing the wound with his saliva to ensure that the vampire taint did not transfer to her. And he'd done the same to the wound on her leg. Perhaps that was the reason she wasn't feeling all there. Blood loss had weakened her.

"I know what you're thinking," he said. "I couldn't possibly know everything you do. But you're wrong. I've trained knights far longer than you can comprehend."

Yeah? So, how long was that? Decades? Centuries? She really wanted to know what the guy's story was and whether or not he was paranormal. But another slap would not appeal to her stinging jaw.

"I've gotten inside your head, Lark. I've lived there while training you, and I remain in the recesses. I know how you function. And I know what it takes to break you down."

"Then you must also know that Gunnar is working with pack Levallois."

"Is that what the vampire has led you to believe? LaRoque has used persuasion on you."

"No, I—"

This time she blocked his slap, and, standing there, her forearm fending back his hand, the two held a stare-down that would reduce any sane mortal to plead for forgiveness and then run for protection. Rook was a master of martial arts and could kill with but his hands. Quickly.

His skin was cold, always so cold. He couldn't be completely mortal. But she'd never dared ask what it was that made him something more, so strong, and at times seemingly able to read her thoughts.

"I can see the truth in you, Lark."

Yes, he'd said that to her many times before. That was the line that always made her wonder if there was something about Rook that allowed him to see a person's truths, like a supernatural mind reader. Demonic?

So why couldn't he comprehend the truth she'd confessed about Gunnar and Levallois?

"The vampire has controlled your mind."

Domingos would never do that. He'd promised he would not. And she hadn't felt the persuasion as she had from Vincent Lepore.

Lark straightened her shoulders and lifted her chin. It was difficult not to wince at the pain in her thigh, but she did not want Rook to learn about that injury. That would mark her as a failure and she might then not leave this office alive. Good thing the other bite was on her breast, safely hidden from his inspection.

"You're thinking about all the times you've been together, wondering how he did it," he put out there. "Damn it! That vampire has ruined you."

Never. But she wouldn't protest. Instead she hoped Domingos was not at the moment thinking something crazy like that she had left him.

The office door opened and in walked a tall man with spiky brown hair and piercing eyes. Lark immediately lowered her head and studied the floor. The man requested that Rook join him out in the hallway.

"Stand right here. Do not move," Rook instructed her, and left to go talk to King.

Lark would not move. Because he would know if she so much as inhaled incorrectly. Why King was in the building was beyond her. He rarely set foot in Order headquarters, choosing to remain an enigma. Knighting ceremonies were about the only occasion Lark knew he visited.

After two minutes, both men returned. Rook followed King, who approached her. Lark lifted her chin, trying to avoid eye contact with King, but also wanting to look at him because he was so fascinating to her. Who was he? How had he come to organize this group of mortals who stalked vampires? Had a vampire harmed his family? Had that been the catalyst? The Order was centuries old. He couldn't be human if he was the actual man behind it all.

He gave her the chance she'd been hoping for. King stepped directly before her, and took his time gazing into her eyes. As handsome as Rook, the man had an angular face that held a chiseled beauty, possessed of a calm sternness. She noted the muscle in his jaw pulsed angrily.

Wooziness stirred with her brain. He was powerful. He was her leader. She had betrayed him.

"How are you this afternoon, Lark?"

"I'm…well." Odd question. As if they knew each other and he was concerned about how she felt. Which she knew was not true. "And you?"

"I'm concerned. Rook has filled me in on your status."

"If I could just—"

A tilt of the man's head gave her pause. She had no idea his level of patience and whether or not he wielded the same lightning-swift reflexes as Rook, and had no desire to test him.

"The vampire LaRoque," he said in a level, deep tone as he laid a palm on her shoulder, "persuaded you, Lark. Do you understand?"

She nodded. Perhaps he had. Persuasion was a vampire's sneaky way of getting into a mortal's mind and influencing the person's thoughts. Had Domingos persuaded her compliance? Her love for him? Because really, a hunter falling in love with a vampire? What kind of crazy had she imbibed? The vampire was insane, and he must do what he could to survive—like tearing open her artery to get to the blood.

King tilted his head, his gaze not veering from hers. She trusted him. He would not steer her wrong. He was old and wise.

"You do understand," he said decisively. "Good, then."

With a curt nod, he turned, said something she couldn't hear to Rook, then strode out of the office.

When the door closed, Rook filled the spot King had just stood in. This time he clutched her upper arms gently, reassuringly, with his cool hands. "You're our best knight, Lark. I've got another assignment for you, but it hasn't arrived at the warehouse yet. Wait in the chapel for me, will you?"

A private entrance to the chapel stood at the back of Rook's office. With a nod, Lark dismissed herself and hustled into the chapel. When the door closed behind her, she released her held breath.

Her lover had used persuasion on her?

"That bastard."

She fell to her knees upon the hard fieldstone floor, clutching for her breaking heart.

King waited for Rook outside his office door. Rook joined the man he'd known for what seemed like forever and they strolled down the hall toward the elevator. They took it down a floor, not speaking. The tension was thick, but it didn't make him uncomfortable. Rook felt no need to speak until King prompted his thoughts.

The elevator doors opened to an underground private parking area. Once outside, King glanced toward the security camera and motioned Rook aside to stand in the blind spot near the concrete wall.

King was a thoughtful man and never spoke unless he had something to say. "After all the centuries I have devoted to the Order of the Stake, I will not allow a pack of werewolves to bring us down."

"I believed her when she said Gunnar was working with Levallois," Rook said. "She had no reason to lie about it."

"That is incredible. But yes, I agree with your assessment of the female knight. She is trustworthy, despite her siding with LaRoque."

"What do you want me to do?"

"Gunnar is out."

"Before midnight, I assure you."

"And LaRoque gets the stake." King added quickly, "But make sure it's done by the right knight."

"Of course. Also to be completed tonight. What about the pack?"

King's jaw pulsed and he clasped his hands together before him for a moment's thought. "You and I will have to dig out the silver bullets. It's been a while since we've shared the hunt, eh?"

Rook slapped his hand into King's, sealing the agreement. "I look forward to it. Let me deal with the immediate stuff first. I'll ring you when it's done."

With a nod, King strode over to a waiting black BMW.

The driver opened the back door. King had never learned to drive, nor had he expressed the desire to do so.

One of these days, Rook decided, he was going to take him out to a pasture and teach him the necessary driving skills every twenty-first-century man should know.

Lark waited in the chapel three hours before Rook poked his head in and, with a nod, gestured for her to follow him down the hallway to the elevator. They rode that down to the parking garage where a car waited. She was glad he was a man of few words; she didn't want conversation with him, anyway.

She was conflicted about Domingos and hadn't been able to stop arguing with herself while sitting in the chill calm of the chapel. But really? No, she was no longer conflicted. Clearly the vampire had persuaded her. How dare he?

And yet some inner niggling seemed to want to grasp that idea and rip it to shreds. But why would she believe such a thing if it wasn't true?

The vampire had good reason to use persuasion on her. It had kept her from killing him, hadn't it? And he'd gone so far as to have sex with her, many times. That was the part that didn't jibe with her rationale. It made sense that he'd persuade her not to kill him, to think of him as an ally and try to get away from her. But why lure her into his bed?

Wouldn't any man do the same if he had the supernatural skills of influencing women into his bed? *Hell, that first night without protection.* The thought sickened her.

Most men were not sexual predators or physically violent toward women. The vampire was a unique predatory breed that relied upon blood and sex to survive. And he'd bitten her.

Had he also persuaded her to believe he'd sealed the wound to prevent her transformation? Could the vampire taint be coursing through her veins as she sat here?

She eased her hand along her inner thigh, wincing at the pain that did not seem to lessen. It had been a deep bite. She had bled almost to the point of passing out. Of course it would take time to heal. Why hadn't he persuaded her to forget he'd done that? To perhaps instead make her believe it was an injury she'd taken during a struggle with another vampire while on the hunt?

Domingos had been playing with her mind; she had no doubt about it.

"He bit me," she blurted out to Rook. "I think you need to know that. I— If he used persuasion on me, then I'm not sure if he was telling the truth about not transforming me. I could change. Oh, God."

"You'll be fine," Rook offered, his attention toward the front of the car, not even glancing at her.

How could he know that? Was it that weird innate truth meter she suspected he possessed that told him she hadn't received the vampire taint?

Hell, now she was starting to lose it. She didn't want to become a vampire. She had only wanted to represent the Order and serve them well. Live to serve. Serve until death. Die fighting. A simple motto to follow.

And what had happened to her desire to avenge her husband's death? Paused at number seventy-two? That wasn't her style. She never gave up on a challenge.

But somehow she'd decided to stop serving and to cease her quest for vengeance. Instead she had succumbed to the dangerous allure of a vampire.

You're smarter than that, Lark. You love him.

She twisted her head toward the window and scrunched

her eyes closed. No, it couldn't be possible. She could never love a man who was like those who had killed Todd.

But they didn't kill him, you *did. You were the one to plunge the stake into your husband's heart.*

"We can forgive this transgression," Rook said in the quiet of the backseat, seeming to sense that she needed reassurance. "You were manipulated. You have to understand that, Lark. You were under the vampire's persuasion."

She nodded, silently accepting.

Yet her heart screamed like those screeching violins in Domingos's head that it was all wrong.

She didn't know what was right anymore.

The Order owned a concrete-walled warehouse in the thirteenth arrondissement. No windows, and only one access door that led up strong iron stairs to an upper floor reinforced by double walls. Sounds made inside were never heard outside. No matter how loud the scream.

Lark followed Rook up the stairs, not questioning what this task was he had planned for her. It would be a trial, for sure, something to prove to him and the Order that she was still on their side and unworthy of banishment.

Hell, anything would be better than another day lying prostrate on a cold stone floor.

Her thigh pulled with each step. A reminder that her determination could be contaminated. Stupid mistake, that.

She moved her left shoulder, and the tugging brand seared into her skin reminded of her dedication a year earlier when she'd entered the Order. Focused and ready to learn. Blinded by grief and the desire for vengeance.

Use it now, a tiny voice whispered at her. *Don't make another wrong choice. You know your truths.*

She couldn't understand her conscience until the door opened and inside she heard the struggles of a man against two others. He was held with thick ropes wrapped about his chest and arms, while another man beamed a small UV light at his eyes.

Domingos yowled and fought against the ropes. The skin around his eyes smoked and burned.

Lark's heart thundered. She took a step toward the knights, wanting to tear them away from the tortured vampire—and then Rook's hand fell onto her shoulder and he said, "The job."

Chapter 21

"Release him!" Rook called. "He's not going anywhere now that you've blinded the pitiful creature. Come in, Lark."

At the sound of her name, Lark noted that Domingos stopped struggling and lifted his head, tracking the thud of their footsteps across the concrete floor as they moved closer to him. The ropes dropped away from around his chest and arms and he stood, unbound, in the center of the room. The three knights stood close, but had assumed a militant pose, on guard, as Rook passed them and they stopped ten paces away from Domingos.

"He give you trouble?" Rook asked one of the knights.

"Wasn't an easy bag. But we didn't let him get up on the rooftops, like you warned us. He'll be a good little leech now. Won't you?" The knight kicked the back of Domingos's knee, and he almost went down but managed to stay upright.

Lark assessed that he'd incurred no injuries during the struggle. Not on the outside, anyway. But he couldn't see. Though his eyes were open, the pupils filled his irises and Lark knew he was blind for at least an hour. He looked pitiful, standing there alone, his shirt hanging on his shoulders and torn at the buttons, obviously during the struggle. Fangs cut over his lower lip and blood spattered his chin, likely his own.

What had she seen in this man that she'd allowed him to touch her, to kiss her, to make love to her?

She shivered, remembering the trace of his hands over her skin. So gentle and reverent. She'd seen into his soul. He'd granted Lisa freedom and she, in turn, had given him back his music. Had it all been a lie?

Apparently. What skills this creature possessed to have gotten into her brain to manipulate it so.

Rook produced a titanium stake, twirled it once and paced before Domingos. "I admire you, LaRoque. You certainly gave us good chase."

"Did you tell him about the werewolves and Gunnar?" Domingos asked Lark.

"She did," Rook answered smartly. "We'll take care of the matter."

That was the first time Rook had acknowledged that he'd taken Lark's words to heart. Good. No matter what theatrics went down here in the warehouse, she had confidence Rook would see to Gunnar's punishment and cease collusion with the werewolves. If she did any good for the Order today, it would be to expose a dirty knight.

"Fine day when the Order of the Stake colludes with werewolves," Domingos teased.

One of the knights behind the vampire stepped forward, ready to punch Domingos in the kidneys from behind, but with a castigating look, Rook stopped him.

"No, he's not for us, boys," he said. Turning, Rook approached Lark. He slapped the stake into her palm. "This one's your kill."

Domingos's heart stopped when he heard the leader's chilling announcement. He'd left the Shangri-La the moment the clouds had moved over the sun. Waiting not a block south of the hotel had been the black van filled with knights. A little off already with his thoughts jumbled about Lark, he hadn't been prepared for their strike, which had come swiftly and with four men and hadn't given him much chance for escape.

Now he could not see. When he opened his eyes the world was painfully white and it felt as if the UV rays still seared his eyeballs. But he could hear. And the slap of the titanium stake into Lark's hand cut through his dark and tortured heart and tore it wide-open.

She would not do it. Could not.

And yet she must. She was a knight. Slaying vampires was what she had been trained for. And if she did not wish to lose the respect of her superior and fellow knights, she mustn't blink to follow orders.

He'd always known it would come to this.

Domingos had been right to guess that she'd left him this morning. For good. Had fled his madness and returned to the life she'd managed to fit herself into this past year. He didn't think it was a good fit for her, slaying vampires and killing without thought, but he had no say in her life now. She'd escaped while getting out had been possible.

At least he could be thankful for the few days he'd had with her. To hold her and get to know her. To feel the touch of her soul brushing against his. To experience moments away from the madness and pain. It had been beyond exquisite. He could die peacefully now.

But he couldn't imagine how difficult it must be for her. He wished he could look into her eyes and convey how much he loved her. She must know. He wanted her to know, despite her rejection of him.

Lark's footsteps tracked the concrete floor until she stood before him. With his sight gone, his sense of smell increased. He smelled the luscious sweetness of her skin, underlaid with a hint of rice pudding and rum, and champagne. Sex tinted that perfume and he decided it was the best smell a man could know before he died.

And now he was thankful he would not be able to see the stake coming toward his heart, or the tortured look in his lover's eyes. Twice now, she had been forced to stake the men she loved.

Or would she smile as the titanium stake pierced his heart?

"Bastard." He heard the softly uttered word, and winced. So she did hate him. Unless…? Of course, she had to put on a facade before the Order. "You used me."

"Used? No, I—"

He could not deny biting her thigh had been cruel and unusual. If he could take it back he would. But he'd thought she'd understood it had been beyond his control.

"I've been under your persuasion all the time." Her voice wobbled and he thought he smelled a salty teardrop.

"No, Lark, I told you I would never do that."

"Liar!"

The blunt end of the stake landed hard upon his chest. The warmth of her fingers wrapped about it and slammed against his body, permeated his skin.

Why did she believe he'd persuaded her? He had not. It was something he reserved only following the bite, and he'd never used it after biting her because she had given him permission—

Hell, had the Order convinced her of this? She was too strong for such underhanded tactics. No matter how she felt regarding his betrayal of her trust, she must not believe he could ever persuade her against her will.

"How did they do it?" he asked. "Make you believe that lie?"

"This is tiring," Rook said from somewhere to Domingos's left. "Reduce him to ash so we can get out of here."

"You would not grant a dying man a last wish?" Domingos tried, unsure what, exactly, would be his request, but it was a time buyer.

"That's not the way we do things," Rook answered.

But Lark said, "Tell me. What the hell do you want before I ash you, longtooth?"

The heat of him was intense. Standing so close to him, Lark could feel the essence of Domingos race all over her body. The stake remained, right over his pounding heart, ready for termination. She had only to squeeze the paddles. He did not smell like rum and champagne—they'd had sex less than twenty-four hours earlier—so he must have showered. Yes, she'd left him in the shower. His familiar smoky scent instead rose to taunt her.

At the time they'd made love, she had felt in her body, in control and that she was doing exactly as she wanted, and not being coerced. Maybe? Sorting out her thoughts was difficult now that she knew he'd persuaded her.

And now he had the audacity to convince her the Order was lying to her? Idiot vampire.

Today she would claim kill number seventy-three. No matter that déjà vu rattled inside her brain, threatening to bring up tears. Twice now she'd been forced to stake a man she had thought to love.

You did love them. Both of them!

She slammed the door on Lisa Cooper. Lark was who she had become, and that woman didn't need tears. This staking was going to be much easier than the last time.

The vampire had requested a last wish, which he did not deserve, but she did want to hear what he thought was so important before she ashed him.

Her finger twitched on the titanium shaft. "Tell me!"

Domingos spread out his arms, not seeing her, yet his dark eyes seemed to look right through and into her soul. "I go to my grave willingly and gladly knowing it is my lover who wields the stake. I had hoped it would be this way, if it was to ever come to this."

"Stop stalling and tell me your last wish," Lark demanded.

She didn't want to listen to his pretty words, in his voice that strafed along her spine and melted into her soul, *becoming her.* Was this more vampiric persuasion?

"Very well." Domingos bowed his head toward hers and nuzzled his nose aside her ear. She stiffened, knowing Rook watched keenly. As well, the other knights stood but a few paces behind the vampire. "Kiss me," he whispered. "And then kill me, because your kiss will devastate."

Lark stepped back, drawing the stake away from him, and looked down and aside. Kiss him? What a ridiculous request. She would never.

You must! He is the man you love.

Twisting her head against the intrusive voice, she had the thought that the vampire's madness had worn off on her. Hearing voices? Was it possible Rook had lied about the persuasion? How could she believe it so deeply? Yet if she struggled for that belief, then something must be off, yes?

Hell, she was confused. And her heart seemed to clatter against her rib cage, while her hands had grown clammy. If she delayed much longer she'd find herself back on the kitchen floor, kneeling over a man who begged for the stake to be free from the threat of vampirism.

You don't need to go there now. Domingos makes you strong. Trust him!

"Give the vampire what he wants," Rook announced from behind her. "It will serve you, our wayward knight, fitting punishment to kiss the enemy."

Lark shook her head, refusing. She gripped the stake so hard her bones ached. She could not. She would not. Not after his betrayal—

And yet how she desperately wanted to kiss Domingos one last time. To perhaps learn from his kiss the real truth.

You know the truth. Don't lie to yourself.

He's never lied to you.

"Please, Lark," the vampire said so softly, she thought she might be the only one in the room who could hear. And something about the tremble in his voice cleaved to her core and rattled her need to remain the unattached machine who had slain dozens of creatures without so much as a blink.

Sighing, she stepped forward, but inches from the vampire, and decided a quick peck on the cheek should fulfill his absurd request nicely. Yet when she leaned in, Domingos's mouth found hers and without touching her elsewhere he held her there, endlessly. The world receded. The knights standing nearby ceased to exist. In fact, the Order no longer existed. She was merely Lark—or perhaps even Lisa Cooper. Taking what she was given, and answering back with a desperate need.

Freedom. Don't sacrifice it again.

And she fell, deep into Domingos, nestled by his darkness, and sighing into his madness. A vampire whose bite made her crave and plead for yet another and another bite. Not her enemy. Simply a man who had been wronged in such an evil way his very soul had been contorted.

And there, deep within his kiss, she remembered that she loved this man because he was kind and gentle with her, and had allowed her to see beyond the foolish need for blind revenge. He had given her hope, and in turn she had given him back his music.

And she knew, against all reason, this man had not manipulated her. Why she believed otherwise was a mystery she would solve. But until then…

"I love you," she whispered into his mouth.

Domingos grabbed the stake from her hand. With his other hand, he wrenched her body around, gripping her hard up under the neck. She allowed it, not wanting to fight, not wanting to put herself back on the side of the man who glared at her now, the one who had trained her, the one who had lied to her.

How had he made her believe the lie?

King, her conscience screamed. It had been his doing.

"Back!" Domingos demanded. "Or I stake her in the heart."

He shuffled backward toward the wall, and remembering his blindness, Lark made a slight adjustment in his trajectory by easing him to the right and toward the door.

"Let him go!" Rook shouted to the knights who approached their escape, hands reaching for their stakes and weapons. "Idiot longtooth won't get far. He's blind."

"She'll lead him out of here," Debraux, one of the knights, protested.

"Maybe."

Lark met Rook's eyes and couldn't read him. Was he giving her a head start? Or merely playing with her? She knew it was the latter. He would let her and Domingos get outside, yet while it was night, she wouldn't get far with a blind vampire. The knights would be on them in minutes.

Minutes were all she needed.

Gripping the door, she opened it and tugged Domingos through. He slapped the stake back into her hand as she directed him to take the stairs down. Using the wall as a guide, he stumbled once, but made it to the ground floor with ease.

"You can't see anything?" she asked as she tugged him down the street and turned abruptly into a narrow, dark alley.

"No, but you lead well. I can hear their footsteps clattering down the stairs."

"Then we're going to silent mode. Trust me?"

"I do."

"I love you," she said, and wanted to explain about why she'd believed he'd persuaded her, but there was no time and it was too risky to make any noise.

"Love you back."

And that response fortified her need for survival.

Dodging behind parked cars, as they passed, Lark scanned inside the interiors for keys. They wouldn't be so lucky. Grabbing Domingos's shirtsleeve, she ran with him alongside her, not moving as fast as she'd like, but not wanting to risk him stumbling.

His hand slid down to clutch hers. He'd trusted her, even when she had been prepared to stake him. Somehow he had known that, by asking for a kiss, she would remember. Or perhaps he had not, and simply loved her that much.

Ahead queued a row of brick buildings, most in disrepair and with boards nailed across the glassless windows. This section of town was undergoing construction, and the sidewalk dropped away to exposed dirt. She clutched his hand tightly and did not slow her pace.

Pulling him into the abandoned brick building, she tugged him down against the wall. "You need blood," she said. "So you can see."

"Yes, but there's no way—"

She pressed her wrist to his mouth, stopping his protest. "Do it."

He gripped her wrist with both hands and shook his head. "I've taken too much from you, Lark. Mercy, but I almost killed you at the hotel. I have no right—"

"Don't argue with me, vampire. If you love me, you'll save us both by getting back your sight and strength. I need you to win against the knights."

Fangs entered her wrist in a painful piercing. Lark moaned with the pain and pleasure of it, then pressed her face to his shoulder to muffle the noise. He sucked greedily from her. It felt so good that she struggled not to sink into the giddy coil of orgasm that always accompanied his bite. Never had she thought an orgasm could prove a threat. There'd be time later to reason out that strange thought.

When they heard her fellow knights' footsteps pounding across the packed dirt and construction debris outside, Domingos tore away his mouth from her wrist.

"Christ, it's dark, but I can see now. My sight is back, and so is— Fucking cats!"

Upon hearing Domingos's outburst, the knights clattered toward the building. And while her lover began to bang his head against the wall, raging against the madness within, three knights with stakes appeared from around the corner.

Chapter 22

Lark was impressed that Domingos stepped before her, trying to protect her as the knights approached. But the two of them could work better as a team, so she stepped up alongside him and twirled her stake. She winked at her vampire lover.

He winked back and nodded, indicating that she take the floor.

"Boys," she said to the knights who stood before them. "Three against two? Those odds will work for me. What do you say, Domingos?"

"Not even a challenge."

"Traitor!" Debraux yelled, and charged toward her.

The other two knights, Moore and Dumas, headed for Domingos.

Stepping before Domingos, and hooking her arms back and within his, Lark levered up from the ground and he supported her as she kicked Debraux in the jaw and sent him reeling toward the other two knights.

"Should have had on your fancy boots with the blades," Domingos said as he set her down and went for Moore. The vampire punched the knight in the gut and deftly dodged the swing of the stake.

Much as Lark worried a stake was going to eventually end up in someone's heart—and she prayed it wasn't Domingos's—she couldn't keep an eye on him and win this fight. So she abandoned that worry and charged into the fray.

Dumas's arm clocked her across the chest, forcing the air from her lungs. Gasping, she maintained her footing and slashed around with her fist, squeezing the paddles to release the stake, which cut across his scalp and sliced a crimson line above his ear.

Bending forward and swinging her leg up high, she clocked the knight who now clutched his ear right across the face, hearing the cartilage in his nose crunch. Dumas went down, cursing her with a nasty oath.

Domingos's shoulder crushed up against her back as he stumbled away from a punch. He rolled through the hit, somersaulting backward over her and landing on the ground before her. Another wink reached through the darkness and tickled her heart. God, she loved that vampire!

Domingos's smirk quickly dropped and he charged toward her, grabbing her by the wrist and swinging her out of the way just as Moore's body collided with his. Lark landed before the other knight, who stood holding the stake in challenge.

"You would side with a vampire?" Debraux asked. "Typical woman."

"I'm not typical of anything." Lark kicked high, knocking the stake from his grasp. Landing the move, she spun and swung up her fist, clocking him aside the jaw and dropping him in a blackout at her feet. "Was that typical, buddy? Yeah, I don't think so."

Domingos yelled. She turned to see Moore toss a handful of dirt at the vampire's face. The dust cloud disoriented Domingos. Moore swung the stake toward her lover's chest and planted it with his fist.

"No!" Lark stepped over Debraux and landed on Moore's back. Her hand grasped the fist he had wrapped about the stake just as the paddles were depressed. The repercussion pulsed up both their hands, away from the vampire's chest—yet the stake did not cut through muscle.

Domingos charged Moore, bringing him down, with Lark still clinging to his back. She landed on the ground hard, her breath chuffing from her. The two men scuffled while she lifted her head to assess the other two. Still down, though Dumas was groaning, and would be up soon enough.

She saw Domingos form a spade of his hand above Moore's chest. The same move he'd made before ripping out the werewolf's heart.

"No," she said, but it was only a gasp.

If he killed a knight, he'd start a war. The Order would not rest until it had hunted down Domingos LaRoque and made him suffer.

But who was she to demand he restrain himself? He fought for his life. And hers.

Grabbed from behind, Lark grunted as Dumas landed beside her and yanked her arm, twisting her body about so she sat up to face him. "Say goodbye to your vampire," he said with a sneer.

"You say goodbye to Moore."

The vampire struck, plunging his hand toward Moore's chest. Lark and Dumas watched, frozen in a defiant hold against each other. And when Lark thought Domingos would rip out Moore's heart, instead the vampire released a primal yell and shoved the man aside. He stood over Moore and delivered a hard right fist to his jaw, knocking him out cold.

Relieved, Lark exhaled. Domingos stalked toward her and he grabbed Dumas. Another iron fist took out the knight and left him sprawled on the uneven dirt ground.

"Let's get the hell out of here," he said, pulling her up.

Gripping her by the back of the head, the vampire pulled her in for a hard kiss. He tasted like dirt and blood, but she only held him tighter and kissed him harder. Here was where she belonged, in the arms of the one man who would never betray her, and whom she trusted completely.

"You didn't kill him," she said.

"I have no beef against him. Any of them. Unless, of course, they had managed to kill you."

"I'm still in one piece. And they are starting to rouse."

He tugged her out of the building, and the twosome ran into the night, elated to have escaped what should have been sure death.

Rook and King stood in the shadows beneath an eighteenth-century limestone building that had once been a patisserie yet was now a bookshop that offered explicit tales bound between discreet covers.

Rook had preferred the patisserie, even though he hadn't been into all that sugar and frilly decorated sweets.

He felt sure King had fond memories of the shop; he had dated one of the shopgirls for a while.

"This is his favorite spot?" King asked.

The man leaned against the wall, arms crossed over his chest. He rarely worked in the field, and the fact that he'd worn a white shirt over gray slacks tonight proved as much. Not so easy to blend while wearing white.

"Every week, intel reports." Rook nodded across the street. "That's him."

The Levallois principal exited the Noir nightclub across the street from the bookshop, a sexy redhead squeezed into a tight pink dress under his arm. She stumbled, stepping out of one of her überhigh heels and drunkenly floundered to get it. Remy, probably not too drunk, stood back, watching her with a lascivious grin. Order intel reported the pack principal was a known womanizer.

Although he understood King had more intimate knowledge of the wolf, Rook wasn't sure what that implied. Friends for a long time—hell, they considered each other brothers—they still didn't tell each other everything.

Rook hadn't the patience to watch this drunken tête-à-tête, and he sensed the same impatience from King's ready posture. Clad in black, Rook blended with the shadows as he moved in swiftly, slamming the werewolf against the graffiti-littered wall of the nightclub, just outside the line of streetlight that beamed across the garishly painted wall.

The idiot woman asked what was going on.

"Get out of here!" King ordered her, and she turned and ran back inside the club, muttering something about always picking the wrong man.

"We have unfinished business," Rook said to the wolf,

who did not struggle, but he could feel the man's strength beneath his hands and knew if he didn't maintain authority the wolf would overtake him.

"You did not slay the vampire," Remy said. "You're right. We do have unfinished business. Never thought the Order was so inept. You must be King. We have a connection, and you know it."

"We are connected in no way," King said calmly. He nodded at Rook, and Rook understood the order implicitly.

He squeezed the wolf's neck, wanting to rip out veins, but cautioned his anger. He never let his emotions get out of control, because when they did, bad things emerged—literally—from inside him. "What I want to know is why you didn't have your own personal knight do the job instead of coming to me."

Remy snickered. "I wanted to do things properly."

"More like you didn't want me to know you have Gunnar in your pocket."

"I had hoped you'd assign him to the job, but...alas. You assigned me a knight who preferred to deputize the very vampire I wanted eliminated as her own personal sidekick. And an ineffective female, at that. Watch it, knight. My talons are itching to come out."

"Keep them sheathed."

Rook let the wolf go but did not step back from his imposing stance. He peered into the man's heart, and what he saw there made him sick. This man's truths were ugly and vile. He would not suffer him to walk away unscathed, but he would neither kill him. This wasn't his fight.

And yet he couldn't decipher what Remy had meant by him and King having a connection.

King stepped forward, his shoulder paralleling Rook's. The man spoke calmly, as usual, "You make a wrong move toward the Order and we will retaliate. Hard. From this day forth, the Order severs all ties with pack Levallois, you understand?"

"Does that mean I lose my own personal knight?"

While King had requested Rook to send a knight to terminate Gunnar, he never agreed with destroying a perfectly capable, smart man. Gunnar had gotten involved in a side job, and it went against everything the Order believed in. He could no longer remain a knight. But he'd not bought his death.

"Gunnar Svedson has been banished," Rook provided, knowing he'd answer to King later for that executive decision. Perhaps that would be an opportune time to discuss King's connection with this wolf. "He's your problem now. And I will charge you with keeping him in line. If Gunnar, or any in pack Levallois, sets foot near the Order's knights, you remember our promise of retaliation."

"What makes you think I'll comply? I don't take orders from mortals, not even the ones who eliminate the occasional fang in my side." Remy stared hard at King. Something was going on between the two men.

Rook lifted the hefty wolf against the wall, and the man's bulky biker boots left the ground. Rook squeezed his throat and stared into his eyes, a much sharper read than he got by studying a man's heart. Inside, that other part of him scowled at the vile thing he held in his hand.

"I can see your truth, werewolf. You are fearful and unsure, and you don't want to find out what I can do to you if truly angered."

He dropped Caufield and stepped back, thrusting back

his shoulders and lifting his chest defiantly as werewolves often did when standing down each other.

The werewolf, noticeably shaken, huffed and tugged down his diamond-cuffed sleeves. He looked at Rook, shivered, but daren't meet his eyes for more than a split second. "What are you?"

Rook smirked. Wolves did have a sense that detected the otherworldly. "I'm Rook. And we'll never speak again."

Remy spat to the side and nodded agreement to that. But again he had the audacity to capture King's gaze. "But the two of us…well, those letters are my get-out-of-jail-free pass, yes?"

"Indeed," King replied, exhaling quietly. The man's heart was racing, which Rook determined was because he stood so close—and that was unusual. "We're done here."

With that, King walked off. Rook followed immediately, not wanting to appear as though he had no idea what the hell was going on—but what the hell was going on between the two men?

Sensing the werewolf's need to chase after them, but knowing from the strong fear scent still clinging to his hands that was the last the Order would see of any from pack Levallois, Rook adjusted that innate knowledge to a possibility.

When they'd turned a corner, King paused. Headlights rushed past them on a main avenue. Across the street, a vendor sporting plastic lit replicas of the Eiffel Tower hustled a crowd of enthusiastic tourists.

Rook nudged a shoulder against King's arm. He felt his old friend shudder; out of character. "What's going on between the two of you?" he asked.

After a thoughtful silence, King provided, "I told you about the letters."

Letters? Rook searched his brain that stored centuries of details and conversation and—ah, yes, the letters. A remarkable mistake that King would pay for one day. Foolishly, neither of them had thought that day would ever come.

"You plotting a means to get those back in hand?"

"As we speak," King replied.

They didn't stop running until they'd reached Domingos's mansion and passed through the wrought-iron gate. Both trundled up the sidewalk and they landed at the front stoop beside an overgrowth of purple-blossomed nightshade and fell into each other's arms.

"Love you," Lark said, and kissed him.

Domingos bracketed her face and bowed his forehead to hers. "Love you back."

"I'm so sorry I treated you like that in the warehouse."

"What was that about? Did you really believe I could have been so cruel?"

She sighed and settled against his chest, and he cradled her there beneath the moonlight. Not at all exhausted after their fight, and then the long run home, she was actually exhilarated.

"Rook and King made me believe you'd used persuasion on me. I have no idea how they did it, but it worked. I thought for sure you'd betrayed me. And yet—" she turned in his arms to find his adoring gaze "—something deep inside me wouldn't allow me to believe without questioning. It kept prodding at me. And then your kiss won me over. I knew you couldn't possibly have done such a thing."

"Did they use drugs on you?"

"I don't know. Well, yes. They tranqed me outside the Shangri-La, but I don't know if that had an effect on my thoughts and made it easy to plant that belief in my mind."

He kissed her mouth and she abandoned the worry with ease. In Domingos's arms, everything was more right than any of her wrongs had ever been. And she intended to never look back. Never.

"I thought you'd left me when you didn't return to the hotel," he said. "You had every right to."

"Never."

"I hurt you."

"It wasn't you. It was the madness."

He nodded and propped his chin on her head, his fingers stroking her hair down her shoulder. "It'll always be a part of me."

"I know. Maybe. I think with music, you'll get stronger."

"Possibly. You make me stronger. But I don't want to rely on you to be a functioning vampire. And I can't continue to bite you. The more blood I take, the more I want. Lark, I'm every kind of wrong for you."

"Exactly." Now she straddled his legs and sat on his lap. Moonlight glinted in his eyes, glamorizing them. She touched a scratch on his cheek, likely from the fight. It would heal, but not so fast as it did for other vampires. "You're my wrong, which is really right. Let's not even get into this again. We belong together."

He stroked a hand along her thigh where the wound hurt from running. "I don't ever want to hurt you again."

"Then we'll figure something out. Some kind of protection plan, yes?"

"You do have your stake."

She tugged the stake from her pocket and tossed it into the shrub beside the house. "No, I don't."

"Hunter," he chided, "it's not so simple as that."

"Why can't it be?"

He exhaled and shrugged. Within his gaze, Lark watched the moon dance and flicker, and finally, he smiled. "All right, then. It can be simple. We are an us."

"It makes me happy to hear you say that. Race you to the bedroom."

He grabbed her hand and pulled her down as she attempted to stand. "Thank you for knowing my heart, and yours."

She nodded. "Thank you for touching my soul and putting me back in touch with my heart."

They weren't there. The whispers. The crazy music that normally pounded and scraped against the inside of his skull. Not even a meow from a cat whose tail had been run over by the crazy train. His head was clear. Only Lark's purrs as she lay beneath him entered his thoughts. Such a gorgeous sound.

He'd hilted his cock inside her and, hands bracketing her torso, rocked above her, not taking his eyes from hers. Though it was dark, the curtains were pulled aside to allow the moon to join in and increase their coupling to a glittering ménage à trois. Silvery light slid across Lark's breasts and twinkled in her green eyes, and it bejeweled the baubles of perspiration on her skin.

She felt so good. Hot and squeezing. He could live inside Lark. He wanted nothing more. He probably didn't deserve her, but he wasn't going to question this relationship anymore. He'd almost walked away from her, thinking she couldn't possibly love a vampire who had tried to kill her.

And when she had been forced to kill him—she could not. In that moment when she had kissed him in the warehouse, Domingos knew she was his forever. Now he had to rise to that challenge and be the best man he could, madness be damned.

Because they were now an *us*.

Her fingers glided down his chest, pinging his nipples in a painful sweet twinge. Domingos gasped and increased his rhythm inside her. She wrapped her legs about his hips and drove him harder against her body, demanding he give her every last atom of himself.

An easy sacrifice.

"Be mine forever?" he asked.

"Oh, hell yes, lover." She giggled then and pulled him down to kiss her. "I want to move in with you. Be with you night and day. Leave that tiny apartment behind."

"I wouldn't have it any other way. I'll even let you redecorate with some bright colors."

"Not here in the bedroom. I love you in the dark. You are mine, darkness and strength."

"Lark, I can feel you squeeze me with your muscles. You're so strong."

"You're thick and hot, like molten steel. God, that feels good. I don't think I will ever tire of making love with you."

He bent and kissed her breast, then nibbled it, but kept his lips over his fangs. To feel her skin against the fangs would ratchet up the need to bite her even higher than it already was.

"I want you to go to FaeryTown," she said.

"What the hell for?"

"You mentioned that faery dust might heal your wounds? Maybe it could do something for your madness?"

"You are already a balm to the voices and clatter in my head."

She pouted sweetly.

"Fine," he said. "But what if I become addicted to dust?"

"We'll make sure you don't. I just want you to give it a try. You deserve to be whole."

"Okay. Ah!" He reached the pinnacle, and his body growing rigid and shuddering above Lark, he came inside her, hard and fast and endlessly.

Collapsing on top of her, he buried his face against her neck and champagne-and-rum-scented hair. Bright and bold, his pretty little hunter, had given him back the light.

He'd won against the werewolves after all.

Lark placed the backpack filled with titanium stakes, blades and silver bullets on Rook's desk. The Kevlar vest and Order coat was also stuffed inside. As well, the folded picture of Todd. She didn't need to look at it. Memory kept him, along with their unborn child, tucked securely in a place that she could access when she wished.

She stepped back and waited for the man to speak.

The risk in returning to the Order's headquarters was great after her escape with Domingos, and their taking out three knights, but she figured her resignation might be the only thing that now allowed her to stand before him and still draw breath.

Rook launched around the desk and gripped her across the shoulders, wrenching back her head and placing a blade at her throat.

Regarding her condition of breathing—maybe not.

"I've had a long day, Lark," he said aside her ear. "And I do not find this ploy particularly funny."

"I'm resigning from the knights."

"Doesn't happen that way." His cool grip tightened painfully on her shoulder. "You want out? You die fighting."

"Is that what happened to Gunnar?"

He released her and stepped back. She had no clue what had become of Gunnar, but a small part of her had hoped the dirty knight wasn't around anymore to draw breath. Normally when a knight was ousted—meaning killed—it was witnessed by the entire organization. That had happened once since Lark had been a knight.

Rook strode to the desk and opened the backpack, removing a titanium stake and holding it between them. "You know I designed this weapon?"

"You're talented. It's a remarkable weapon."

Yet she thought it had been used since the inception of the Order, which dated back to the sixteenth century. That couldn't be right. Not if he had designed the thing.

"You and King own a fine organization, and it provides a good service to innocent mortals not the wiser to the vampires who walk this earth, but I can't—"

Slamming the base of the stake against the marble desktop, Rook said, "Never say can't, Lark. You can do whatever you set your mind to."

A mantra he'd frequently drilled into her brain while training. It had worked. Until she had met a man whose influence had touched her very soul.

He spun the stake and landed it sharply in his grip. "You fell in love with a vampire?"

She nodded, and did not bow her head in shame, instead defiantly and proudly holding the man's gaze. "By killing the wolves Domingos LaRoque was doing what he needed to do. The pack had tortured him."

"I get that. And I took a job on behalf of the Order and promised to fulfill it."

"Some jobs aren't worth the money," she offered.

"No, they're not."

Surprised by that admittance, Lark held her breath to keep from admonishing him for the mistake.

"We've worked with werewolves in the past," he said, "but it's never been a common thing. King and I intend to rethink any future alliances with the breed." He held out the stake to her, and she reluctantly took it. "Can you love a vampire and still pursue those of his breed who would bring harm to others? The job the other night—you were able to complete that."

"Yes, but…isn't it an Order rule not to fraternize with the enemy?" There was no manual, but Lark was pretty sure she'd had that tidbit drilled into her skull during training along with the doing-anything mantra. "And if you think I could ever use Domingos to get to other vamps—"

"What I know is that I don't want to lose a talent like you, Lark. It is unfortunate that you've taken up with La-Roque, but that's from my perspective. Yet the truth I see in you now? I have to admit, it dazzles me."

She pressed a palm over her heart, feeling dazzled as well by the love she had found from the least likely source. And the surprising reassurance from her leader.

"How can you see people's truths?" she dared to ask. "Are you mortal?"

He tilted his head, giving the question some thought. Then he wandered around behind the desk and tapped the computer keyboard, bringing something up on the screen Lark could not see from where she stood.

"King wants you eliminated," he said. "I've convinced him you're worth the save."

So he was going to avoid the question she most wanted an answer to. She'd give him that. He was sparing her life.

"If," he added, "you'll remain with the Order."

"I'm not sure," she said. "You need to tell me one thing before I decide."

"I can't answer the question you most want answered."

"It's a different question." She waited for him to lift his gaze to hers, and when he did, she felt no fear. "How did you convince me that Domingos used persuasion on me? He didn't do any such thing, Rook. I know it."

"I did no such thing."

"But I believed," she protested. "For a while there, I was ready to stake him."

"Sounds like you've got some inner demons that still need facing before you commit completely to a vampire. Anything else?"

The man was a master at avoiding the truths that he claimed to read so easily in others. Maybe that was his actual truth: others' truths were clear to him, while his were blurry as mud.

"Can I get a week or two off to think about all this? I confess, I do believe I excel at my work, and I feel I'm only getting stronger. And I want to help those who cannot help themselves, but…"

"Two weeks," Rook said, gesturing for her to retrieve the backpack from his desk. "Report back in with a phone call. I'll be waiting."

She grabbed the backpack and headed toward the door. As she gripped the knob, Rook said, "I warn you that Domingos LaRoque had better walk the straight and narrow. I will not hesitate to send another knight after him should he prove a danger to mortals."

"He won't," Lark said, and left.

Epilogue

Months later

Lark slipped around the side of the building, eyed her prey and scampered forward, light on her feet, despite the extra weight she carried. Stake in hand and ready for action, she ran toward the vampire, who had wrapped his hands about a young mortal man's throat. Choking him before the bite? That was a new one.

But not according to Order intel. This vampire liked to take his victims home with him and torture them for days before finally draining them completely of their blood and then tossing the body in the Seine.

"Time to die," she growled, and made a leap for the back of the vampire. She hooked an arm around his neck, sharply jerking back his head.

The vampire took the surprise with skilled reaction. He dropped the male, who scrambled away, screaming.

Slamming his back toward the wall of the building, the vampire crushed Lark between his body and the rough bricks.

Air gushed from her lungs. Her stomach revolted, shifting miserably. She felt a sharp tug at the base of her spine. A kind of *not right* pain.

As the vampire turned with a fist prepared to slam into her gut, he suddenly paused, staring at her huge belly.

"You're pregnant!"

That was the distraction she required. Slamming her fist against his chest, she did not pause to compress the stake paddles. The weapon entered flesh, bone and muscle. The vampire yowled, then dusted before her, hanging there in a distorted shape of his body for seconds, before dropping to the tarmac at her boots.

"And you're dead."

The sharp pain in her spine attacked again. Dropping the stake, Lark winced and doubled over the pile of vampire ash. She eased a palm around her eight-months-pregnant belly. Something was going on in there.

"Not due for another three weeks," she gasped.

Clutching for the wall, she was shocked to feel what she suspected was a labor pain, a tight, clenching squeeze in her uterus worse than any PMS cramps she'd ever experienced.

Three weeks after telling Rook she didn't wish to leave the Order, she'd learned she was pregnant. That first time with Domingos had been the kicker. Thing was? Domingos had been standing right there with her, watching the pink line appear on the stick. They'd both cheered to see it, and then had hugged each other in joy.

No doubts. No regrets. This baby was a miracle they were ready to welcome with open arms.

She wasn't sure she could make it home if the pain

persisted, and home was three quarters away. She'd have to call Domingos, and he was going to be angry she'd gone out on a job. She'd promised him to take it easy the last trimester, but this particular vampire had burned her ire. And Rook had trusted she had the skill to complete the job, despite her rounded girth.

"And I did it," she managed between wincing breaths.

Practicing the breathing technique she'd learned in Lamaze class, she closed her eyes, yet kept her ears honed for approaching footsteps. According to intel, the vampire had acted alone, but she would never let down her guard.

"Oh!" A fierce shock of pain squeezed her innards. And suddenly her water broke, gushing down the inside of her Kevlar-lined pants. "Hell, it's time."

She fumbled for the cell phone in her pocket and dialed up home. Domingos answered immediately, as he'd taken to carrying the cell phone she'd bought him in his pocket the past few weeks. He had suspected the baby would come early because she was so round. Weird vampire instincts? Who could know?

"Lover," she said on a gasp. "Can you come get me?"

"Where are you, Lark? Is it the baby?"

She nodded, and knew he couldn't hear her nod, but another labor pain forced her to concentrate and focus on what was going on inside her body.

"It's the baby," he said, guessing. "I've got you on GPS. What the hell are you doing in the seventh?"

"Just come get me, please."

"I'll be there in ten minutes."

The ride to the hospital was a little tense—Domingos hadn't been able to hide his anger that she'd gone out on a job—but more so, fraught with anticipation. By the time they pulled before the emergency doors, Lark already felt the urge to push. Domingos paid a nurse to park the car for him because he didn't want to leave Lark alone, and she was thankful for that as they wheeled her toward an O.R., her lover's hand firmly clasped in hers.

Twenty minutes later, Lark admired Domingos, who stood near the window in the quiet birthing room, moonlight spilling over his face, as he looked over the scrunched little face of their newborn boy. Tears spilled down Lark's cheeks, and she attributed them to hormones, but knew they were from pride and love for the new little man in her life, and the steadfast vampire who would be in her life forever.

She'd done it. She'd carried their child to term. It was such a relief after having lost one child. The second semester had been fraught with fear of losing the baby, and she hadn't taken more than two slaying jobs then. The relief was immeasurable. But more so? She had given Domingos a family.

A family they both desired.

"He looks like you," she whispered, not so much exhausted from labor and maybe even exhilarated. "That thick dark hair is precious."

Domingos swept his palm over their baby's black hair, which stuck up a good half inch all over his head. "Why are you so good to me, Lark?" he asked plainly.

"What do you mean?"

"Look what you've given me. A tiny creature that we made together. He's so perfect." The vampire sniffed back a tear. "I never thought myself capable of creating something like this. This. This goes beyond music. So innocent." He swallowed, his smile slipping. "I don't want him to grow up with a crazy daddy."

"He won't." They'd been looking into using faery dust to cure Domingos's madness, and it seemed a possibility. But they'd wanted to wait until after Lark gave birth because it required some intensive sessions that would push Domingos toward addiction if not carefully monitored. "We'll make you better."

"This sweet little boy already makes me better. I wish he didn't have to face such an unsure future."

A child born of a mortal and vampire may or may not become vampire. They wouldn't know until the blood hunger appeared at puberty. They were prepared for either outcome, but who could ever be ready for such a thing?

"Stay here in the now," she said, patting the bed beside her. "Come sit, lover. Let me see what we've made."

He sat beside her and gently lowered the baby into her arms. He was so tender with the infant, Lark felt he was handling parent duties better than she. She'd never held babies much and didn't want to drop the little tyke.

"What's his name?" she asked. They'd not discussed names, mainly because of her fears of losing the baby. "I want you to name your son."

Domingos cupped a hand over their child's head and kissed his tiny nose. "Kindred was my father's name."

"I love that."

"I love you." He kissed her and then turned to lie beside her on the bed, and together they cradled Kindred LaRoque. "Let's get married."

They had tossed the idea around during the past few months, but neither wanted to do it because it was the thing to do just because they were bringing a child into the world. And getting married because she was pregnant had echoed of Lark's past marriage. She felt as though she would love and live with Domingos forever, and he felt the same. So a contract written on paper had seemed unnecessary.

But linking her fingers with Domingos's now, Lark went with what her heart wanted and said, "Yes. I will be your wife."

"And lover." He kissed her.

"And friend."

He kissed her again. "And my soul. You and I and Kindred, one happy family composed of vampire, hunter and who knows what the future will bring our son?"

"I only hope that he is happy, no matter what he becomes. When we go home tonight, will you play him a song?"

"Only if you accompany me."

"We'll give him our love for music."

"It's already in his soul," he said, and he kissed Kindred's forehead, then nuzzled against Lark's shoulder.

"Love you," she whispered.

"Love you back."

* * * * *

A sneaky peek at next month...

NOCTURNE™

BEYOND DARKNESS...BEYOND DESIRE

My wish list for next month's titles...

In stores from 19th July 2013:

❑ Phantom Wolf — Bonnie Vanak

❑ Daysider — Susan Krinard

In stores from 2nd August 2013:

❑ Dark Rival — Brenda Joyce

Available at WHSmith, Tesco, Asda, Eason, Amazon and Apple

Just can't wait?

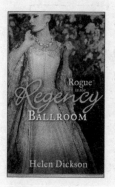
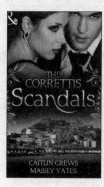

The World of Mills & Boon®

There's a Mills & Boon® series that's perfect for you. We publish ten series and, with new titles every month, you never have to wait long for your favourite to come along.

Blaze®
Scorching hot, sexy reads
4 new stories every month

By Request
Relive the romance with the best of the best
9 new stories every month

Cherish™
Romance to melt the heart every time
12 new stories every month

Desire™
Passionate and dramatic love stories
8 new stories every month

Where will *you* read
this summer?

#TeamShade

Join your team this summer.

www.millsandboon.co.uk/sunvshade